It's only when the rain comes sissing down in those long and loose slanting lines that a different kind of courage finally gives you that impetus you need to drive you through the doors of the pub – those doors that have held you in both fear and fascination for the last half hour.

So, in you go, then! Open the door and keep your walk slow, and don't look around too much until you get to the bar at the far end of the room. Try to look nonchalant, as though you're just dropping in for a casual drink after a cocktail party or something, and don't want the night to burn out so quickly. Try and find someone you know well enough to talk with, but someone that won't get you tied up into something you don't want, and won't try to tie himself up with whatever you do want.

The classic novel of homosexual love.

Neville Jackson

No End To The Way

CORGI BOOKS

1985.

NO END TO THE WAY

A CORGI BOOK 0 552 12621 7

Originally published in Great Britain by
Barrie and Rockliff (Barrie Books Ltd.)

PRINTING HISTORY
Barrie and Rockliff edition published 1965
Corgi edition published 1967
Corgi edition reprinted 1967
Corgi edition reissued 1985

Corgi Books are published by Transworld Publishers Ltd.,
Century House, 61-63 Uxbridge Road,
Ealing, London W5 5SA.

Made and printed in Great Britain by
Hunt Barnard Printing Ltd., Aylesbury, Bucks.

For
JOHN and "JOOP"
wherever either of you may be

Oh eyes, no eyes, but fountains fraught with tears;
Oh life, no life, but lively form of death;
Oh world, no world, but mass of public wrongs.

THOMAS KYD
The Spanish Tragedy

Part One

THE WAY IN

I

YOU know all too well that you just have to go in, that it will be impossible for you not to go in, because it's Saturday night and, as the song goes, Saturday night is the loneliest night of the week.

So here you are, outside the most likely pub in town where tonight's adventure might be waiting for you, and yet all you can do is walk up and down, up and down, risking a glance at the doors whenever they swing open, and then looking quickly down again at the jagged little bits of your own reflection, with those hermit-crab eyes of yours flapping back at you from the puddles in the pavement.

Sometimes there's a gust of wind, and when it comes it's always cold, a slap in the face from the chill hand of winter, as physical a thing as if it was a cold and wet dead fish that had hit you. You've walked past those doors now not once or twice nor even three times, but probably thirty-three times. So what are you going to do? Walk past them another thirty-three times?—until the pub closes and you won't be able to go inside, won't be able to find someone for the night, or possibly the whole week-end? The hell you will!

But it's only when the rain comes sissing down again in those long and loose slanting lines that a different kind of courage—or rather, a *lack* of courage—finally gives you that impetus you need to drive you indoors, in through those doors that have held you in both fear and fascination for the last half-hour. Another half-hour and it will be closing time. So, if there *is* your 'cup of tea' in there among all the usual ducks and drakes—and there are always so many more ducks than drakes in the flock, far too many nellies for the neddies—you'll just have time to pick him up without having to drink too much.

Tonight almost anything could be your cup of tea, it's been nearly a month since that second officer off a Swedish freighter —sheer hell with the language, of course, but a wild thing in the cot; about the best slice you can remember in years. You'd picked him up here too, in the old Palais Grande, saloon bar for men only, the most dependable place in town.

So, in you go, then! Open the door and keep your walk slow, and don't look around too much until you get to the bar at the far end of the room. Try to look nonchalant, as though you're just dropping in for a casual drink after a cocktail party or something, and don't want the night to burn out so quickly. Try and find someone you know well enough to talk with, but someone that won't get you tied up into something you don't want, and won't try to tie himself up with whatever you do want.

And there are just the ones you need: young Roy and Andy, a pleasant enough couple, especially now they're been *married* to each other—what is it?—five, six years? They're always safe so far as competition is concerned; never want anyone else but each other. They only come in Saturday nights to 'see what's what, and with whom, and what's new on the market.' 'Just for the kicks,' they always say, 'otherwise married life gets a bit dull at the edges.' Besides they're always glad to see you whenever you do come in. So Roy and Andy it is, even if they are in their twenties still, and you can give them a good ten years or so. Roy's quite grown-uppish at times; it's only Andy that's still like a little trish in his teens. Sweet enough kid, though. And they make a good couple, despite the disparity in their jobs—a school-teacher and a shop-assistant. Got a nice flat with a spare room for the loners, like yourself, who need it occasionally, just for the price of a few bottles of beer. Yes, Roy and Andy it most definitely is, now that you've had a chance to take another quick look around.

So—"Well, girls?" you say, as nobody gives a damn what you say in this bar, and the barmaids all love it anyway.

And Roy comes back with, as usual: "Get you!"

"How's tricks?" you ask them.

"How are your own!" Andy quips. "*We* don't *do* that sort of thing!"

"I know what *you* do, honey-boy, and it's just what I'm after," you say, enjoying yourself with them. They're always the same, whether you haven't seen them for months or only yesterday. Good types and a lot of fun. "How about a bit off the side, Annie, when your husband here goes bush or something?" 'Annie' is Andy's camp name, naturally. Funnily enough, Roy never seemed to get one.

"Ooh, you *dreadful* man!" Andy minces, and Roy gives one of those slow, shy smiles of his, and says: "Hop in. I need a bit of a rest." Joking-like. He'd probably scratch your eyes out if you did try something.

"What you both look as though you need is another drink," you say, catching the questing eye of one of the barmaids. "Those empty glasses look as though they might evaporate, in those hot little hands of yours. What's it to be, beer?"

"Beer it is," Roy tells you.

So you order three beers and, now that that's over, you can start operating.

So this is life in the barnyard! The three counters of the rectangular bar are all crowded, sometimes two and three deep. Some that can't fit in pose carefully in small clusters in the middle of the large, high-ceilinged, old-fashioned room. Lots of tired mirrors in gilt frames, ornate pillars with paint peeling off like sun-burn. Rows and rows of bottles, mostly fancy liqueurs that rarely get opened from one year to another. Beer and cigarette ads and some dried flowers stuffed in a vase. Toy dogs or dolls that the barmaids get as gifts from some of the more gushing types, and keep for mascots on their tills. All a bit tatty, and not entirely clean. The kind of pub the gays always seem to pick out and make their own, the world over. A bit tizzy, but not too flash to keep out the rough trade, like sailors and that.

This one is a bit handier than most. If the cops come in to scour round, it always looks respectable enough. And the rest of it's a very respectable pub, one of the city's best. Just a bit old and in need of a face-lift. Country people use it a lot, in the residential part. And the lounge is pretty fashionable for the squares with their wives or girl-friends. Only not all of them are as *square* as they and marriage—*normal* marriage, that is—would have it. There are a couple of doors and a very convenient corridor leading to the 'gents' from both the lounge and the bar, and some of these so-called squares like to take a look or two, and maybe size up something for later on. All kinds of visiting firemen—bankers, commercial travellers, visiting M.P.'s, Government wallahs, a farmer or two, professional sportsmen. You never know who's going to take a speculative squiz through the place next. Some of the biggest nobs in town—or other towns. A lot of people would get one hell of a shock if they ever heard who. But these are the hunters, like yourself, and so of no personal interest. Neither are the nancies, or the obvious ones. It's the ones that *aren't* obvious that you want, that most everybody wants; what's called 'rough trade' or, if it's not so rough, just 'trade'. Casual adventurers. Or week-end dabblers. Sometimes only once a month, once a year. And bisexuals. There's no end to the variety of types in the game.

So back to the bars you look, and almost straight away you see Sid Needham, squashed—or rather squashing himself—in between two groups where it's easy to see he's got a prospect in each, and hasn't yet made up his mind on which to pounce. Amazing, but for nearly twenty years he has looked pretty much the same. The small lean types often do, till suddenly one night, overnight, they turn fifty and look it. That's what'll happen to Sid one of these years, and maybe not so far off either.

But right now he still looks the same as ever, dapper under his wavy hair, forever grinning those intimidating leers of his, his eyes skidding and plundering around the room all the time. Yes, he's definitely looking at you, and what's more he's caught *you* looking, so there is nothing else to do but to conceal your mutual contempt behind a mask of cordiality. Impossible to think that he was the first one to seduce you, when you were just eighteen, almost as many years ago. The first one after Uncle Kev, that is.

But Sid is nearly always the first to seduce everyone. It's his speciality. Takes 'em once—or maybe twice or a few times, just to make sure they're far gone in the game they'll never get out of it again—and then he tosses them into the circle. It's his speciality, all right, picking the new ones, the ones that unmistakably have it *in* them, but don't yet know what any of it's all about. A few nights with Sid and they *know* what it's all about all right, and as soon as they are 'made', as he calls it, he launches them, like debutantes, in a new crop every year.

So you sidle your eyes away from Sid Needham, wondering which of the two young and oh so shiny-new prospects he'll make out with; your eyes slide slowly along the bar like a slow-motion film, and you start thinking: No, there's nothing here for you tonight after all.

Then suddenly it's as though your whole chest has caved in from a blow in the ribs. You try not to give yourself away, but it's as though the whole room is swimming crazily around you, and it's not for a while that you realize you've been holding on to the bar so tightly your knuckles are white, and the insides of your fingers hurt against some sharp edge.

That's it. You haven't seen anything quite like it for years. The very look of him, every mannerism, every gesture, is perfectly normal; and anyone, camp or square, would swear it was all man and had nothing else on its mind but women. About twenty-eight. Big shoulders, big hands, and hips so narrow they wouldn't even know how to sway. Dark. Well-dressed in a plain dark-grey suit that hasn't got a trace of swish. No tizzy jewellery or anything like that.

He's just standing there listening as though everything being said around him was the most interesting conversation in the world, and not trying to talk over the top of everyone else like all the others do. He just stands there, smiling a little. And listening. His eyes always look squarely at whoever happens to be talking, and not skating around the room all the times as everyone else's always do. He just doesn't seem interested Which makes sense, because he looks the type that wouldn't even know about it, and wouldn't be at all interested even if he did. And yet he must do—be interested, you mean; or at least know about it—otherwise he wouldn't be here.

Well, that's for you, all right. So you compose yourself, or try to, and watch him, staring so hard that you almost will him to look back at you. And you think he'll never look back at you. through all those slow crawling minutes, each marked by great ponderous thumps of seconds that synchronize so ruthlessly with your own sudden and riotous heart-beats, uncontrollable. You're about to give up, turn away. You've made a mistake. It's just an accident that he's here. And then suddenly, for a moment so brief that you can hardly tell whether it really happened or not, his eyes lift, meet yours for just the one fleet second, and then turn back to his own group again.

You can't really believe it; but yes, he looks again. A little longer this time, though still so quickly that no one else could see it. But it's long enough for you to have seen, and especially to have seen the eyes narrow just ever so slightly in acknowledgement and—could it also be acquiescence?

You're sure it's a sign, an agreement. Every fibre of your being goes singing out into that crazy, noisy, smoke-swilling, impossible room; and you stand there in a sweat of anxiety and anticipation until, thinking he has deliberately turned away from you with the inevitable brush-off, you suddenly realize that he is gazing into the mirror to take a better look at you. So you give him a nod, one of your quite unmistakable nods, half-fearing he'll turn away from you again with one of those unbearable looks of disgust. If he does, the whole night will come crashing down on top of you, and you'll give it all up again—well, for at least a week or two anyway. You almost expect it; can almost see it before it even happens. But no. No, not at all. What does he do but raise his glass and, still looking squarely into that distant reflection of your own importunate eyes, drains it in a silent toast.

You've forgotten Roy and Andy, forgotten the barmaid and

the very bar itself, forgotten everything but that look of promise and that silent, so private, so intimate gesture meant for you alone. Nothing else exists. The little wheel has spun, stopped, and the night is set. Nothing else matters at all. You're not even aware of anything else until, dragging you back from all those delirious speculations, those vivid anticipations, you realize that someone else alongside you has said something, and at first you think it must be either Roy or Andy. But it's not; it's Sid Needham of all people. And of course he has seen it all, and he's grinning just as though he had also been able to see everything that's been going through your mind.

"Like it, don't you?" he leers. And that smile of his is really the precise shape of a hiss. His is the kind of evil that oozes from every pore of his body, insidious. You try to sound off-hand:

"Yeah. It's not a bad slice."

"Not a bad slice!" Scoffing is not just second nature to Sid; it's his first. "Want to meet it?" he sidles.

You shrug, still trying to be off-hand.

"Oh, I think I can manage my own arrangements, thanks, Sid."

You hope that puts him in his place. But——

"It won't work, brother. On *that* one, I assure you, it just won't work."

"Oh?"

How much longer can you hide all your anxiety and trepidation from someone as indefatigable as Sid Needham?

"No. He just won't be picked up, that's all. Doesn't like it. He doesn't like anyone else to see it. You've got to be introduced. Then as far as he's concerned, it *might* be O.K. No, wait"—and one freckled little-old-maid's hand clamps on your shoulder—"I only said *might*. He's pretty fussy. But of course, my dear, anyone with *those* looks can afford to be."

There's nothing worse that you can think of than to become indebted in any way to Sidney Needham, but you can see, now, that it's inevitable. One glance back across the room is enough to tell you that all he says is probably true. Someone like that just wouldn't like being picked up. So you've got no option.

"All right, Sid," you say, still weighing the pros and cons of it, but knowing the scales are already tilted, "and what little name and address do *you* happen to want, in return?"

Sidney puts on his look of pained indignation, and it's all you can do not to fold up laughing.

"*Nothing*, darling. Nothing *at all*." And the upraised hands are the hands of the eternal usurer.

So—"Come off it," you say.

"I *assure* you, darling. Just say the word, and Mrs. Needham's little boy Siddie will take you *straight* over to the apple of your eye. Or no—I think it would be better if I brought *him* over *here*, away from all that bunch. By the way, his name's Cor."

"What?"

"Cor. He's Dutch. He landed on these fair shores while you were away in Europe, darling. And he drinks gin. So order one for the apple of your eye, and a tiny Scotch and water for little Siddie, and I'll be right back."

"What's in it for you, Sid?" you demand.

But again, the unctuous indignation.

"*Nothing*, darling. *Nothing* at all. I just think that you're two nice people who should get together, that's all."

You're about to make some retort but he is already gone, easing himself slowly back into the group he had left, and then you can see him sidling up to the one and only person in the room who matters, this Dutchman—Cor, was his name? Yes, Cor. You've heard it before: the pianist, Cor de Groot, also Dutch. Sid is talking to him now, and he nods, looks over, squeezes his eyes slightly and puckers that sculptured mouth into another fleeting expression of acknowledgement. And you can't bear to look any more, so you turn to the barmaid, only now realizing that Roy and Andy have joined another group going on to a party. So you order a gin, and a Scotch, and another beer.

Sid's clammy little hand on your own, and you turn and hardly know what to say, hardly know if you'll be able to say anything at all, as Sid makes the introductions with incredibly good behaviour, snaps up his drink and, even more unbelievably, goes. There is only tonight and this great hunk of Dutchman left standing before you.

"What do you have in your gin?" you manage at.last.

"Nothing, thank you."

His accent is what you might call thick. Dutch. Mannish.

"Nothing?"

"No. I'm Dutch."

"I know."

"We drink it neat."

"Well, it's *your* liver. Cheers!"

"*Proost!*"

"Pardon?"

"*Proost*. It's Dutch for 'cheers', I believe."

"Oh. Well, *proost!*"

So that's how you meet, as easy as that, as casual as that. And you can't help wondering: Will he also be as casual a lover? And you remember someone once telling you: You ought to have a permanent affair; nothing much comes out of casual affairs, you know, except casualties. It's strange that it should occur to you now. Superstitions, premonitions—is there something in them after all?

Will you ever remember what you talked about?—filling in those empty, anxious minutes until you could bring yourself to ask the one question you wanted to ask. You must have talked about something. The weather, maybe. No, football. He bought a round of drinks and you talked some more. Then it was your turn again. But when you went to call the barmaid, he said:

"I don't think we need any more. Do we?"

"No?"

"No. Too much is not good."

Even in English, his g's are those hard Germanic gutturals, you think to yourself, at the same time wondering if you can make the necessary arrangements with Roy and Andy. But before you can say anything else, he says—

"Shall we go?"

"Where?"

So important; your place, with parents, is definitely out. But——

"My place," he says.

There is the pressure of his hand on your arm, the firmest and yet gentlest of squeezes, restful, reassuring. And then you find yourself weaving across the crowded room and, almost in a kind of daze, stumbling out into the night.

2

ANYWAY, it's a promising start. He's got the place and you've got the transport. But as you walk down the steep hill to the car-park and look at the night-streets not so busy with traffic now, going downhill with your shoe-heels hitting hard on the pavement-blocks, and your soles flapping weightless just a split second afterwards, going down towards the dark gulf of the river with here and there lights knifing and plunging through its own dark private depths—it's then that the doubts and misgivings start to set in, as always.

In one sense you can hardly believe your good fortune in having someone like this Greek god—no, *Dutch* god—this *Cor*-fellow striding alongside you with his eyes deep in his own thoughts, it seems, and his hands even deeper in his trouser-pockets, because it's cold and he isn't wearing an overcoat. Maybe it's this one very simple fact, of his not having an overcoat on such a cold night, that sets the other sense going. Maybe he *is* rough trade, and only does it for money; and if there's something you can't stand, will never lower yourself to doing, it's paying someone to go with you. If they don't go with you because they like you, then you don't want them to go with you at all. Everybody's got to draw a line somewhere, you reckon, and that's where you've drawn yours. You're dead serious about it. More serious, perhaps, than about anything else in this so-called 'double life' of yours. Double? More like two twisted strands so closely interwoven that you can hardly tell which is which at times. It would be nearly impossible to try to separate one from the other, even if you wanted to—which you don't. And if you tried to cut out one strand, then the other would be too weak, too meaningless, to be looked upon as a life. You just wouldn't be *you* if you did. No, you just couldn't do it. All that you *can* do is to try and reconcile one way of life with the other as much as you can, not letting one intrude into the other. And in one direction it's necessary anyway, because there's a law against it; at least in this country there is. And even if there wasn't, you wouldn't want your normal friends, family, to know about it, because they don't understand; to them it's still something dirty, or depraved, mentally deficient, disgusting. Like those men who like women only when they're having their periods, or little girls. And what could be more disgusting than that! Prostitution, for another thing. Which brings you back to what you were thinking about in the first place.

Maybe this Dutchman alongside you, who makes every nerve and fibre of you twitch and quiver with desire, maybe he'll want money for it, either to earn a bit extra than what he gets from his ordinary work, or more likely just to blackmail his own conscience. *I-only-do-it-for-the-money* kind of thing. There are lots like that. And they really do seem to kid themselves with it, dumb idiots. But they must have some awful moments with themselves at times. Which is one thing you don't. You've got that old saying which, however flippant it may be, is nevertheless true: You're perfectly adjusted to your maladjustment!

So you look at him again, striding alongside you with his steps in time with your own, and you're not sure, not at all sure, whether it's him keeping in step with you, or you with him. And if it *is* you with him, then you haven't been at all conscious about it. If you're in tune with someone, perhaps you automatically find yourself in step with him too. It's an interesting thought, and you wonder if it happens with normal couples, a man and a girl, even though there is normally such a difference in just the length of their steps.

Yes, you look at him again and see the firm forehead beneath the silhouetted hairline, short-cropped, and yet almost like a plume, the way it flows back over his head so smoothly. His eyes are deeply entrenched, as though sheltering themselves from some kind of hostility. It's a good nose, too, long and straight. And you've already noticed the mouth. It's the first thing you did notice, as usual. Mouths are so important to you. You don't know why, but they are. Some people like eyes, or hands, or teeth, or the backs of heads. But with you it's always the mouth you notice about anyone; whether it's a slice you want to make or just any normal person outside of that sphere entirely, you always look first at the mouth. And it's usually this that makes you decide whether you like a person or not. A mouth expresses so much, particularly when it's not expressing words. And this mouth is firm and yet generous, 'sculptured' was the first word you thought of, as though some genius had just carefully and lovingly chiselled it. Beneath it is the chin, firm and well-shaped too, and—oh God another weakness of yours!—with a cleft in it. He could get money for a face like that, all right. Any time, anywhere. He wouldn't need to have the body to go with it, which it looks as though he has anyway. Yes, he could easily be for money. Usually, if they are, they make quite sure you're going to pay up long before you get this far, and he hasn't said anything about it yet. Hasn't said another word, matter of fact. He just walks there beside you, looking straight ahead of him, and all that you can see of his eyes, which might give you a clue if you could really see them, are the occasional little beads of light which they catch and hold for a second or two, catching the light from street-lamps as you go by, or from the headlamps of passing cars. But then those deep eyes of his soon drop these little light-beads again, and there are only shadows left. Darkness. And he seems so withdrawn into that darkness.

Yet, even if he isn't for 'rent', that's not the end of your worries. Maybe he's the beating-up kind. Get you to some place and then not only beat you up but make off with your wallet, your watch, and anything else of value. And what the hell can you do about it? Go to the police and say you picked up a *man* in a pub and then got robbed? *They* say you can, if you can ever trust them. But where does that get you? You know all too well where it gets you. . . .

But now you've reached the car-park, and found your car, and he stands on the other side of it, waiting to be let in, while you fumble with keys in the lock, open the doors, and then find your knees knocking a fair bit when you get in and start to manipulate the gears and things. And then he does say something, at long last.

"Nice car," he says. And that's an ambiguous statement if there ever was one, with all kinds of potential. Appraising the car to gauge how much to ask from you maybe? Or just an innocent remark, something to break the long silence? You won't know for a while yet. . . .

But it looks as though it is just an innocent remark, and a timely one too, for when you say: "Oh, it's enough to get me from here to there, and a few other interesting places in between," he seems to find conversation to come more easily. He starts off by telling you which way to go, just the name of the suburb, and not a bad one either, neither high-class nor low, but respectable, new. Then he tells you about other places he has lived in, that he's been out from Holland for nearly a year now, yes he likes the place, the climate is wonderful, he quite likes his job, and he's earning more money than he could ever get in Holland.

Well, that much is a relief anyway—he works and is satisfied with the money he gets. And as though to clinch the matter, he offers you a cigarette, and you say yes and ask him

23

to light it for you, which he does, lighting two together between those exquisite lips of his, then taking one out and passing it to you. And when you put it in your own lips, it's almost like a kiss. Yes, this pretty well clinches it, all right. It they're for money, they usually smoke only your cigarettes into the bargain.

So now you can ask him what kind of a job he does. And then comes a bit of a let-down. He's a bar-steward, he tells you. And a bar-steward doesn't go too well with an advertising agent, socially or in any other way. Working-hours for instance. But that hardly concerns you at this point of the game, or any other point more likely. All you've got in mind is tonight, or maybe the whole week-end if his place and what he does in bed are congenial—congenital?—enough. You never do want anything more than that, never even look for it—not any more. Three pretty disastrous affairs have been more than enough.

Yet in a way you're still a bit disappointed. He looks as though he should have amounted to something more than a bar-steward, even though he does tell you next that he works in a club, a men's private club, and one of the city's best at that. So he knows a lot of people around town, including people who count. But hardly as an equal; just to serve drinks to. Yes, it's a bit of a let-down, all right. Somehow with a face like that—and not only just the face itself, but also, yes, the kind of serenely satisfied expression it has—you feel that he could have amounted to something better. Something much better. Somehow you have the nerve to say as much to him about it, and when you steal a side-glance at him quickly, you get a lift-up again when you see him smiling quietly, smiling to himself, thinking about himself. Then he tells you that he had studied architecture in Holland for four years, only had a year to go, but then he came out to Australia, and now if he wants to take it up again he has to start from right back at the beginning. Another five years is a long time, he says, even if he could afford it, which he says he can't. In any case, he adds, he'd be well over thirty before he'd be finished, if he did start again. And that's a bit late in life to start earning your own living, he says, with that slow smile of his again, a kind of pain seeping through it all the time.

You don't have to know any more; you can see the whole picture. Hopeless.

"It's a pity you didn't finish in Holland before you came out," you suggest.

But he just shakes his head, no.

"It wouldn't have made any difference," he tells you. "I'd still have to do it all again. Europe's architecture just won't *do* for Australia," he adds. And it's not just sarcasm, but more a kind of light bemusement. "Like medicine and law, and several other things," he goes on, and the whole silly point of it rubs you so raw, you almost hate the country, the way it wantonly makes so much waste of its new migrants and, much more personally, treats people like yourself as some kind of criminal.

But here is the first real point of communication between you, and coming from where it nearly always comes from, a kind of commiseration. You feel it so acutely that, without any precautionary thought, you automatically take your hand from the steering-wheel and put it on his thigh, to give a squeeze of understanding. No more. But you get back much more. You get back so much that it's all you can do to stop from driving up a tree or something, for he quickly takes your hand in his and clenches it firmly. And not only that, but he holds on to it, the fingers intertwined with yours, even more firmly, nothing furtive or feminine about it as there so often is, and your two palms together are like two immense planes of both flesh and understanding, a kind of profound communion, something that is even more wonderful, perhaps, than already being in bed together.

He doesn't let go of your hand, but keeps it there, his thumb gently massaging the back of your wrist, and you wonder how long he'll go on holding it like that, and whether he can feel the way your whole body is trembling at his touch when he himself seems so quiet and calm about it. Then you yourself have to take your hand away to turn down the side-street he points out.

Soon there looms the vague bulk of a block of flats, and he tells you to leave the car on the grass verge between the road and the footpath, under the shelter of a huge old motherly looking gum-tree. But now you're both all stiff and silent with each other again. You don't know what he's thinking, although you know very well what *you're* thinking. For now comes the next thing to worry about.

It's a gound-floor flat he leads you to, with its own entrance. That's another big help, anyway—in case you want to get out again. Not too much fuss or noise, like stairs and lift-wells, doors and things. You watch the way that large hand of his, almost smooth of hair, handles the key in the lock, and this next inevitable fear swells within you. Not really a fear, but rather a kind of tremulous fascination. Yet it makes you feel a bit nervous anyway; it always does. Even if there's no longer anything to worry about—so far as money or getting beaten up, or being robbed is concerned—there is still the matter of finding out whether or not you're both compatible with each other, in bed. The hunt is always better than the actual kill, you always say. But the hunt isn't exactly over yet. It's never over until you hit the cot.

The door opens, and he reaches inside with one hand to switch on the light. But you haven't time to look inside; his hand comes back again and reaches for your own.

"I hope you will like my house," he says, in such tones cf solemn formality that it almost puts out of your mind what you have come for, it's so much a kind of welcome. And that's one thing you hardly ever get from your own kind, Australians. Somehow it's rather Continental, especially what he follows up with: "It's very small. But it suits *me* on the moment." And you notice again how he often says *on* the moment instead of *at* it, or even *for the present* or something.

"It looks fine," you say, still without having taken a single glance at it, because you can't take your eyes away from his face, or forget that his hand is still holding your own. And when he goes on holding it, leading you inside, it's almost as though he is carrying vou across a threshhold.

3

BUT of all things, formality again.

"Sit down and I'll make us some coffee," he says.

And that's just exactly what he does. No who's-your-uncle or anything. But of course you can see the point of it after a while, and know how right he is. Warm you up for one thing, and give yourselves time to get acquainted for another. The kind of touch that makes you feel more for a person than you can ever remember of scores of others. And out of all those, only three of them that you might ever call permanent; even then, none of those lasted. Does it, or will it, ever? But can you ever give up trying? Life is such a lonely business at the best of times, and your kind of life the loneliest of all.

So you sit sipping coffee, feeling it thaw out the chill core in your body, and you nearly spill it, slopping it on to the saucer and saying, no, it doesn't matter, don't bother to re-pour it, and you tip the slopped coffee from the saucer back into the cup, telling yourself that you must concentrate, at least a bit, and not keep feasting yourself on those wonderful hands and that sculptured mouth.

God, you've forgotten his name already, apart from Cor that is. You've got a mind like a sieve. Always did have.

"Van Gelder," he tells you, smiling that slow and almost luxuriant smile of his, whimsical. "Cor van Gelder." Of gold? you wonder to yourself. If so, it couldn't be more appropriate. Then, "What's yours?" he asks.

What's what? Where are you? Look at a picture or something for a minute, to take your mind off *that*. Then perhaps you'll be able to keep your mind on one thing at a time. There's only the one picture, and that's a print of an Australian landscape in water-colours, of all things. Strange; you'd have thought it would have been something Dutch, to remind him of home. Very strange, come to think of it; you can't see anything from Holland in the whole flat. Has he cast off his own country from him altogether? Was something there so painful that he doesn't want anything to remind him of it any more? It would have to be something like that, for him not to have even the one tiniest memento around. For all you can see, the flat could be just that of any Australian, and even then a very impersonal one at that. Strange, very strange. But——

"What's what?" you must ask him.

"Your name, of course."

"Ray."

"I know it's Ray. But Ray what?"

"Oh yes, of course. Wharton." You spell it for him, but then he takes out a notebook, a pen, and hands them to you.

Now is the time, you think. The first step towards a tidy little try at blackmail. But you have only to look at those eyes of his again, at that sculptured mouth, those hands, and you think to yourself: Yes, I can trust him. Instinctively. So you write down not only your name, but also your address, home and office, with telephone numbers. Then he does the same. And that's yet another formality over. Any more?

"I'm going to take a shower," he says. Then, probably because you have looked so astonished, he adds by way of explanation: "I went straight from the club to the hotel, at nine o'clock, and I've been working all day. I don't like to be smelling when I"—and he hesitates, and is that a smile of just shyness, or embarrassment?—"when I go with someone." So at least you know now that he does 'go with someone' as he puts it. How often? How many? But what has it got to do with you, anyway? You're acting the jealous lover already!

"O.K.," you say, and you pick up a magazine, *Esquire* you notice, and start to read. Or rather, you start to pretend to read, for, as casually as if you have known each other for years, he takes off his coat and drapes it over a chair, sits on the chair and takes off shoes and socks, stands again and

28

removes his tie. And then—still so unselfconsciously that you can hardly believe he isn't deliberately posing, titillating perhaps—he pulls his shirt from out of his trousers, and then up and over his head.

Torso. You can't really concentrate on that book, for that torso looks as though it was also sculptured. Body-building, perhaps? Can such chest and muscles and waistline come naturally? When you breathe again it almost hurts, and you swear it can be heard all over the room like a knife searing through canvas. Trousers and underwear go simultaneously, to be folded over the chair with the coat. And it's really too much, much too much, and you just *have* to stare at the short-story headline at the top of the page as well as at those legs and loins just beyond it. They breed 'em well in Holland. But then he steps into the shower leaving the door open to talk to you through it, still as unselfconsciously as ever, and you wonder if it's possible for pure lust to give someone a heart-attack.

How carefully and completely, how lovingly the water from a shower caresses a body. The first drops seem to alight, like tiny transparent birds, on to the parched skin. At first just a few, and then suddenly whole flocks of them, until quickly they merge and mingle, slide down those smoothly cream precipices of skin and flesh, surge gleaming over sheer marvels of muscles, dampen and darken that delicious delta of hair on the lower stomach, and the sparser delta of much finer hair sprouting from the small of that magnificent back, to taper into the sharp cleft of buttocks. Such an ugly word, buttocks, for so beautiful a combination of curves, cleft and columnal thighs. How inept is the English language at times. For as beautiful as breasts they are, and perhaps even more precisely formed, without being marred by the disfiguring flaws of nipples.

By now the drops are rivulets, and the rivulets cascades, flying from wide shoulders and powerful back, down the narrow and so exquisitely designed valley of the spinal column. avalanching over loins and thighs and down the full fantastic length of those languorous legs to feet and floor below. Cascades too, now, of froth and foam, like explosions of surf from some vertical sea or something—and the pleasant tang of the soap he uses. Small wonder there is such a tremendous sale in the U.S.A. (and other countries, too, you suppose) for cinefilms of athletes taking a shower. Yet so few women buy them. Mostly men. Naturally. And of course there are hundreds, thousands, who would more than willingly pay twice as much to see such a thing in the flesh, as a floor-show say, than they would for feminine counterparts in even the Folies Bergères. Guess it'll come to that one of these days—that's if it doesn't exist, surreptitiously, in some places already. Or rather, you should say, you guess it'll come *back* to that one of these days, like Roman baths and Greek games, all that sort of thing. Enough! That's not in the book you're supposed to be looking at . . .

The music of water fades and dies. The shower is turned off. Now there is the sound of rubbing, of towel on flesh, and you can't help but look up again to see how all the flesh glows, almost blossoms, after such passionate ministrations from the towel.

"You would like to have one too?" he suggests.

Why? But why not? Can you offer a body stale and a trifle damp in exchange for one so carefully prepared? Of course not. So you must take one. But you can't quite manage to undress with that same composure as he did. And once you step into the shower recess, even though he busies himself with collecting and washing the coffee things, you unconsciously close the door.

It is only when you too are bathed and dried, fresh and warmed again after the cold night air, that you can see both reasons for the shower—cleanliness, and warmth. But inside that clump of a chest of yours, your poor stupid heart is again a tormented thing, vulnerable, besieged once more by that last fear of all as you open the door. But you have only to look at him as he lies there, waiting for you, watching for you, those calm eyes of his searching so candidly for yours and, finding them, holding them so steadily, almost as welcoming as the one arm extended with its open palm, and you know that everything's going to be all right.

Hand of the eternal lover. Hand of the lover so long desired, through all the ages. Take it, and hold it. be grateful for it—and forget all those ridiculous fears of yours. After all, this *is* what you came for. Well, isn't it?

4

HE SLEEPS. Innocent as a child, with only the mildest of snores—more a breathing just slightly heavier than usual, really—he sleeps. And after all that. Well over an hour, really; or so you find when you can get your wrist-watch into a stray finger of light from the window. Of course, you *were* talking for a while.

His head rests on your shoulder. You can feel his breath warm on the base of your neck, and a curl of hair at your ear-lobe. One arm lies across your chest, his hand cupped around your other shoulder. A leg, warm and heavy, lies crooked over your own. The weight of it has made that old war-wound in your knee ache a little. You try to move your own leg, but the hand tightens suddenly on your shoulder, holding you closer, and he murmurs indistinguishable sleep-words in your ear. Something about a 'henk' or a 'hank'. A Dutch word probably. Then he relaxes and settles again, and you can almost feel his smile. You haven't the heart to disturb him again, so you just lie there, your heart flapping where your sleeve should be, and your soul hanging from somewhere up in the ceiling.

Lying there in a strange bed with this Cor asleep against you, the room, though you know it to be small, seems immense, immeasurable in the darkness. The only pale dim light that you can see, so remote, is from the window where, beyond a blurred segment of lintel, there are a few infinitesimal stars, tiny and wet-looking, cold, barely discernible as they twitch so wanly between cloud and wind-bruised cloud. All you want to think about is Cor, and to marvel at the near-miracle of what has happened between you, to contemplate in awe what he has just given you, so effortlessly and unembarrassedly that, contrariwise, it makes *you* the one to feel ashamed. Ashamed that, in the beginning, spontaneously, you had not been able to do the same for him. It makes you feel inferior somehow. And for the first time in your life you find yourself wanting to give yourself to someone within a few hours of having met him. Despite three so-called affairs, and scores— maybe hundreds by now—of casual encounters, this is the first time in your life you've ever felt that way. You feel it so much that you almost want to wake him up and have him do it. Yet somehow you can't. There is a kind of trust in that calm and innocent sleep of his, a trust you can't bring yourself to break, nor even disturb. No matter how much you want to, you just can't do it. You have to wait. Wait until he wakes himself and then, if he moves that way, that will be the time to give yourself. Right now it will be another kind of gift by waiting till then, restraining yourself. And already you recognize this as the tenderness of a lover, impossible in common lust. You recognize it and you know it, know it as well as you know your own name.

And that's why you're sunk.

No matter what happens between you afterwards, you know that things—life—will never be the same. You'll never again be able to think of anything, anyone, even life itself, without Cor. As the saying goes, you're in love, right to the end of the line. Hook, line and sinker. Sinker? Yes, you're sunk all right. And could you be happier about it? Have you ever been happier about anything in your whole miserably empty life before? If this is happiness, then by God you're almost bursting with it.

And quietly, gently, you move up your hand to close it

around the one on your shoulder. Squeeze. Under your fingers, those other fingers seem to squeeze too, sleep-drowsy. He moves a little. Closer towards you, if that's possible. And again there is something undiscernible murmured in your ear.

Sleep is beginning to swim round you too, like a slow, slow current of warm black air. Like the night. Mystic as the clouds sliding so sudden and silent against the sky. Distant, and eternal, like those cold wet stars.

Sleep . . .

5

SHRILL of alarm-clock and, faintly, far away, immediate derision from a rooster.

Your eyes fly open. And in those first few unknown seconds, of another world, you expect the day to fly in. But it's still dark, or almost. Beyond the window-sill the stars have also fled; and between great ragged patches of cloud, the sky is grey as a bruise. Dawn comes dank and wintery these days, reluctant, like the realization of where you are. But then, just as quickly, in a split second as it were, you know exactly where you are, for on one side of the second's split you have seen your car under the motherly gum-tree, half-dark as it still might be; and on the other side of the split, which holds you now in a kind of gripping disbelief, you see only Cor's face leaning over you. Unlike that of most bed-fellows you have known, there is no sourness on his breath, though you can only wonder about your own. Yet it must be all right, you think; for he lowers his head, smiling, and kisses you. Now is the time, you think to yourself, to show him that you *can* give as much as he. But no. Throwing back the bedclothes—and reluctantly, tenderly removing your hand—he says:

"I must go to work."

"What! On a Sunday?"

He smiles, stretching his body as though it has an armour of it own against the chill morning air. But then, you remember, he *is* from Holland; and winters there are much colder than here, so these cold mornings from which you yourself shrink probably mean nothing to him.

"Especially on Sundays," he says. "It's the busiest day at the club."

"Of course." And you wonder why you hadn't thought of this before. "But surely you don't start so early? Doesn't the club open at ten?"

"Yes," he tells you, and you marvel at how quickly he can dress, depriving your eyes of that body of his. "But"—and he smiles again, almost as though he is having to give some kind of instruction to a child—"there is much to be done before the bar can be ready. In fact, the hardest work of the week. I must be there by seven."

So gone are any ideas you might have had for spending the day with him.

"Oh, God!" you say. But it's really such a selfish thought. The morning is beginning to wash round the room, like greasy water slopping in a bucket. You don't quite know what you want to do. Stay here alone all day? Or go out somewhere alone all day? Either way, away from him, it will be alone. Lonely, and longing.

"Tonight?" you ask. "What time do you finish? I'll meet you."

But he shakes his head, crouching with bent arms over bent leg to tie a shoelace.

"I'm sorry, Ray"—how he seems to drawl your name, almost lovingly, almost with a diphthong instead of a vowel—"I'm afraid I have an appointment. You see, I did not know."

"Of course not," you concede, and you try hard not to look like a small and petulant child. "Oh, well——"

"Can I call you?" he asks. "To tell you when I'm free?"

What else is there?

"Yes, that's best. You have my numbers, don't you?"

"I know them by heart already," he says.

He is nearly dressed, and you know you must hurry if you are not to keep him late. You can drop him off in the car before going home; save the time spent in his catching a bus.

"You can stay here a while longer if you like, Ray," he says, when you suggest driving him to the club. "It's cold, and you look tired. Why don't you sleep again, and go when its warmer. You can let yourself out."

Rather the cold than the loneliness. No, you'll go.

"All right, then," he says; and as though you're not far enough gone as it is, he has to make one of those friendly, oh so intimate jabs at your shoulder with a playfully clenched fist. "I'll make us some coffee while you're getting dressed. I'd cook you some breakfast, but I don't think I have anything in on the moment."

'*On* the moment' again. But you wouldn't correct him; wouldn't want to change it for worlds.

"No, thanks," you call out to him as you start looking for clothes, shoes. "I couldn't eat a thing just yet. I'll have it at home, later."

It's true, you find; you just couldn't eat a thing right now.

Out in the car, what a queer world it seems. The streets so quiet and empty, only half-lit, and eery somehow, so early on a Sunday morning. Roosters still crowing, talking to each other from their own private horizons; quite a conversation they can have when the rest of the world still sleeps. Not everyone: a late milkman still delivering bottles. Glass-rattles as he runs. And now and again an old woman, or a youngish one, a youth, a man, or a whole family, all in church clothes hurrying echo-footed along hollow-sounding pavements. It's really not so quiet after all. Church bells. Wind whispers. You can hear quite a lot if you listen, when you think there's only silence. Silence is rarer than you think. Cor has it, just sitting there, saying nothing. And yet is it really silence? It's really as though he's talking to you, saying without words all that can

35

only be said without words. And you feel the same way. Even distances have shrunk. It's no time at all before you're back in the city, dropping him outside the closed, still-asleep doors of the club, and he's saying:

"Thanks for the lift, Ray. I'll call you. Monday or Tuesday."

You watch him let himself in with a bunch of keys he has taken from his pocket. Every movement is decisive, manly. No one seeing him now would ever think . . .

A wave of the hand, and he is gone.

Strange, but this city street is quite deserted. Not even a dog. Makes you wonder if any of it really happened, or if it was all just a dream, a dream turned into some kind of wishful sadness, now that you're awake. And it's over. You don't know why, but you find yourself looking down at the seat beside you, where so short a while ago *he* was sitting . . .

Well, that's something; it's not empty after all. He's left his wallet there. Accident? Or does he mean to make certain that he does see you again? You *could* take it in to him. Just knock on the door and hand it to him. But no. If it is an excuse he's made, then it's good enough for you. So you slide the wallet into your pocket and, feeling much happier about things now, drive away into that milky milkmen's morning.

All the same, it'll be a long day today, for any Sunday. And longer still till tomorrow, or Tuesday. Maybe by then you won't be as sunk as you think you are. But that's a silly thought, too. You know you're sunk all right. What's more, that's just how you want to be.

Well, it'll give the old folks a shock, you guess, but it looks like gardening for you today, my boy. Do you good to get into some digging, while you think about whatever may be ahead of you—if anything. So home with you, wherever it may be . . .

6

IT'S one of those days when there's not much sense in doing anything else anyway, overcast all day by the look of it, with now and again a bit of fine drizzle, like an inward weeping. No sun and too cold for the beach, or even tramping through the bush. Not enough rain to drive you indoors all day, or even to drink.

So the garden it is. Digging's good for you, anyway. Always was, ever since when you were a kid, about five or six you suppose, and your Uncle Kev—your father's youngest brother, about sixteen he'd been then—had taken you down behind the grapevines and undone his trousers and showed it to you. And you, knowing somehow there was something wrong about it, if only because of the furtive, secretive way it had to be done, instead of openly and somehow naturally like everything else, had nevertheless been fascinated by it. It had seemed such an impossible thing to grow from a little thing like your own, till you remembered how big a man was compared with the little baby he grew from. Fascinated, you were. Warm like the hot-water bottle your mother gave you, winter nights. Unbelievable. Would yours grow big like that one day? You could hardly believe it; looked at it every day, in the bath and in the lavatory, to see if you could see any difference from the day before. But there never seemed to be, and sometimes you despaired of it ever growing up like Uncle Kev's.

Yes, you'd known there was something wrong about Uncle Kev showing it to you, and you looking at it, but nevertheless you'd wanted to once you'd seen it. And it didn't take much persuasion—about the good fairies not bringing you anything for birthdays and Christmas and so forth, if you didn't—for you to touch it like Uncle Kev had wanted you to. Seeing is believing, they say. But not for kids and babies it's not. They want to touch everything, just to prove to themselves that it's really real. And Uncle Kev had had a packet of lemon drops, so it was inevitable. How strange and wonderful it had been, with the grapevine leaves sometimes half-transparent in the sun or darker in the shade all rustling around you, rising and rippling, falling again, like little waves on a wind-wrinkled sea, sibilant. Even now, you still get excited at the smell of grapevine leaves, so pungent they are when you crush them between your fingers.

"Don't tell anyone," Uncle Kev had said, putting it away again and cleaning you up with his handkerchief, and that's the smell you always half-hope to smell again when now you crush grapeleaves in your hands. But you need an Uncle Kev for that. And you kept your promise because, as kids do, you had crossed your heart and sworn to die, and because you had liked your Uncle Kev so much, and also because you had known your father or your mother would have done something awful to you if you had ever told them; they wouldn't have understood. They hadn't ever talked much to you about the good fairies and the wicked fairies and so forth like Uncle Kev and even Grandma had. But also why you didn't tell them, more than the rest, was because you had known Uncle Kev came every month, and it had been a big and wonderful secret between you that you hadn't wanted ever to end.

That's when the digging had started, gardening. About the third or fourth time—it's impossible for you to remember now—your mother had come out to call you, and had looked a bit funny at you both when, after a while, you had to come out from behind the grapevine, and she'd asked you what you'd been doing, and of course you couldn't say, even if you hadn't promised not to. But it was Uncle Kev who had found the answer.

"Oh, he wants to have a garden of his own," he'd said, just as though that was what had really happened, "and I've been

38

finding a place for him, right down the back there, where it won't matter if he makes a bit of a mess."

How clever, how wonderful it had been of Uncle Kev. For your mother, and your father too, had been very pleased about it, and every now and again they had even given you plants and things out of the big garden in the front to put in your own garden behind the grapevine. So of course there had to be a garden, and you had loved it, having one all of your own. You had loved it even for the garden's sake, it had been so interesting to watch the little plants you put in it grow up and have buds and things and then—oh, marvels that they had seemed, because they had been your very own—burst into flower. Yes, you had loved that little garden, even if it hadn't been so that you and Uncle Kev could then stay behind the grapevine as long as you wanted to.

How long did that go on for? You can't quite remember. Years maybe. And no one—no one at all—ever knew. It was just between you and Uncle Kev, because, as he said, the two of you were *kindred spirits*. Eventually, Uncle Kev grew to look like a real man, but it still didn't change things as far as you were concerned, and you were really very proud when people said how wonderful it was the way he loved you so, and you loved him, and none of them really knowing how much. Uncle Kev grew to look like a real man, all right, and got a girl-friend and became engaged to get married. But it didn't make any difference to you. In any case, you hadn't expected it to, then. After all, he didn't get married. The engagement was broken off; and only you, really, knew why; and you hugged the secret of it all to yourself even more than that first secret between you, it was all so wonderful. And you were growing up, too. Of course you soon noticed it, it all seemed to happen so quickly. It seemed to start growing within a few weeks. And of course Uncle Kev noticed it too, and did for you what up till now only you had been able to do for him.

Your mother and father were going away for a holiday, and taking your little brother and sister with them because they weren't yet going to school, and you were. So you were going to have something better, they told you. Even they didn't know how much better it was than they would ever have thought. You were going to stay with Grandma and Uncle Kev, and it seemed only natural that Grandma should make up a bed for you in Uncle Kev's room. Now you didn't have to go behind a grapevine or anything.

Uncle Kev didn't wear any pyjamas to bed. This had seemed kind of shocking to you at first, you always wore pyjamas. But when you saw that Uncle Kev didn't, then you wanted to be a man too, so you took yours off, first the trousers, under the blanket, and then the coat. But the coat hadn't been so easy, in bed. Uncle Kev had laughed, watching you, and then he had come over and taken the coat off for you, and you could see he was getting *that* way again. So it seemed quite natural that he should get into your bed with you, to cuddle you a bit, and whisper secrets like when you had still been small. Him so warm and close beside you, and you talking baby-talk again. But it was such a small bed, and Uncle Kev's so big, that you were glad when he suggested going over to his bed.

How he cuddled and kissed you! Much more than your father had ever done, or even your mother. How you wished that Uncle Kev could have been your father, so that he could sleep with you every night and cuddle you, all warm and close together with your skins touching. And it seemed as though you had almost become a part of Uncle Kev. You thought you would die of your happiness, until Uncle Kev had started to ...

You didn't think it was possible. And it hurt. You started to cry and asked him not to. So he stopped for a while. But then he started again, and his arms around you were too strong to get away from, and if you struggled too much it hurt all the more, and you cried and cried. He kept on saying "Ssssh!" all the time, "Grandma will hear." And you wanted Grandma to hear, yet at the same time you didn't want her to hear, then did want her to hear. But she was deaf, Grandma was, and sleeping in her own room on the other side of the house. You could have screamed your lungs out and she wouldn't have heard. And in any case it was better for you not to struggle. So you just lay there, still, and then suddenly it didn't hurt any more. Besides, Uncle Kev was really a part of you now.

"You've got to do it to become a man," Uncle Kev had told you. And you'd believed it. You had believed everything Uncle Kev told you. So you believed this was what you had to do to become a man, and you wondered who had done it for Uncle Kev. Had he had someone as nice as Uncle Kev himself was? All the same, you were glad when it was over. You thought you'd never be able to go to sleep, but you did.

In the morning you had looked at yourself to see if you had become a man, but you couldn't see any difference. You'd wanted to tell Grandma about it, but it was always so difficult to tell Grandma anything, she was so deaf. Besides, Uncle Kev had told you not to, otherwise it mightn't work, and you wouldn't become a real man. And you had wanted to become a real man more than anything else in the world, like some of the really big boys at school were. And what Uncle Kev had said must have been true, because you knew that some of the big boys also did that to each other, and to some of the smaller boys too, in the lavatories at the far end of the playground. Sometimes one of the young teachers did it; you've forgotten his name now, but he'd been very good-looking, youngish. You hadn't seen it for yourself, but Georgie, your friend, had said he had seen it, and you had half-thought that Georgie had been the one the teacher had done it to, though Georgie wouldn't admit it.

After that, you couldn't wait for night to come, to be with Uncle Kev. Every night. And no one ever knew. No one. You cried like a baby when it was time to go home, but Uncle Kev promised he'd ask your father if you could come and stay every week-end, or nearly every week-end. And that had made you feel better. You didn't tell anyone why. Not a soul. Not even Georgie at school. Somehow it had been something just between you and Uncle Kev, you had loved each other so.

But Uncle Kev hadn't kept his promise. He hadn't been able to. That very first week he had been killed on his motor-cycle.

And no one, not your mother or your father or your grandma or anyone, had really known why you had cried so much, night after night, week after week. And you couldn't bring yourself to believe that Uncle Kev was dead, not even when you had gone to see his grave in the cemetery, and it had had his name on the tombstone to prove it. You had felt sure that Uncle Kev would come back, that he'd only gone away for a while and would soon come back to you. He couldn't leave you like that, for ever. He just couldn't.

But he did. And never again was there another Uncle Kev. Even now no one knows what was really between you. No one ever will. Would anyone ever be to you what Uncle Kev had been? And you had never again let anyone do what Uncle Kev had done with you, even though at times you wanted it so much. But that had been just for Uncle Kev alone. No one else.

After that, you had worked a lot in your garden. Not only your first little one at the back behind the grapevine, but in the others around the house. At first just at the back of the house, and then the front. And soon your father had let you do all the gardening. The whole garden had become your own particular province, as it still was.

Digging there. The grapevine was huge now. Joke—it could hide a football team! But don't think about your Uncle Kev any more. That was all years ago, way back in the past. Dead. Dead and buried. Just like Uncle Kev. And now *you've* become another Uncle Kev. But not with any nephews of your own. You couldn't. Besides, there aren't any. Which is probably a good thing. No, it isn't Uncle Kev you think about from now on. Cor . . .

7

ALL day Monday at the office, and no call. Monday night at the house, and you stagger the family by staying home and watching the telly for once. Tuesday at the office; but again nothing. He's not going to phone; he's just not going to. Every nerve and bone shrieks it at you. *He's not going to phone.* He couldn't have lost the phone numbers. Easy to look them up in the book anyway, even if he can't remember them like he said he could.

So what'll you do? Ring him? Not till Wednesday, maybe Thursday—if you can hang out that long. Must show a bit of indifference too; pretend you have been busy. Don't let him know how eager you are. Eager! About half out of your mind . . .

No, he won't phone; that kind doesn't, you tell yourself. But then, on Tuesday night, at home, just as you're going to bed, he does. And you have to make the call short and not even sweet. Pretend it's from a business colleague or something, with the old folks and the kid sister half-listening. Can't say any of the things you really want to, not even when *he* says them. But you can tell he's calling from a public phone-booth. There's nothing much you can do, except make an appointment for Friday night, because he says he can't make it on Saturday. He doesn't even mention the wallet, and you forget all about it until he's rung off.

So Friday it's to be, not Saturday. Convenient in a way. Just so happens that Bruce Farnham—Professor Bruce Farnham, that is, in charge of the biochemistry department at the university—asked you for dinner next Saturday, and you were a bit hedgy. Now you can accept. He's got a 'visiting fireman' or someone over from the east, some big-wig in the government, nicknamed 'The Duchess' in the circle. Might be worth your while to meet him, you never know. And you can talk to Bruce about Cor. That'll rock him, you tell yourself; you on the steady again.

8

IT's almost as though he's brought you luck. On top of the usual rush programme, you land a new contract (for men's underbriefs, illustrations to use live models; that'll tickle the rest of the girls!) and you're as busy as hell all the week, lining up models and photographers, sketching roughs for the new sponsors, layouts. It's always the same; they take weeks, months maybe, to make up their minds, then want everything dropped in their laps within a few days—minutes, if they could have it their way. Yet in a way it's a good thing; keeps your mind busy. Even so, the week goes slowly enough; seems almost to go backwards at times, or have a few extra days thrown in just for the hell of it.

Then it's Friday, and you find yourself having to rush like hell just to be able to make it at eight. No time to go home to change. Have a shower in the office building, put on the same tacky clothes. Not so bad though. Good job it's winter; summer would take the bloom off them a bit. Reminds you of your own deodorant ads. Still, you can always have a shower at Cor's place again no doubt. In fact, that's half of what you're looking forward to. Maybe you'll have it together this time. Christ, ten to eight already. You'll just make it if you hurry, and if you're lucky with the traffic lights.

He's not there. You've made it on time, all right; your wrist-watch tallies with the town-hall clock. But he's definitely not there. Have to go round the block again; no parking space. Second time round and you just about sink through the flooring, clean on to the road; for he's still not there. You're about to go around again when, out of a chance flick of the eye, you spot a taxi pulling in at the kerb, someone getting out of it, paying the fare. And sure enough it's Cor. Navy-blue blazer and grey flannel trousers, and again no raincoat or anything. Looks quite sporty, as though he's going to a gym. Just seeing him makes you feel like you've won a lottery or something; on top of the world. You toot the horn and he looks up, waves —just as though he's known you for years. It's only a few seconds between when he has paid off the taxi and he comes over to you, but it seems ages.

Then: "How are you on the moment?" he says.

On the moment again.

"Fine."

He smiles. And you had almost forgotten the leisurely slowness, almost an opulence, of that smile of his.

"That's good," he says. By which time he is in the car beside you and, keeping his hand well below the dashboard, he reaches out to squeeze your thigh. Squeeze of the eyes to go with it. He dosen't have to say it, but it looks as though the week has been just as long for him as it has for you. Then, just before you pull away from the kerb, you hand him his wallet.

"So that's where I left it," he says, and he seems genuinely pleased to have found it again. Which makes you think that his leaving it in your car might have been purely an accident after all. "I thought I might have," he added, "but I—I didn't like to ask you about it."

"Didn't like to! Why ever not?"

"I—well, I thought that—you see, I——"

And it suddenly dawns on you, he thought you might have taken it. Or, not quite so bad, just kept it after finding it in the car. After all, you didn't say anything about it when he called you on Tuesday. Oh, the irony of it! The pure farce of it! And it's as though you have both just seen the whole joke of it together, and you both laugh, and it seems to set the evening off at a wonderful start.

"And I thought *you* would want money," you tell him.

At first he is incredulous, almost shocked.

"You didn't!" he says. And it's almost a protest. "What on earth made you think that?"

"You just don't look the regular type. The little nancy-boy, I mean."

"Is that what you're supposed to look like, just because you want to love another man?"

He is so serious about it, it makes you feel almost ashamed at having treated it as some kind of joke. So this time it's your turn to reach over and squeeze his thigh.

"No, Cor," you say, and you mean every word of it. "You don't have to look that way at all. In fact, if you did, I wouldn't have wanted you in the first place."

"It's the same with me," he says simply.

"Matter of fact," you go on, wanting to keep the conversation going, without lapsing into one of those silences of his you remember so well, and also to find out a little more about him in the process—"I often wonder why the nellies let themselves get that way. They ought to have enough sense to know that they defeat their own purpose by acting like girls. And not even decent girls at that. The sillier ones. Little spoilt and pretentious bitches. Once they let themselves get like that, even dressing up as women sometimes, I wonder who in the hell ever wants to go to bed with them. I reckon if a bloke's really homo, he wants to go to bed with another man, not a parody of a woman."

"Parody?"

"Sorry. An imitation of a woman, but an imitation in rather bad taste."

"I understand. And what you say is right. I too want to go to bed with a man, and to have a man of my own to love. If you want something that looks like a woman, then you should go with a woman."

This is a little blunter than you usually get, this woman-talk, especially when it sounds as though he means it.

"You've been to bed with women then?"

"Plenty. Of course." He says it as though you have merely asked him if he has ever eaten dinner out or something. And you know it's no bluff, no idle boasting. He means it, all right, which surprises you in a way. And yet, in another, it doesn't at all surprise you. Besides, you know all too well that a lot of Continentals, even the self-proclaimed homosexuals, are bisexuals. So it shouldn't at all surprise you with someone like Cor. But what does rather set you back is his next question—after another rather devastating statement, that is:

"I think I've been to bed with many more women than I have men," he says. "Haven't you?"

You can't see the sense in lying to him already, even if you wanted to. So you say:

"No. No, I haven't."

"You've been with more men than women?" he asks, almost incredulous.

There's still the opportunity to avoid the issue, even if it is such a small lie that hardly has anything to do with the two of you. But somehow you can't, not with Cor. So you take a good deep breath and come out with it.

"I haven't been to bed with a woman at all," you manage to say. "Never. Only men." And now that's over with. But you might just as well go the whole hog. "And I don't think I ever will. To tell you the truth, Cor, I don't think I can. I don't think I could do anything. So in that respect, at least, I guess you could call me a virgin. And I'll probably stay that way."

He doesn't say anything for a while. And you can't tell whether he's incredulous, or perhaps despising you a little. Maybe he's the type, like so many, who are really normal, but like a dabble on the other side of the playpen occasionally. And they're the type you think you hate most of all—the occasional dabblers, just for the hell of it, but never daring to admit to themselves that they really like it, have a craving for it.

47

Can't face up to themselves, mostly. They're also the most dangerous types, the ones to sneer at you if ever an issue is made of it, among squares, and the first ones to talk about you in normal circles. They're really more like bitches than most of the little nellies can ever be. So, is that what you think Cor is ? Well, if he is, you'll have to change your mind about a few things, that's all. Or else lower your own standards a bit. For if there's one thing you do know, it's that you're too far gone with him now even to try to pull out.

But it's not that way at all. After being so quiet about it, and for so long that you know he's still thinking about it, you're not at all surprised when he says:

"I'm afraid I haven't been as good about it as you have, Ray." His voice is so low, you have to listen carefully to catch the words.

You try to think of something to say back to that, but you can't. And after a while you realize that it's not really necessary to say anything at all: probably spoil it if you do. So you just button up for once, and say nothing.

You stay quiet again for you don't know how long. But it's Cor who speaks next. For once you haven't been trying to find something to say, you've been so busy thinking how well the evening has started between you, despite what you might have been afraid about during the week. But——

"Where are you going ?" Cor says suddenly.

"Your place, of course," you tell him. "You know we can't go to mine. All the family's there."

And then the beautiful beginning is all over. The doubts and difficulties set in, right from that very moment. For——

"Oh, I'm sorry, Ray," he says. "We can't go to—to my place tonight. You see, I—I share it with a friend. And he—well, he wouldn't understand this—this sort of thing."

That's busted the caboodle all right. Pull up to the kerb and sort yourself out with the gears; slip yourself back into neutral.

"He was away in the country last week-end," Cor explains, "so it was all right. But he's back again on the moment, so we can't——"

"I understand," you find yourself saying, and then you also find yourself saying what you have to say, to get things clear right from the start. "This, er, friend of yours. You're living with him? I mean, as a lover or something?"

Now wait for what comes out of that one. Reassurance? Or a neat little knockout drop? But——

"Oh no, Ray. Nothing at all like that. It's just to—well, sort of cut down on expenses, until I get myself on to my own feet. I couldn't afford such a place on my own on the moment, so we——"

Breathe out again.

"I understand, Cor," you say. It's not necessary to know any more. Of course he'd be likely to share a flat with someone. And that someone, for a person like Cor, couldn't possibly be a little nellie or something. With someone like Cor it would be bound to be a square—not only to keep up appearances; he probably prefers it that way, no matter the disadvantages at times.

Well, that's that. Now you've got to think of something else. But of course: Roy and Andy, and their spare room. Pick up a few bottles from a pub—a *square* pub, not the Palais tonight, thank you—and then drive out there. Pity they're not on the phone. It'd be just your luck to find them out. Still, your chances are better on a Friday than they would be on a Saturday; they'd be bound to be out. Now all you can do is hope that they're homeloving types, Fridays.

Then it occurs to you that maybe Cor wouldn't like it. So you have to ask him, tell him about Roy and Andy, assure him that they're good types, won't want to butt in or anything, although maybe they'd like a peek at him in the bathroom afterwards, specially Andy. You're half afraid he's going to say no when you've explained it to him, but he seems to take it all right. So out you go.

Your luck is out, all right; they're not home. You can't think where to go next; can't take the risk of booking into a hotel, not in this town, not even if you took two singles and spiffed the expense. That's just the kind of risk you can't afford to take. But maybe Roy and Andy will come home again, if you wait a while. You can only try; it's about your only hope. So you open a bottle and you sit there, talking, and drinking from the bottle, quietly, and you don't really care how long you have to wait, it's so good just to have him with you again.

When the first bottle is finished, and you find that only a quarter of an hour has gone by, you begin to wonder if perhaps Roy and Andy aren't somewhere at the back of the flat, doing some painting or something, and haven't heard the bell. So you go back again, knowing full well it's mostly wishful thinking, and you're really not at all surprised when, this time, you see a note pinned to the door. Striking a match, you read: No Milk Till Monday, Thank You. And then you know they've gone away for the week-end. Pity you didn't think of asking them before; you could have had the whole flat to yourselves. But it's too late now. Just your luck.

By now it's also too late to go to a movie or somewhere, and yet much too early to take the risk of going to a park. In any case, you don't at all care for doing it in the car, it's so damn risky—and uncomfortable.

The funny thing is, Cor doesn't seem to mind at all. He just sits there, smiling most of the time, you can only suppose with happiness. But at times when you look at him, sideways, that grin of his makes him look almost idiotic. It's not a very comforting thought. Queer, they call us, the squares do. And sometimes you can see why; the behaviour of some of you *is* so damned queer. But then you remember what it was like the first night with Cor; and if anyone seemed less queer, then it was he. Must be just a trick of the light perhaps. Anyway, you've got to think up something else now.

Then you could beat your brains out! Why on earth didn't you think of it before? You've got a key to the office door as well as to your own. No divan or anything, but glasses for the beer and a carpet on the floor. And it couldn't be more convenient, right in the heart of the city, and you can park the car right outside as well so that, if anyone should see it, they won't at all wonder what you're doing there. You can't help it, you just burst out laughing, and it's some time before you can stop yourself long enough to tell Cor the joke. And then b)th of you are laughing almost all the way back to the city.

Electric radiator and everything; what more could you ask for! A roll on the carpet right alongside the desk in your own office. Toilet, hot shower and all. Not as good as at Cor's place, but it'll do; could be much worse. Never thought you'd enjoy your office so much . . .

Afterwards you think that, in a way, it's a good thing you haven't got a place to stay all night. Cor has to work in the morning, and a good night's rest will do you good too. Again you're so happy about things, generally, even happy about having to wait for another week, that you don't think anything of it when Cor asks you if you wouldn't mind dropping him off at another address, instead of at his flat, he'd arranged to stay with a friend of his, he says, to give his flat-mate a chance to entertain his girl-friend.

The suburb is an old one this time, yet still within a mile of Cor's flat. This other friend of his lives in one of those houses that should have been pulled down after the war, but will probably stand till the next one. Solid enough, but so damned ugly. Pinched little rectangle of a garden, neglected by the look of it, before a pinched little rectangle of house-front. Pretty dark street, too. Dark enough to kiss each other good-night without having to worry about it, or even hurry it up. And when he has gone, you find yourself singing all the way home, at the top of your voice, the car's engine humming a sort of accompaniment. Just a big happy kid.

9

SATURDAY you start having crazy thoughts. Unless you really do something about it, it doesn't look as though you'll ever have much of a life together, you and Cor. And that's how it's got by this time. You can't stop yourself thinking about it, about having some kind of a life together.

Your own life is mostly working flat out all during the week, from Monday morning to Friday night, and most nights into the bargain, either really working on some new plug or something, or else just meeting clients, having drinks with them and getting new contracts. It's essential.

So that leaves the week-ends. You've always made a point of keeping those to yourself—to your real self, that is. Otherwise you'd go clean off your rocker.

But Cor doesn't have any free week-ends. In fact, that's his busiest time—naturally, in a private club. The members are more often there over week-ends than during the week. So from Saturday morning till Sunday night Cor is having to work flat out. True, you can meet him late, Saturday nights. But that's hardly fair on him, he does need *some* sleep. And his one free day is Monday, when you yourself have to work, and an afternoon during the week whenever he feels like it, but when you still have to work. So when do you see each other? —apart from just a snatched hour or two, which is really no kind of a life together. Pretty sordid, come to think of it—like a series of quickies.

The only answer is to get a place of your own. The family's house, naturally, is out. So is Cor's, with his friend living with him. And it's not very likely that he can just ask his friend to get out, just like that. No, that's impossible. Without some real reason or other, the bloke'd be bound to think there was something a bit fishy somewhere. And if he snooped around enough, he'd soon find out what and get nasty maybe; those types often do. Or else he'd just gab it around the town, and that's be a pretty kettle of fish!

No, a place of your own is the only answer. At least, then, you'd have nights together. And that would be a bit more like some sort of a life of your own. It'll hurt the old folks, though. Still, they ought to understand; a bloke's got to break away from the old apron strings some time or other. To get married, normally; then they never even question it. But this is different; even if it does, in a way, amount to almost the same thing. But you can't very well tell your own family you're leaving home to go and live with another man. They'd throw a fit. But what you *can* say is that you need to be nearer to the office and have a place of your own for entertaining business people. They should understand that all right. You can't ask people back home because the old folks always go to bed so early. And anyway, it's not their kind of life at all. In a way, it would be an intrusion into their home, bringing back business acquaintances. Especially some of them.

No, that's the answer, all right. And you guess Cor can soon think up some reason or other too. The same excuse, you reckon; he wants to be nearer to town because of the late hours he has to work sometimes. So a flat right in the city is the answer, for both of you. And there are hundreds of blokes —gays *and* squares—who share flats to cut down expenses.

Yet there's still that bit of a difference in your social status. A bar-steward doesn't sound so good, living with an advertising agent. But yes, you should have thought of it before; you can always say that he's really an architectural student. After all, that's what he did in Holland. Come to think of it, that's not such an empty idea after all. Right from the start you thought that he could amount to something better; in fact that he *should* amount to something better. Well, maybe he still can. If he's so much happier in his personal life, then perhaps he'll want to go back to his studies, spare-time. And then he would amount to something after all. It may not necessarily have to be architecture, which takes such a long time; if he's got the talent for that, then he might also have the talent for your own line. It's a bit of a wild one, but you could always sound him out. And if he does have a flair for it, then you've always got room for an assistant; maybe even a partner, later on. Of course, his language might be a bit of a handicap. And yet that's just a lot of nonsense, too, He may have a bit of an accent, but he can talk with you about almost anything at all. And Barbara, like any good secretary, has to clean up even your grammar and syntax, or whatever it is; so she can do the same for Cor. On the other hand, he may have some rather bright ideas, coming from the Continent. And God knows, local advertising could do with some bright ideas.

The more you think about it, the more everything seems to be fitting into place. If two people really want each other, then they've just got to make it possible, that's all. You don't get anything in this world handed to you on a silver platter. Nor even a brass one. Not usually, anyway. Getting Cor is about as much as you could ever ask for. The rest is up to you— same as ordinary normal people, you suppose.

Anyway, one thing about it, you couldn't be happier thinking it all out, planning it all out. When you really think about it, you can't remember having ever been happier in your whole life before. You don't even want to remember what life was like before you met Cor, and you certainly don't want to go back to it. You can't even contemplate any more what it would be like without him. Life just wouldn't be life, that's all.

So now you can start looking for vacant flats in this morning's paper, right now.

10

DINNER with Prof. Farnham. The lot. Drinks first, till you're nearly pie-eyed with Scotch. Then soup, fish, roast, sweets, coffee and nuts! You don't know how he does it. No help. Does the lot himself. Cleans his flat as well. Where does he get the time for it, let alone learn how to do it all? Yet the flat is spotless, dinner as though it's been cooked by a professional chef. He just doesn't look the type that turns into a housewife. Six foot three in his socks and built like a Trojan. Must terrify the sailors when he's marauding the docks! He doesn't look at all life a professor, with lectures and work at all hours of the day and night, and those learned theses or whatever they are he writes. You just don't know how he does it. But old Bruce does it, all right; what's more, he seems to revel in it. He even makes home-made chocolates with liqueur centres that you can't buy anything like in the shops. And if the flat needs curtains or cushions or something, or a chair needs re-upholstering, then he does that himself too. Drives his car like a professional racer. Water-skis and plays tennis and squash, swims all through the year. Catches interstate and overseas planes like anyone else would catch a bus. Looks more like some professional sportsman than a professor; or a mountaineer like a second Hillary. You doubt if anyone would ever pick *him* for a nancy!

"Glad to see yer, mate," he drawls, as always, and his voice doesn't go with either of his personalities, professor *or* gay. He's one that's way out if there ever was one. A handshake like a rock-crusher, yet as tender as a chicken in the cot, they say. But not your type to find out. Just a good friend. A very good friend. One of the best, reliable. Always reliable.

His guest from the east is fattish, fortyish, with red hair going bald, freckles. Bruce tells you he's the chairman of some sort of governmental tribunal, just visiting the state for a few days before going back again. They've been friends for years, Bruce says, and you can't imagine why, he seems to have so little of interest, personally or—very definitely—physically. He puts on a bit of a pompous act for a while, for the first five minutes or so. But he soon starts to unbend once Bruce gets his camp cackle going. Unbend? He unbends so much he gets as limp as a dead lily. All the grandeur and pomposity has gone with the hairpins, and he's just another aging and rather sad old aunty. And you can't help wondering what the rest of the tribunal would say if they could see their chairman now. Never believe it, of course.

More Scotch and lots of mad chatter; seems as though they've both been around the world not once or twice but dozens of times. Makes your own one jaunt seem like a weekend in the hills. But at least when you travelled, you did travel. Quite a good tourist even if you can't help yourself from sneering at things like organized tours and so forth, like most of the gays do. But you did see the things that everybody should see, if they ever get the chance. Things like mountains and cathedrals, museums and art galleries, life in the cities above the seams. All that these two seem to have seen are the same gay clubs, camp bars, notorious pubs, streets, parks, public lavatories and pissoirs all over the globe—which rather surprises you from old Bruce, but maybe he's only talking about such things because his friend seems to have nothing else to talk about. It's the kind of talk, and that part of gay life, that makes normal people hate the camps. And you can quite understand why. You hate it yourself. Despise it. It's all pretty disgusting really, and you can't understand the people who can find excitement only in that kind of thing. And yet you have to admit that you've got to resort to it yourself every now and again, when you get a bit desperate for a slice and you haven't got anything steady. But that's all over with now, you tell yourself. All over and done with—now that you've found Cor.

You're itching to tell Bruce about him. But somehow you can't bring yourself to talk about Cor, or anything that means anything at all to you, in front of this tired old aunt. So it looks as though you'll just have to let it slide. But as it turns out, around midnight or so, Auntie says she must get herself back to her hotel, or she'll find herself out in the streets chasing the milkmen. And besides, she says, she has to get her beauty sleep. She always refers to herself as 'this old girl' or 'tired old sheila' or something. Something you also hate, that kind of talk. And yet you've already started thinking of him as 'her' yourself. You should offer to drive him—her—into the city, you suppose. But you just couldn't stick twenty minutes of that inane yabbering in your ear all the time, so you just keep mum. Anyway, it's really up to old Bruce to offer first. And it's not till Auntie had finally gone, 'whisked away in a tiny little old taxi', as she says, that Bruce tells you his car is in dock for the week-end. That's why he didn't offer to drive Auntie into the city. And he didn't suggest you might do it as he wanted a chance to talk with you.

"We might even do a little sortie around the old harbour lights, eh, mate?" he says, nudging you in the ribs and pulling that wink of his, not only with the whole of one eye, but also with half his mouth as well. And that covers quite a bit of territory on old Bruce, his mouth being one of the largest you've ever known.

But now that he's suggested you do over the docks together, as you used to every now and again in the old days, you've got the chance to tell him that doing the docks and all that sort of thing is out now so far as you're concerned. Out altogether from now on. You mean to lead up to it slowly, teasing him like, knowing how his curiosity soon gets the better of his patience. But somehow you can't. You find yourself not only bursting to get it out, but goddamn it you're blushing into the bargain. So there's only the one thing for it. You just have to blurt it out, just like an overgrown kid.

It's funny to watch old Bruce's face. You can see that he's quite taken aback by it, the way his chin almost sags to the floor. All the features of his face sag. The dark patches under his eyes drop so much you think his eyes could slip out of their sockets. Then he recovers himself; becomes serious and solicitous; pats you on the shoulder and says: "Well, good on yer, mate. Christ, I'm glad to hear it!" Then, of all things, he's damn near blubbering over it; takes out his handkerchief and has to give that great long beak of his a blast that almost raises the roof three storeys up. "Wish I could find someone myself at times, old cock," he says, making a few more little bleats from that old nose of his. And then, nearly recovered again, he gives one of those wryly comic smiles that remind you a bit of some movie actor in the old silent films, you can't think who, but you can remember it as though it was only yesterday. Anyway, he makes this wry little grin of his, and says: "But it wouldn't work, I know *me* all too well. Everything'd be just *bliss* for a week or two, and then I'd get the old itch again. I'd be back on the beats, old thing. And whoever had shacked up with me would be suing for divorce! No, old mate," he says, slapping your back and making that wryly sad little smile of his again (little for a mouth his size, that is), "I love to see it happen for someone else, but I reckon it's just not for me. Your old mother here has got too used to her little old comforts, Ray me boy. All me gentlemen callers!" And so its titters again now. But yet another change comes, just as quickly. As you expected, he's all eager for the details. He's almost like an excited old dowager, knees close together, but with all that length of legs somehow doubled up under him at what looks the most awkward angle. And leaning forward, he clasps his hands on your knee and says: "Now, tell your old mother *all*. *Every* word of it. Do I happen to know the lucky slice? Have I *had* it by any chance?"

You can't help laughing, he's a real pantomime.

So you tell him. Not Cor's name for a while. You keep that for the end, as a sort of climax. Just give him all the details of how and where you met, and when, what it was all like. He'll want to know it all anyway, sooner or later, and he's really enjoying being kept on edge about it, waiting.

But eventually you've told everything you can think of, and there's only the name left. You know that that's all there *is* left to tell, and if you hold out any longer it will seem only ridiculous. And it's only then that it occurs to you that most people, if they could see such a scene, and hear such a conversation, between two men, would not only think it ridiculous, they'd say it was unbelievable. But there'd be nothing much ridiculous about it, if the whole secretive part of it wasn't necessary. It's that which makes it sordid, or absurd.

You can see old Bruce is getting a bit impatient, a bit puzzled. And then he must realize it; for he gives your knee a little poke and says:

"Well come on, for God's sake! Tell your old mother or she'll split a gut."

Then you're really at ease again, and you don't have any difficulty in telling him after all.

You expected one of two things: either he'd sort of shake his head, as though he was trying to place the name and description out of the thousands of 'bits', as he calls them, that he either knows or has had, and would joke about it a little and say he doesn't know how it managed to get through his net; or he'll suddenly slap his thigh and say something like: "Oh, *that* one, darling! Well, your old mother *is* surprised! But a very nice little slice it is, *too !* Very nice *indeed !* Makes your old mother quite *sick* with jealousy!" Or something to that effect. You can almost hear the words and the way he'd say them.

In fact, neither of the reactions you expected from him is what comes; nothing like it at all. Instead, to your own surprise, consternation almost, his face again sags just like it did at the very beginning, and something inside you seems to sag with it. Before he says a word, before he even makes another move, you know that something is wrong. Or rather, you know that *he* knows that something is wrong. For the very first time it suddenly occurs to you, in a split second, how you've rushed into this whole business without even thinking about it, without even getting to know the boy or find out something about

59

him. And seeing old Bruce's face, you know instantly that there *is* something you should know, that you should have found out before you went leaping to a lot of fancy conclusions.

Bruce screws up his face and is all serious and sort of perplexed again. "Are you *sure*, old thing?" he says. "Or rather, what I mean is—do you *know* what you're doing?"

It's as much as you can do to say anything at all. But eventually you do manage to say: "What do you mean, do I *know* what I'm doing? If you mean about going steady again, then of course I know what I'm doing. I mean, I know the other times didn't turn out like I hoped they would. But I'm willing to overlook all that, have another go. I mean, there just isn't anything worthwhile in life unless you do. What the hell do you live for, if you're not going to find someone eventually, and make some sort of a go of it? Or at least try to . . ."

It's been quite a speech, for you. You're not altogether unaware that it might be mostly the Scotch talking, though you mean every word you said; and for once the words all seem to have meant something. You couldn't be more serious about anything if you tried. But at the same time you suddenly know you've really been just kidding yourself. You knew all the time that this wasn't what old Bruce meant. You know what he means, and you just sit there, helpless, like a sitting duck waiting for the rifle to go off.

Bruce is shaking his head. All commiseration and, goddamn it, even patronizing. And then he says:

"Don't you know *anything* about that boy, Ray? Don't you know anything at *all?*"

You've pretty well prepared yourself for whatever might be coming. It's going to be something of a shock, you know; something pretty nasty. Old Bruce wouldn't look like that if it wasn't. So maybe it won't be so much of a shock, now, after all. Maybe, if you already expect the worst, whatever comes won't seem so bad; it might even put a bit of an edge on things. But what does come is quite a good deal more than what you had ever bargained for.

"Don't you know, Ray boy," Bruce goes on, still with that same painful and sort of screwed-up look on his face, "that that boy's *married?*"

The word drops into the room like a stone into a pond. You can hear it hit, and then ripple around and around, all around you. Unbelievable word. He seemed so genuine, Cor; about the most genuine type you've ever met. You just can't believe it. He looks the square type all right, but not the two-timing type. Not married and doing it on the side, on the sly. It just doesn't seem like Cor. And then, only then, when you feel so convinced about it, it suddenly occurs to you that old Bruce here is just pulling your leg, enjoying himself. And if he is, he's doing it darned well.

"You're kidding," you say.

But no, he's not kidding.

"Listen, boy," he says, with that quiet and companionable intensity of his, whenever he's talking about something that matters. "He's married all right. I *know.*"

You still can't believe it. Yes, one part of you can, almost. But the other part can't believe it at all.

"*How* do you know?" you ask him; or rather, it's almost a demand. It sounds it, even in your own ears. Just a trifle absurd. But you can't help it; you've got to know. You've just *got* to know . . .

"Listen, boy," Bruce is saying, "you know I've been around this town, clean inside and out again, and through it backwards if it comes to that. I *know* this town, I tell you. And I *know* that boy. I also know he's married. I made it my business to find out. He's a dish all right, a dish if there ever was one. Christ, they don't come like that every day of the week. I was pretty keen on him myself, I can tell you, the first time I laid eyes on him. No, not *hands* for once, old thing. So that's why I made it my business to find out. His wife's a nurse, also Dutch. They came out just after getting married. What's more, she's *pregnant*, boy. She's so pregnant, last time I saw her, she must be five or six months gone. I'd say Cor was just doing a bit of philandering on the side. Some types often do, you know; only they don't do it with women. That'd be straight-out infidelity. Some warped sort of sense evidently convinces them that they're still being faithful to their wives if they just do it with another man . . .'

"You're kidding," you say again. It's all you *can* say.

But—"I'm not kidding, boy. You know me, Ray. I wouldn't kid anyone about a matter like this. Especially not you, old thing."

You nod your head. Yes, you know it. You know old Bruce well enough for that, all right. He just wouldn't do it. So what he tells you is true. It must all be true. You just have to sit there, numb inside and out, and let it sink into you, swill all around inside of you, like a pain from some inward bleeding. From anyone else, you'd have to check up on it yourself, or just ignore it altogether as another bit of bitchery—a Sid Needham bit of bitchery. But not from old Bruce; never from the Prof. So it must be true all right. And so now where's all that wonderful brave new world of yours?

But then, when you think about it a bit more, when you think a bit more about Cor, and what he was like that first time, and even more about what he was like the second time, it's almost as though there's been a whole lifetime between you already. It can't be just a sideline, something temporary and on the sly, just for the hell of it. Something would have shown if it was, and nothing had. He was genuine all right; he had wanted everything as much as you had, if not more. You've got no doubts about that—no doubts whatsoever. So—take another look at things . . .

Even if he *is* married, you know that he has at least got some sort of a need for you, and a big need at that. You couldn't contemplate sharing him with another man, but maybe a woman's different. A woman certainly couldn't give him what he wants. Maybe he has the two needs, one for a woman and one from a man. Some do, you know. You know it quite well; you're not all that naïve. Well, if he needs a man as well as a woman, you still don't mind being the man. The woman doesn't count. It's not only as though she's another life of his, it's almost as though she's another world, nothing to do with you. And nothing to do with Cor either, as far as his being with *you* is concerned. Another thing—although you have to admit it does sound a bit on the crafty side, on your part—his being married could be a good thing. It could be a very good thing, a perfect alibi. People could hardly think things, if he's married and a father into the bargain. Come to think of it, it could be just about the most perfect solution of the lot. Thinking about it, you suddenly feel lifted up again, revived, and you can almost feel your determination creeping back within you like some physical thing. You'll still go ahead with it all right, it makes no difference. More, it's even better. Yes, you'll go ahead with it no matter what. All the more to bind you together. Much better. Much better. The future's all straightened out again, like a long straight road after a bit of a curve—a curve that wiped the road out of sight for a while, but it's behind you now.

But then, just as you think you've got everything all pat again, then comes the next blow. And this one really does set you staggering; there's not much getting up again from this one. For old Bruce suddenly goes on, quiet like . . .

"And that's not all, old thing," he says. "This Cor of yours has also got a boy friend. Or rather, hardly a *boy* friend: he's a good deal older than either of us. Pushing fifty, I'd say. You'd more or less say he *keeps* Cor, especially in all those fine clothes and so forth . . ."

This you can't believe; you just can't. The words aren't true. They're not even happening. It's all a mad crazy dream, or you've had too much Scotch or something, and soon you'll come to and just laugh at it all.

But it's no laughing matter. Bruce is saying: "This old boy's name is Hamilton—Ron Hamilton, I think! I'm not sure. Could be Bob for Robert. I just know his initials, R. W. He's the manager here for one of the big stores, an interstate show. A pretty big shot in his way, although I must say he doesn't look it. Sort of an ordinary bloke. He's got a big house—company house, of course—overlooking the river. Two cars. Owns a racehorse or two. And boy, that all takes dough. Apart from that, he rents a small flat, I'm told, somewhere on the other side of town, where he and Cor can go. Cor lives about a mile away, with his wife. They're in one of those old-type houses. You know, all squeezed up like a box. I believe they even share it with another couple. Dutch, too, I think. It's all low rentals there, but sharing it would really be doing things on the cheap, especially when both of them are working. Although I suppose his wife will have to give it up any old tick of the clock now. She'll soon need a bit of nursing herself . . .'

It's all true, then. You don't want to believe any of it, but you can't deny it. It's all, all true—coming from old Bruce for one thing, and the little you've seen for yourself for the other. The flat you first went to, nothing in it Dutch, and yet so impersonal for even an Australian. Now that you think of it, it couldn't be anything else than what it's used for—a nest for the occasional night.

"I *think* I've got some coffee," Cor had said. You hadn't thought of it at the time, but surely he would have been *sure*—had it been his own place.

And the second thing, the house where Cor had asked you to drop him off last time—Christ, only the *second* time—exactly answered the description Bruce had just given you. It all fits like the wheels in a Swiss watch—the lot.

"Oh, shit!" you say. It's all you *can* say, and you must be showing your feelings as plain as Christmas, for old Bruce doesn't say anything more—that is, nothing more after he just says: "Sorry, old chap. I hate to do this to you. Especially to *you*. But it's better you know from the beginning——"

Beginning? You've just had the end slapped in your face. You can't say anything more, can't do anything more, except make some kind of gesture that you've got to go. But old Bruce seems to understand, lets you go, sees you out without saying another word. Just pats you on the shoulder again. The whole fucking rotten stinking game. You wish to God you could get yourself out of it, but you can't. You know you can't.

You're stuck with it—stuck, as the saying goes, like shit to the proverbial blanket.

For the moment, just get yourself out of here. Anywhere. Not home. Not yet. Anywhere else, but not *there*. Just *any-where*.

The night is all cold and wet, dark, without street-lights now. Only the car headlights knife ahead into the wet dark of the road, like the twin knives you feel that you've just had thrust and twisted clean into you. No, don't go on with things like that. Melodramatic. Hysterical. And that's the last thing you want. Just drive, boy. Just keep on driving. Drive the whole goddamn night if it's necessary. And don't even think that it's your *eyes* that are misting up, blubbing like a big kid. Kid yourself it's the rain, weeping down the windscreen. Brush it aside with the windscreen-wipers. Keep on driving. Anywhere. The rain's almost a comfort. Anywhere. It doesn't matter a sweet hell where you go—plenty of petrol. You can drive the whole goddamn night if you want to.

And then you find yourself *there*. You don't know how you got there, but you're there all right. The tree. So park the car, take your torch. Everything's dark, no lights. Must be later than you think; you must have been driving much longer than you think. It's easy to do, keep on driving when you're just thinking the same unbelievable things over and over.

You lift up the torch, flash it on for just a split second, and see what you knew all the time you were going to see. Letter box for flat number one. Name—R. W. Hamilton.

So now you can go home. Now you can go *all* the way home —as you've said before, wherever it may be.

II

ANOTHER Sunday digging in the garden. The folks'll begin
to think it's a regular thing. But how different from the previous Sunday! Today it rains and blows in great wintry gusts.
It's almost like a professional boxer sparring with you, trying
to give you a few not so playful smacks on the jaw. And when
it rains, it comes down like an ocean has been emptied on
you; it really does. Your family say you're crazy to go out in
it: why don't you watch the TV or something? And they
know if there's one thing you can't stand, it's TV. See too
many damned ads on it for one thing, a lot of them your own.
Most, of course, come from other agencies, or have been made
in other states or even overseas. But they're all phony. They're
all so phony they nearly make you puke. But that's what the
sponsors want. Morons, the lot of them. No, that's the last
thing you want to do, look at commercial TV. So you put on
your oilskin mac and the oilskin sou'wester that goes with it,
your fishing outfit—whenever you do go fishing that is, which
is not so very often any more—and out you go into the garden.

Half of your Paris geranium has been smashed off by the
wind. Could even have been hail last night, after you eventually got to bed, and to sleep. You hadn't heard it, but by the
look of the ground, all stippled with heavy little imprints like
old-fashioned leather, it looks as though it must have hailed.
Which would explain the broken Paris. And just as it was
getting to look a real beauty. It's always the way.

A bit farther along, you find one of the azalea bushes also
smashed. But it looks as though it's been done by a cat this
time. Damn cats, they even go around tom-catting on a night
like last night. But can you blame them? After all, weren't you
out in it all too? But not tom-catting this time, for once.

When there are two of anything, there's usually a third coming up. It's an old superstitious saying of your mother's, and all your mother's family. You must have a bit of it in you too, for you find yourself looking round, half-expecting to find a third plant smashed up somewhere, half-expecting it and also, you have to admit it, half wishing for it. And you're really not at all surprised when you do find it: a picket blown off the fence and smashed clean across half a dozen snapdragons. The third thing, and with a vengeance. Funny thing is, there must be something in it. Look around the garden where you will, you can't find anything else—just those three things.

And that's not the only matter in which it adds up either. Just as you think you've got over last night, and you've made up your mind that you'll forget the whole stinking business—never see Cor again—you suddenly remember that it was two things, not just one, that smashed up that big brave new world you were planning. Two things—a wife *and* Hamilton. Is there a third on the way with this too? And if so, what's it to be—a nice little piece of blackmail, for instance?

You can't stop yourself, you think of him all the time. There was a time this morning when you woke up and it was only just after six and so you went straight off to sleep again, but not before thinking to yourself: He'll be getting up now, going to work. And goddamn it if you didn't wake up again just after seven, and you thought to yourself: He'll be at the club, starting work. And you could almost see those hands of his, letting himself in with the keys, the door opening and closing, and you wondered: Is he thinking about you too? Is he thinking that he's not only got one old man to keep him, but another younger one that's good for the cot while the wife's preggo, and might bring in a bit of extra kitty as well, if he handles it right? Is that what he's thinking? Well, you've got another think coming, Cor old chap, you tell yourself, or else you'll be a Dutchman!

And then, oh God, did you have to crack a joke like that? Of course, you did it without thinking; it just came naturally.

But you can't even crack jokes any more. You'll be a Dutchman! Even a stupid thing like that is enough to set the whole lousy set-up going round and around again.

Someone calling?

"What?" you shout back, through wind and rain, or under it more likely rather than through it. "What?" you shout again, and yet you know all too well that you really heard the word. Or if you didn't exactly hear it, then you kind of felt it. Telephone.

So you have to go in to the back veranda, strip off the wet oilskins, take off your muddy boots, and by the time all that's done you half expect whoever is calling to have hung up. At least the room is empty when you go in and pick up the receiver. It's probably Bruce, you think, ringing up to see if you got yourself home all right, after the state you were in.

"Hello?"

Whenever something happens twice, it'll happen a third time, mark everybody's goddamn moronic words! It's Cor. The third knife. In, and then twist. Twist it just a little more and you'll be a screaming idiot ready for the nut factory.

"I can't wait till Friday like we said," he says. "I know you said it's best not to ring you at home, to wait till you're at the office. But Ray"—you'd almost forgotten the way he drawls that name of yours—"I just *had* to ring you. What? Yes, I'm at the club. Can't talk long, it's pretty busy on the moment"—and even that silly little word seems to smack you clean between the eyes—"but Ray, are you free on Tuesday? I can't wait till Friday again. And I can make it on Tuesday."

You're an idiot, all right. You find yourself saying: "Of course."

"At your office then? About eight?"

You can still say no, for God's sake; call the whole idiotic thing off. But what do you find yourself doing?

"Sure." And even then you have to make it worse. "But why wait till eight? Can't you come at six? We'll have dinner." He'll have to find an excuse, you think to yourself, to tell his
68

wife—his goddamn Dutch *pregnant* wife. What a pretty set-up
it all is!

But—"Wonderful," he says. Then: "Ray, it's really wonderful, just to hear your voice again. I mean it, Ray. But I've
got to go. Till Tuesday, then. At six, your office. Look after
yourself, Ray."

So that's that. Well, you're an idiot, all right. If you really
want to take up masochism that crazy, why in the hell don't
you just go and stretch yourself out over an ants' nest or
something . . .

12

TUESDAY, and you're so damn busy with a new account,
local biscuits, you clean forget the time. You have Barbara
taking down blurb copy until well after five before you suddenly remember—Cor coming at six. You have to bundle her
off so that it's almost indecent, as though she might guess at
what you want to get rid of her for. But that's crazy, she
wouldn't have an inkling; thinks you're mad for the women,
the line you shoot. But it's all necessary—it's all necessary,
God only knows. And you reckon you put it over so well that
if anyone was to swear on a Bible to her that they knew you
were queer, she wouldn't believe it. After all, she's had the
occasional brush of the tit and slap on the bottom to prove it.
You've made sure of that.

As soon as she's gone, you start rehearsing to yourself what
you're going to tell Cor. All the questions you mean to ask, or
maybe just state the bald facts. After all, you know the lot—
and he can't very well deny it; he can't very well deny any of
it. You practise doing it all haughty-like for a start, but that
gets a bit hysterical. So you try it the off handed way, all aloof

69

and you-don't-give-a-stuff sort of thing. But that's as false as a plastic tit anyway. So you settle for doing it straight, quietly and seriously, like a gentleman; after all, that's the best way of doing anything. And then, quite literally, you'll show him the door, and good-bye to all that. Then you can go join a nunnery.

You think you've got it all pat by five to six, but then all the doubts set in. You don't know if you can carry it off. If only you didn't have to *see* him, all that hunk of everything you've ever wished for in a life-time. Up for sale, sort of; but no dice. You're not at all sure you can carry it off. In fact you're pretty sure you'll make a balls of the whole thing and finish up blubbing like a great kid again. You should have been a waterworks engineer; you're already shaking all over. Pull yourself together. Never for one moment let him see how it's really got you. Just pull yourself together.

And you think you've just about got yourself right again when, bang!—right on the dot of six, the night door-buzzer goes and you have to go over and let him in. You can get yourself over to the door, but where in the hell have all those pretty words you thought up gone to . . .

"Hello, Ray."

He's in about the shabbiest lot of clothes you've ever seen— old, and too-small looking, as though he'd just bought them in a jumble sale or somewhere. Shirt collar frayed, and the top button won't do up under his tie. What the hell! This some new technique? Something like: I'm so poor, couldn't you give me a hand-out sort of thing? Shoes clean though and—maybe you never noticed it before—he's wearing a plain gold ring on his wedding finger, like you know a lot of Continentals do when they're married.

You've got a bottle of sherry waiting, to oil things up a bit in the hope they'll go more smoothly. And you've also got every word and movement planned and timed. You know exactly what you've got to do, every step of it. But he goes and throws things clean out of plumb right from the start. You hadn't expected anything like this to happen. For he says:

70

"Just a little something for you, Ray. Nothing much, just a little something. Gosh, I'm glad to see you. Seems weeks. How's it been on the moment?"

For one thing, you hadn't bargained on his talking first, and you'd clean forgotten what a neat little incision every word could be. And for the second thing, you hadn't expected any packet to be pushed, almost sheepishly, into your hand, and then him to go walking across the office and pretending to see for the very first time the picture on the wall you yourself painted.

For a few moments you can't make up your mind whether or not to open the packet; it might be something that's pertinent to the whole matter. Or should you just put it down on the desk, ignoring it, and go ahead with your little act? But curiosity and the cat again; you open it.

It's a pair of cuff links, plain gold, not over-expensive, but not cheap either. And when you can clear your eyes again, you see that they've been inscribed. So you have to look, and that really does it; on one link are your own initials, RW, on the other his, CvG. Why don't the walls cave in, or the ceiling fall down on you? Your fingers shake so much you can hardly lift the links out of their box. And when you do, you see that something else is inscribed on the other pieces of the links, the undersides that go on the inner parts of your sleeves. It's a date, by the look of it. Yes, it's a date all right. And then you realize the date is of just over a week ago. It's the date of the very first Saturday night you met. So now what do you do? Your whole act has gone clean out of your mind. And even it it hadn't, how could you ever go ahead with it now . . .

You'll have to give them back, of course. You've never in your whole life had a present like it, that says and means so much—or at least you would have thought it says and means so much, if you didn't know better. It's the sort of thing you couldn't have even thought up yourself. And now—now the irony of it! The one present that could have meant the whole world to you means nothing at all. All you can do is just give them back—no alternative—unless you can really make yourself as hard as nails and keep them as a memento, a little lesson in experience, a warning against being a damn fool again in the future. But no—a lot of things you might be able to do, but that's not one of them.

You know he's waiting for you to say something, naturally; and of course everything you've prepared has gone with the winds now, or almost. There's really only the one thing you *can* say. So you say it; no use in beating around the bush.

"Cor, they're—they're very nice. Very nice indeed. But—but I'm afraid I can't really accept them. You see, I know—I know everything. About your being married for one thing, and Hamilton for another."

There, it's done with. Could it have been shorter? Or less sweet? You wait to see his face. Or maybe he won't show anything. Maybe instead there'll be useless denials, lies even, perhaps even recriminations and so forth. It'll be interesting to see just what kind of an act *he* can put on. . . .

He's still looking at your picture. Stock still, he is. But then, slowly, he turns. And of all things, there's that calm and steady gaze of his, intent from deep down in those oh so deep eyes of his, eyes that look almost oriental. And that's not all—he smiles. He actually smiles, that slow leisurely smile of his that fits his face so smoothly, so incredibly smoothly. And——

"I thought you might," he says. "Sooner or later you'd have to find out."

Gone again—everything from underneath you is gone again, cut completely away. Is there no end to it? No end at all?

"But why didn't you tell me, Cor?" you hear yourself saying. "Why on earth didn't you tell me?"

The same gaze the same smile. It hasn't stopped, any of it. The devil! Just how *can* he be so self-composed.

"The first night," he says, "there was no point to it. I thought it was just, well—only for that night on the moment. On that way, why should I say anything? I thought you'd be gone after an hour or two, or at least by the next morning. So what would have been the point?"

He is so right—so terribly right. No point at all.

"But, Cor," you go on—you have to go on. "The second time, after a week? Why didn't you tell me then?"

"I—I still wasn't sure that it was worth while," he says, just as calmly as before. "At least, not until after you'd left me. And it was too late then. Besides . . ."

But he just trails off. And at last his eyes are averted, looking all around the room, looking as though they want something to clutch hold of.

"Yes?"

What a cold little word that can be at times! So cold and remote, like a star when you're lonely.

"Besides," he goes on, "I knew then how I felt about you." He hesitates again; then: "Ray, if it means anything to you, I love you, Ray. That's all. I was frightened if I told you, about my wife and that, you wouldn't want to see me any more. I was afraid I'd lose you. You don't know how afraid. I still am . . ."

And now there's nothing left that you can say; you can see that he means every word of it. No one, not even the best of actors, could have put on a show like that and not mean it. So now what do you do? But you don't have to do anything. He starts to say something again.

"Ray, it was only last Friday night when I saw you last. To get this—this little present for you, something to sort of prove what I'm trying to say—I had to get some time off on Saturday morning, to order them. They promised they'd be ready by Monday, and that's why I phoned you on Sunday. I know how people talk, Ray—and there's plenty about me for them to talk about, if they want to. I just hoped I'd get in first, that was all. Tonight. But of course,"—and he shrugged his shoulders, as though he had just staked everything he had in the world on some silly gamble, and had lost—"I was just a little too late. I'm sorry you had to find out from someone else, Ray. I—I suppose—I suppose you don't want to see me any more. Do—do you want me to go now?"

Words! Where are just a few words for you to say? You

can find them easy enough for copy and ads—why not now? But all you can find are: "Oh Jesus, Cor!"

And then you're both suddenly half-laughing, half-crying, holding and hugging each other. And the walls and ceiling don't need to cave in after all. Sherry. Sitting on the floor, of all things. And you looking over and over again at the cufflinks, wondering what you can ever think of to give him in return. Sitting almost on top of each other, still half-laughing and half-crying, silly as a couple of children. Only a few sips of the sherry, and then you both need each other badly. Then even that close together is still too far apart. God bless the office for having a carpet and a shower . . .

13

NATURALLY you want to know all the details and, now that your lovemaking is over, now seems as good a time as any, just lying there, together, the electric radiator bathing your bodies with warmth. That wonderful rosy glow makes Cor look like some fallen statue in rose quartz. Raining like mad outside; but with the radiator, the sherry, and Cor so close alongside you, it's almost as though you're in some kind of spaceship, looking out on some alien and hostile planet—which the world pretty well is.

He tells you his wife's name is Mia. They were born in the same little village just out of Amsterdam, about thirty kilometres or so. They practically grew up together, went to the same school and everything; that is, when they could go to school. The war had made a bit of a mess of that, he said. A lot of the time they were out looking for food together, and watching the German troops whenever they went through the village. Times like that, he said he was glad he and Mia weren't Jews. The Germans were always looking for Jews, hunting them out like rats and sending them off in trains to labour camps in Germany. At least, everyone had *thought* they were being sent to labour camps, at first; but it wasn't long before they found out that most of them ended up in the gas chambers. He hadn't liked Jews much up until then; in fact, he was often getting into fights with them, fights he himself often picked. But when he found out what was really happening to them, he didn't pick fights with them any more. Neither did the other boys. He felt really sorry for them after that, horrified, and a bit ashamed of himself for having fought with them, mostly just for the fun of it. A *bit* ashamed? No, it was more than just that, he said. Sometimes he used to lie awake and cry about it to himself, nearly all night, thinking of the mean things he had done to them, just kids some of them, who were now being taken off to the labour camps—and the gas chambers. Instead of hating the Jews, he had hated the Germans then; he had hated the Germans more than he had ever hated the Jews or anyone before. He still did, not as much as he had then, but he didn't think he could ever get over hating the Germans after all that they'd done.

Because it wasn't only with the Jews, he said; it was with the Dutch as well. Someone had knifed a German soldier on guard duty, outside a warehouse where food was stored. So the Germans had taken eleven of the young men in the village whom they suspected of having been in the vicinity at the time —not necessarily right at the place itself, but just in the vicinity, seeing no one would admit to the killing. The Germans lined the eleven of them up against a wall, without any bandages over their eyes, not even with their hands tied. And they made the rest of the village stand on the other side of the street and watch. Then they shot them, all of them, the whole eleven of them. Cor's older brother had been one of them, and there was a cousin of Mia's. Mia had been standing with him, holding his hand, and they had both tried not to blurt out crying with the Germans watching them. But after a while he hadn't been able to help himself, especially when his own mother had started to cry out and then sink to the ground. He hadn't wanted to cry, but he hadn't been able to help it, he said. In any case, he was still just a kid at the time, and so he supposed it was really only natural. But he had felt a bit ashamed of himself all the same, though Mia had cried too, she hadn't seemed to cry quite so much as he had. She had gripped his hand so tightly, it was as though after a little while their two hands had become almost one. When they had gone home again, Mia had stayed with him all that day. They hadn't said much to each other, with his mother weeping and crying out all the time in the next room. They had just stayed together, till it was getting on for curfew time and Mia had to be taken home.

The village had built a memorial on the spot after the war. It had a plaque with the eleven names on it, including his brother's. And afterwards a statue had been added, depicting a young boy just standing there, waiting to be shot. There was no soldier aiming a gun or anything, he said, but nevertheless you could just see it, as though one was there. You could see it in the way the face of the boy-statue just stared straight ahead all the time, the way his brother had stared, he said, without trying to look for his mother or his father or any of them. He had just stared straight ahead of him as though it was all just some kind of game, and he couldn't possibly be about to die. That was what Cor could remember about him now, he said. When he told it to you, you felt a cold slag of horror seep through the whole of your body, like a kind of death. And you knew he must be feeling it too, the way he shivered suddenly. So you just lay there for a while, holding each other, and you sometimes squeezing your hand tighter on the curve of his shoulder.

Then he started to go on again.

When the war was over, they had gone back to school. Mia had been in the same class, so naturally they had always gone to school together, and walked home together. He didn't really love her, he said, although he did love her of course in some kind of way, more as though she were a sister or a very good friend. He supposed that Mia had always been his best friend. He didn't seem to fancy any other girl at all, so it was just naturally supposed that he and Mia would get married; even he himself expected it. And not only both their families did, the whole village did.

Then had come the time for him to study architecture. He had had to go to Amsterdam for that. He took a small room, an attic really, near the technical school where he studied. He lived as cheaply as he could because his father had to find extra work, at night, to be able to pay for him. He always went home week-ends. He was about eighteen then. He used to hitch-hike to save even the bus-fare. Sometimes he walked, nearly all the way.

It was one evening when he was walking, in the autumn, when a car had stopped to give him a lift. It had been a new sports car, and the fellow driving it was about twenty-three or -four, on leave from working out in the Far East, in Java. His clothes were very expensive and the car seemed a sheer wonder to Cor, something he himself would never be able to afford, not before he was forty or so anyway. But the biggest wonder of all was the thought of someone having a whole six months to themselves, just for holidaying, with fares paid and everything. That, to Cor, had seemed the biggest luxury of all. They hadn't been driving for very long when Cor had said he felt as though this fellow was some kind of young god, he seemed to have everything: money, car, good clothes, wonderful personality, all that time for holidaying—and to have travelled all that way and seen so much of the world for another thing. Cor said he just sat there beside him, his mouth half-open all the time, like a real country oaf.

They were just driving along through the fields and farms, cows and windmills, sometimes a small village now and then, and Cor said he had felt as though he was really on top of the world, even if it would only last for just an hour or so, and not for ever. And then the car had broken down. It wasn't a flat tyre or running out of petrol or anything crummy like that; the car had just sort of choked and stuttered, shaken all over, and stopped. The fellow had got out and tried to see if he could do something; they were some way from one village and a fair way past the last one. It was already dark and getting cold. They had both tried to see what was wrong, trying everything; but neither of them had known much about cars. So after a while they had given it up, it was getting so cold, and got back into the car for warmth and to wait until another car or someone came along.

But nothing had. He had asked the fellow where he was going to, and the fellow had said something that had really seemed astounding. He had said he was going nowhere in particular, just driving around, he had nothing else to do and he liked driving anyway. Cor had thought: Who wouldn't, with a car like that? And then the fellow had said he had intended to take Cor all the way to his village, once he had picked him up, and then drive back alone to Amsterdam; it would give him something to do, some place to go. But now the car had broken down, and he was sorry that he wasn't able to take Cor all the way after all. Cor had been so touched by this, he had got out of the car again to see if there wasn't something he could find to make it go. But of course he just didn't know where to look; neither of them did. And after a while, when still nothing had come along, they had got back into the car again; it was getting really cold by that time.

And then, Cor said, it had happened—or at least the start of it had. At first, Cor said he had been a bit shocked, this fellow had seemed such a regular sort of guy, not like a *'flikker'* at all. He had wanted to get out of the car and go when the fellow had first started, putting his hand on Cor's leg in a way that Cor knew could only mean the one thing; he wasn't all that dumb, like most country yokels. But the way this fellow did it, it was as though it was the most natural thing in the world for them to do. Somehow he still seemed a regular sort of fellow, and Cor found himself fascinated by it. He had always been a bit sexy, he said; he and Mia had tried it when they were only fourteen, and they had been doing it ever since. All the boys at the school mostly did it too, even with each

78

other, mostly just playing around of course. Oh, he was no prude, he said, let alone an angel, and so he had just thought to himself what the hell, and let the fellow do what he wanted. He had even enjoyed it, he liked the fellow so much; and somehow it had seemed a sort of way, a very personal way, of showing just how you felt, or of expressing something. And so he himself had done just as much as this fellow had, or as much as could be done in a small sports car, which wasn't so very much after all, he said, not considering what he knew now.

In fact is was hardly anything at all, and he had to admit he had been a bit disappointed when the fellow had stopped, just as he was getting used to the idea of two men kissing each other and so forth. But then this fellow had said it was silly for them to be just sitting there in the car, they'd freeze to death and it was so damned uncomfortable anyway. Then he had suggested that they walk into the next village and put up at a hotel if they could find one, and see to the car in the morning. By that time Cor said he knew he would have agreed to anything, it had all been so much an adventure; something anyway that he had never done before.

And so they had gone, walking about three kilometres to the next village. And there *had* been a small hotel, and they'd been able to get a room there, only the one, a double room with one of those big old-fashioned double beds. Real Dutch, Cor said, smiling. And then everything had happened, things he hadn't even known were possible, although he'd heard that they were. He's always thought of it as something sort of dirty before, he said. But again it was the way this fellow did things, it seemed the most natural thing in the world, and as though things like women didn't even exist. The part which had affected Cor most of all though, he said, was finding that it excited him much more than anything he had done with Mia—much more. It was this that had dismayed him more than anything. Although he hadn't been able to admit it, even to himself, for a long time afterwards, he said he supposed he would always look back upon that night as one of the most

wonderful nights in his whole life. Nevertheless, he had known
—deep down somewhere inside him he had known—that it
was true . . .

Now he is silent again, once he has said all this. And you
can't help it, you feel suddenly and terribly jealous; envious
too in a way, but mostly jealous. And you can't help holding
him closer, even though you know you haven't a hope of ever
trying to create the same sort of impression on him yourself.
You know that something like that only happens the first time
—Cor with this fellow, you with Uncle Kev. So you relax
again; he's starting to tell you something more anyway.

In the morning they had found a garage and got a man to
go out with them. It was dirt in the petrol, the man said. It
hadn't taken him long to clean it all out, but they'd never have
been able to do it themselves. The main thing, Cor said, was
that he had seen that the car breaking down had been genuine
all right, and not just some sort of pretext. It was this that
had made him like this fellow even more. In fact, he said, he
was beginning to feel an impossible thing—impossible because
he didn't think such a thing *was* possible, not between two
men. And he was trying to tell himself that it wasn't really
happening to him at all; it couldn't; but he knew that it was
all the same. One part of him said that such a thing was quite
impossible, the other that it was not; in any case, it had
already happened—he had fallen in love with another man.

So then he had asked him to come and stay at his home for
the week-end. It had all seemed quite natural, and it still had
when he had told his family how they had met, how the car had
broken down and everything. But no, not *everything* of course.

Only Mia had been upset about it. In fact, he said, she had
been furious about it. She had already started training for
nursing, and now their week-ends at home didn't coincide very
often. They had coincided this week-end, and so she was
furious at having to share Cor with someone else, and a
stranger at that. Yet it was more than just that, Cor said; much
more. It was almost as though Mia could sense what had
happened between them; it was as though she knew, in some
80

kind of impossible way, because of course she couldn't possibly have known. Anyway, she was so furious about it that she had walked out and left them to themselves. And it had been weeks, months maybe, before he had seen her again.

In fact it *was* months, he said. He could remember now, because this fellow had spent the week-end with him, becoming almost one of the family the way his mother and father had taken to him. And early on the Monday morning they had driven back to Amsterdam together. After that they had practically lived together, this fellow either going to Cor's place one night, or Cor to his another. They even had a week in Paris together. Cor had never been to Paris before; in fact he'd never been out of Holland before. It was all new and strange and sort of dazzlingly wonderful for him, and he felt as though it could never end.

But of course it did. The leave had to come to an end, and although Cor had somehow thought his lover would never leave him, the fellow just wrote him a note one day. He had sailed that very afternoon from Rotterdam for Java. There hadn't even been time for Cor to go and see him off, even if he'd been able to.

But that was the point, Cor said; he hadn't been able to. He hadn't been able to do a thing for weeks, he was almost out of his mind. He didn't go to his classes or anything, just stayed in his rooms and stared at the four empty walls. He couldn't tell anyone about it; he certainly couldn't tell his family. So they, of course, just didn't understand. They thought he had been studying too much and had had some kind of breakdown. They took him home and he stayed there for a while. When he seemed all right again, he went back to his room and his classes. But he couldn't study. He couldn't concentrate on anything except that one thing. He was left alone—one might almost say *jilted*, he said, smiling.

But when he and this fellow had been together, he had got to know about one or two bars where he could go. He found that there were other men, mostly older men, who liked him and wanted him to go with them. So he went. He'd let them buy him drinks, and sometimes he even took money from them, but only if they offered it. He needed the money for drink he said. He started to drink more and more; nearly every night he was at some bar or another. Nearly every night he found someone to go with, someone to help him forget—or to remind him all the more acutely—of the one person he really wanted to be with, but would probably never see again.

He didn't know how long it would have gone on for if Mia hadn't got to hear about it. He didn't know how she did get to hear about it, but one evening he returned to his room from classes and there she was, waiting for him. She talked to him as though nothing had ever happened, he said, and they just started going with each other as before. Everything was exactly the same as it had been, except that it could never really be the same again.

But there was still the old temptation, he went on. There had to be some nights when Mia couldn't be with him and he would be alone. And then his loneliness, and his memories, would be too much to bear alone. He would have to go out, and he always finished up doing the same thing: going to some bar or other, getting drunk, getting picked up. Mia put up with it—or ignored it—for a couple of years; he didn't know why. It wasn't as though they had ever been great lovers, he said—just very good friends, although he did admit that they both expected to get married, and still did. She was quite certain she would win in the end, he said. She had said it was just a matter of time, as with most everything in this life—just a matter of time. If it had been another woman, she had told him, she would have given up. But she still felt she had a chance when it had been only a man. *Only*, he said.

By the time he had turned twenty-one, he still hadn't got it out of his system. He tried women, prostitutes, even Mia when she wanted it, but if anything, it was worse. He had become promiscuous, going with almost anyone, men or women. Not only that, but he was almost an habitual drunkard. He didn't care about anything or anyone or even what happened to him any more. He didn't even care about Mia, or how much suffering it all might be causing her. It was even more as though the whole world had ended for him, and there was nothing left for him to do but just to keep on as he was all the time, drinking, sleeping with anyone. He hardly ever looked at his studies, so it was inevitable that he should fail his exams. He was told he couldn't go on with the course any longer, so he got a job—as a barman in one of the bars where previously he had been an habituè. He became very popular, especially with male customers.

But Mia was persistent, he said, if nothing else. Somehow she got him to consent to marry her, and so they *were* married. But he had also consented—God knows why, he said—for them to migrate to Australia.

"You see," he said, "homosexuality is legal in Holland, once you're over twenty-one. She knew I'd never get out of it if we stayed there. And she found out that it was still *il*legal in Australia. So she figured that there wouldn't be bars and places where I could go. But she doesn't know the world and its ways," he went on, smiling again, a smile that was almost like a little twist of pain. "It must have been quite a let-down for her, when she found out that there *are* such places here, and that I was soon going to them . . ."

He stops again, and you both just lie there, the whole sordid story seeming to seep slowly into the room, drooping into you through the languid near-darkness. You want to hold him close, to tell him you understand. But even when you do tell him, the words sound empty somehow, empty and futile. Besides, not everything is explained; and as though he knows it, he goes on again.

"But I didn't meet anyone here whom I really liked," he said. "I looked—I kept on looking all the time—but I didn't find anyone. Then I met Rob—that's Rob Hamilton. I didn't like him. I mean, I didn't like him in the way that you *love* a person. But I did like him *as* a person. And he seemed to want me. He wanted me so badly, he promised me the world, gave me everything—well, gave me lots of things; clothes and that sort of thing. And he kept me from going to the bars, from getting drunk and—from just going with anyone So I. sort of just let everything slide. Besides, Mia got to like him too. Or rather, she got to like all the things he started giving her as well. I guess she's got that way that she can't do without them. Good clothes, expensive perfumes, stockings, all that sort of thing. Oh, she knows what's been going on between us all right, but she doesn't seem to care. 'As long as it's not with another woman,' she always says.

"And so there you are. I didn't know I was going to meet *you*, Ray. But now that I have, well, I've told Mia about it. And I've told Rob too. In fact, I've given him back everything he gave me—everything. It was an awful scene, but I couldn't help it. I couldn't keep his things once—once I no longer wanted to go with him. Some people would, I suppose. But I couldn't. I just couldn't."

He stops again. And you lie there, clenching his hand in yours, knowing it's all true, even to the part of giving back the clothes. Tonight he was wearing clothes that were so much older, shabbier, than what you'd seen him in before. And you've only got to think of the cuff-links, and of everything he has just said, and you know you would have to look for years, years, to find another even half as good as he is. As the old saying goes, he's been through the mill all right, well and truly. But no matter what he's been through, there's still something he hasn't lost. Old-fashioned as it may sound, it's his honesty he hasn't lost, not one bit of it. And another thing he hasn't lost is his capacity to love. That's still there too, as much as ever it was; even more, perhaps. What more can you ask for?

So you tell him about your plans, for getting a flat together and so forth. Not too much; you've learned long ago that it's not always wise to make too many promises. You get quite enthusiastic about it, just telling him, so that it's almost a disappointment when he says:

"Oh, Ray, don't go leaving home or anything like that, just for me. Not yet a while, anyway. I mean, I can't leave Mia either on the moment, when she's going to have a baby. You do understand, don't you? I mean, we can see each other quite a lot now, as much as you want to. And we have your office here. Let that do for a while, then we can see how things go. You do understand, don't you?"

Yes, you suppose you do understand. Once again he's probably right, wise. At times it seems almost as though he's the older one instead of yourself. So that's how you'll let things go for the present, just as he says. After all, it's not as though there are only the two of you involved.

Then, suddenly, like a chill that impales you on a winter night, it occurs to you that you don't really know just how many of you there are involved—so far as he is concerned. Mia, you know, for one; and this Rob Hamilton for another. But always, *always* there is that first ghost to lay, that very first love. With you it's Uncle Kev, even though Uncle Kev has been dead a long time now. And with Cor? Even before you ask him, you almost know exactly what the answer will be. You suddenly remember that first night with him, and how he talked in his sleep. And you also realize that he has never told you the name of that first lover of his. He just called him this or that *fellow* all the time. You know it will probably be a mistake to ask him; in fact you can be almost certain of it. But you also know that you just have to ask him, even though you know what the name will be long before he tells it to you.

"Henk," he says.

And yes, that *was* the name he had called out, in his sleep; and so now you can't help wondering just how much that's going to mean.

14

It's after he's gone that you start thinking about all he told you, and it's not a very pretty picture. Yet the way he told it to you, he hadn't sounded at all sorry for himself—not a bit. He was just telling you something, explaining it, that was all. There wasn't any question of his trying to make you feel sorry for him or anything like that. The last thing he would ever want, you reckon, is pity. He'd probably hate you for it if you started to pity him.

So when you start to think over all he told you, you first of all think that this fellow Henk must have been a pretty lousy sort, to just walk out on him the way he did, without leaving an address or anything where Cor could at least write to him for a while. Letters can be a big help, that way. It's only when you write letters to each other that you have the chance of writing everything out of your system. But sometimes this doesn't happen, or can't happen—like you with Uncle Kev, because Uncle Kev was killed.

Perhaps it's a bit like that with Cor and this Henk. Well, if it is, then you've just got to do something yourself to make him feel that the live lover he's got now is much better than the dead one he had before, long ago. Besides, it sort of puts an edge to things, gives you more to live up to. So in a way you can really be glad about it. After all, it's things like that which give you an added zest, to keep working on all the time. Otherwise, without them, things can soon get pretty dull; the edge wears down a little, blunts. And before you know it, you finish up bored with each other, then maybe sort of despising each other.

So you tell yourself that just because Cor calls out a name

in his sleep—it could have been only his father's name, or his brother's—it doesn't necessarily mean that he's still in love with him, and that you don't mean a damn compared with him. It doesn't even mean what you've already been half-fearing all the time, that he possibly uses you as a substitute for the person he really wants, turning his back to you and closing his eyes, pretending that you're not you at all, but the person he really wants to be with. You mustn't even think a thing like that; you'll be all washed up if you do. You know you can't even bear to think of something like that; it makes you sick to your stomach. More, it makes your whole body feel as though it's suddenly unclean, being used like that, then discarded afterwards.

No, it's not Cor and this Henk in the past you've got to think about. What you've really got to think about, to set your mind to, is the future—you and Cor together. And ruthless as it might seem, you've got to forget all the others, forget them completely—forget Mia and Hamilton and everything that's happened to either of you in the past. If you really want this thing to work out at all, that's what you've got to do. Maybe you will even have to keep *on* doing it, all the time.

One thing, Hamilton doesn't worry you very much. Of course you can't help feeling sorry for him; but it can't be helped. Cor doesn't love him, and he does love you—or at least he says he does, and you know how you feel about him. So there's no use in your playing the little gentleman and just stepping out of the picture, even if you could. It would only make the two of you miserable, instead of just one. Anyway, knowing how these things usually go, Hamilton will probably soon get over it and perhaps find someone else. God knows, there *are* plenty of fish in the sea as the saying goes, whether they're legal or illegal.

Cor's wife, Mia, though, is a very different kettle of fish. She really is in a mess, especially with a baby coming. And even if there weren't the baby to consider—which, oh God, is yet another thing—you'd still feel sorry for her—so sorry that you almost wish it had never happened, you meeting Cor. But only *almost.* You know all too well that if you had the chance over again, and you knew all the circumstances right from the beginning, you'd still want it to happen. No matter what it involves, you still want Cor. So if anything at all is love, this must be it. You would do anything to have someone like Cor for your lover. What's more, you know that you *will* do anything, if it's necessary.

But it's a pity that you have to be involved with someone like Mia. From what Cor has told you, she sounds as though she must be a pretty *noble* sort of person. She just must be, to have done all she has for Cor, to have gone through all she must have gone through. This last thing will probably be awful for her—awful. It'd be enough to kill a person, it suddenly occurs to you; and a shiver goes clean through you. You want Cor all right, but you don't really want to be involved with people killing themselves, just so that you can have him. And yet? And yet? Oh God, she might even lose the baby over it; it's been known to happen before, thousands of times. That would really be awful. But what can you do about it? It's not as though her having a baby is your fault at all; that had happened long before you even met Cor. And if he hadn't met you, then it could just as well be someone else he might meet. In fact, with all that capacity to love as he has, he'd all the time be searching for someone. And sooner or later he'd be bound to find him. So if it hadn't been you, it would only be someone else. That's what you've got to keep on telling yourself. You've just got to put all other considerations clean out of your mind—Hamilton, Mia, her baby, everything . . .

15

You've got plenty else to think of, of course. You're so busy in the office, for one thing; and you've always got plenty of other things that you have to see to, like most other people you suppose. True, you do spend a fair amount of time thinking about this one matter; you can't help it. And who wouldn't? But you're sure that there's nothing, nothing at all, which demands as much time as does your work, which is probably a good thing.

In any case, things are going so well, so smoothly with you and Cor now, that you don't need to think about things anywhere near as much as you thought you would. You don't have to make any effort *not* to think about them either, like some people might suppose. They just seem to slide to some place in the background of their own accord, to take up their proper perspective all by themselves. And after a while, it's almost as though you and Cor just haven't got any problems in the matter at all.

In fact, everything seems to work out so easily that sometimes you really wonder what on earth you were worried about. How right he was, about not rushing in and getting a flat and so forth. This way he's able to stay where he is, looking after Mia. And you can stay at home, so that you don't have to upset anything there either. And the office—well, the office becomes something quite different to what you'd ever expected of it before.

What's more, you really do see quite a lot of Cor, especially when he too works during the day. You've both got your nights free then. It's only when he has to work at night it's a bit difficult. But then you find that you can work late too, and you get a lot of work done that you'd never have got through otherwise, while you're waiting for him to knock off and come to you. Of course you don't make love every night; although, come to think of it, it must be very nearly every night. Neither of you ever seems to get tired of it; but sometimes you do just have a cup of coffee or something, a sherry or two. Just seeing each other is enough. Sometimes you're so incredibly happy, you think that one of these days you'll just burst with it, clean in the middle of the street or somewhere.

16

YOU might have guessed that things were going a little too smoothly. There comes one of those days when Barbara has got you booked silly with appointments, says none of them can wait, and right in the middle of it all, without the name registering or anything, she just ushers in someone who's been waiting a fair while, she says, but who insisted on seeing you. Not even a phone-call first or anything, to make an appointment; he just walks in.

At first you think he's the Hamilton from one of the petroleum companies that you've got a big job going for. But as soon as he walks in, you can see it's not that Hamilton, and you start wondering, just for a second or so, just which Hamilton he can be before you pull some kind of bloomer. And then it smacks you clean between the eyes as to which Hamilton it is, and you nearly have a heart-attack.

Thank God he acts normally enough, as though he hasn't got anything like *that* business on his mind. Before you can even register what he actually looks like, you do register how he can at least control himself to look normal, as though he's just called on some regular business matter or other. Especially in front of Barbara; she's been making a few cracks lately. You might have guessed you couldn't use the office as you do without leaving a few traces to give you away, like two sherry glasses left unwashed, or the coffee-cups. She knows what you're up to all right, but the funny thing about it is that she thinks it's with some woman. Well, as long as she thinks that, you're all right.

But now, thank God, she doesn't seem to suspect anything, and Hamilton certainly hasn't given any reason for her to suspect anything. Once she has shown him in, she just leaves again. And there you are, just the two of you, standing, staring at each other as though you're both some kind of animal seeing each other for the very first time. That's really how he looks, now that he's dropped the façade he'd had on up till now—just like some sort of animal, but a frightened, rather nervous one. He's not at all what you've been expecting. Cor's so big and good-looking, you had expected Hamilton to be big too, perhaps even bigger than Cor. You had expected him at least to look a real man for Cor to have been interested in him. But this—this pathetic little mouse of a man, so nervous and self-conscious and even twitching a little—like a scared rabbit twitches—well, he's not at all what you expected. In fact, now that you've really had a good look at him, you wonder what on earth Cor ever saw in him in the first place.

You can't imagine for the life of you Hamilton being a company manager; he just doesn't look the type—a secretary or an accountant, something like that maybe; but not a manager, even for a branch in a small state like the West. But perhaps that's it; perhaps he rose up the scale in the usual way, and then the directors found they had to make him a branch manager; but they didn't want him in any of the eastern states, so they sent him over to the West. That sort of thing happens all the time, among the big companies. And so the West gets all sorts of weird-looking types being sent over—Cinderellas for the Cinderella-state, you guess.

But then again, maybe he has more gumption when he's in his own office, giving orders and so forth. Maybe he feels and looks much more self-confident then, especially when he's got only routine or business matters to deal with. It usually is a totally different matter, for anyone at all, when they have to go to someone else's office, let alone on a matter like this. So you can understand in a way why he should look, now, such an insignificant little ferret. For of course it must be as much hell for him, a matter like this, as it is for you; perhaps even worse.

So, now that you've finished glaring at each other, you try to be some sort of gentleman at least; try to put him at ease. But——

"Wharton?" he says.

"Yes," you say, rather flatly.

"My name's Hamilton. I want——"

"I know," you cut in. "I know who you are. But first of all, won't you sit down?"

That does deflate him a little. You can almost see him shrink, like a released balloon, before he sits down and starts fiddling with the ends of his fingers, picking at the nails.

And then, instead of making a few preliminaries as you would expect from any civilized person, his face sets into an expression like a petulant child and he blurts out:

"You've got to keep away from Cor!" Just like a little child. It seems a wonder he didn't say: 'Give me back my golly-wog' or something. Yes, that's just what you expect him to say next.

"Oh?" you say, taking care, at the same time, to raise one eyebrow, like you had to practise for years before you were able to manage it.

It looks as though you've flattened him with just that much, the pathetic little ferret. God knows, really, what Cor ever saw in him. The way he cringes almost makes you puke.

"Yes," he says, "you've got to keep *away* from him." Still the little petulant child, if not more so. "I mean," he says, and then of all things: "It's not *decent*. Didn't you ever give a thought to his *wife*?"

Well that beats all. You certainly can't let *that* pass.

"Did *you* ever give a thought to her?" you counter. And you couldn't make it more pointed if you tried.

Again, that rather bamboozles him. He splutters, spits all over the place.

"That's not the point!" he says, raising his voice, so much so that, just as though he is a naughty child, you have to say: "Ssssh!" Not loudly, just short and soft, but sharply enough for him to know that you mean it. And he does take the hint; next time he speaks, his voice is back where it was before.

"That's *not* the point," he goes on. "At least I knew how to do things *properly*." And you think to yourself: *Properly*, of all things! Would he tell that to a judge? But he's going on again; *carrying* on, you might almost say. "Cor and I are just very good friends, that's all. And I'm a *very* good friend of his wife's too. I've been doing quite a lot for those two, in my own small way"—mock modesty now, even more pathetic—"setting them up on their feet in a strange country and so on. And then you—*you* have to horn in on somebody else's friendship, and break the whole thing up, and what's more, you, you——"

Oh God, the self-righteous, stupid little prig! A *friendship*, for God's sake! Not admitting anything else ever happened between them—just *friendship*. It's about as much as you can do not to laugh in his face. Why, the silly little ferret will say he's not even *queer* next, and anyone can tell it a mile away. It's too much; really too much. You can't even be bothered talking with him about it. All you feel like doing is just kicking him out and telling him to mind his own business. And you damn near do it, too. You would, if it wasn't for Barbara and perhaps some other people waiting in the outside office. So all you can do is say:

"Don't you think it's rather up to Cor to decide whom he wants, or whom he doesn't want?"

And again he's deflated. But he still keeps trying. You have to hand it to him in a way; in a sort of little *ferret* fashion, he does at least keep trying.

"Cor wouldn't have had to decide any such thing, if *you* hadn't butted your nose in!"

Well, he certainly can produce some humdingers all right. Anyone'd think you'd seduced a *choir-boy*. But by now you've really lost patience.

"Look, Mr. Hambledon, or whatever your name is," you say, knowing full well how most people hate having their names mixed up, "I suggest you take yourself out of here before I bust you wide open"—and you can hardly believe that you can sound so fierce yourself—"and if you think Cor doesn't know his mind about these things, well you're not fit to lick his . . ." But before you finish saying it, you suddenly think, that's probably just what this little ferret-faced runt does anyway. And it almost makes you throw up. So: "Get out," you tell him, and this time you really mean it. "Get out, before I throw you out."

He's out of the chair and over to the door like a startled rabbit, but still determined to have the last word.

"If you don't stop butting in where you're not wanted," he says, or rather almost hisses it, "then there are one or two things I can *do* about it."

"Oh?" Be rather amusing to find out what he has in mind. So: "Such as?" you say.

"Such as I can get his wife to insist on going back to Holland. And with her having a baby and all—did you stop to think about *that*, mister? Well *did* you? Did you stop to think about her having a *baby*, and what it would be like having someone playing around with her husband while she's having it?——"

It's all you can do to hold yourself back. But he hasn't finished yet. Let him *have* his little say—turns always come round.

"Well, she wants to go back to Holland, all right. And I'm going to see that they get there. If you want to know, I've already booked their passages, *and* paid their fares. And if you think Cor'll leave her to go by herself, well maybe *you* don't know so much about him after all!"

That one hits home, all right. You're not at all surprised that this little ferret would want to pay for them to go home; it's just the kind of thing he would do. If he couldn't have something he wanted, then he'd do his damnedest to make sure no one else could have it. Ordinarily, you wouldn't have a thing to worry about; you know Cor wouldn't go. He wouldn't accept the passage being paid for him for one thing, and he certainly wouldn't be able to go if he had to pay for it himself. But Mia, and her going to have a baby, was another thing. Hamilton was right; Cor wouldn't leave her to go by herself. You can be pretty well sure of that, but don't admit it yet. Don't even admit it to yourself. And even if you do, for God's sake don't show it to this little ferret before you.

"And what's more," he goes on, "you seem to forget that I've got a fair amount of influence in this town, with the firm I'm in. I've only got to say the word in a few places, Mr. Wharton, and you'll soon find some of your big accounts going somewhere else. There are *some* people in the world, you know, who don't like dealing with *queers*, once they find out that that's what *you* are."

It makes you so sick, you could almost hit him there and then.

"Get out of here!" is all you can say, and you start going around the desk. But you don't have to go very far; you don't even have to tell him to get out again. He's already gone, pulling the door to hurriedly behind him.

So you sit down, try to calm yourself. It's done more to you than you think; you're shaking all over. Must compose yourself before Barbara shows someone else in. You just must, that's all.

But thank God for some small mercies; she doesn't even come in herself. And when eventually you can bring yourself to open the door and look out, she says that there's no one else to see for about half an hour. Did you want anything? If you don't, then she's got those biscuit blurbs to finish.

So you tell her, yes, go ahead. You've got several things you want to see to yourself.

And that's not entirely a lie either. Yet, when you do go back to the desk, you find yourself just sitting there, holding your head in your hands. Cor *would* go back to Holland, all right, with his wife having a baby. You know he wouldn't do anything else. And he wouldn't just leave her there either, and come back out again himself, even if he could afford to—if either of you could afford it. You know he just wouldn't. And what's more, Hamilton could do just what he said he would. In fact, he *would* do it, smirch your name all around town. And your business wouldn't be worth two pins if he did, you know that. Then, with or without Cor, what on earth would you live on?

17

HALF an hour, Barbara said—time enough to have a drink —and God knows you need one, to pull yourself together. Without thinking, you just walk down the street and go into the first pub you come across. And it's not until you're at the bar and have ordered a double scotch and soda that you realize you're looking at those old familiar mirrors and pillars. Of all places to pick, the Palais—where you first met Cor. But you're here now and you've ordered your drink, so there's nothing much you can do about it. What the hell difference does it make anyway! One thing, there's not many people here, no one you know; just the one bunch all together in the far corner.

Your drink comes, and you gulp it, almost the whole lot of it in one throw.

And then you see that you were wrong about not knowing anyone there. One of the men from the group in the far corner slips out of it and comes over towards you. And of all people

—of all the people you just don't want to see at the moment—it's Sid Needham. That sidling sort of walk, the inevitable leer.

"Well, if it isn't Mrs. Wharton's little boy Ray," he says, smirking wider than ever. "And how's the big love affair going?"

It's the kind of thing that makes everybody hate Sid Needham; makes you feel as though you want to hit him. But of course you can't; he always covers up that sarcasm of his with a pseudo-innocent smirk. You can hardly bear to look at him, let alone talk to him. So you pretend he's just caught you in the middle of swallowing your drink.

"Now don't tell me," he goes on, "that you've forgotten it was little Sid Needham here who introduced you to your big love, have you? Why, how could you! And how *is* Cor, by the way? Still the big heart-throb?"

It's as much as you can do not to hit him, especially with the way you feel after Hamilton. But of course that would really be a scene, so you've just got to control yourself.

"He's fine," you say, mumbling it into your glass. But then, no, you think; there *is* something you can say. So:

"Tell me, Siddy boy," and you try to sound off-hand, "just why *did* you go to all that trouble to introduce us? Now don't tell me you did it just for the good of your health. And don't tell me you did it for the good of *my* health, either. It just won't wash. I think I know you a little bit better than that."

"Do you?" he counters, and the leer never falters for a moment. "Do you? Well then, *if* you do, then maybe you should have thought of that before."

"Oh?"

"Yes." Insinuating, but what?

"Well, why did you?"

"Why? *Why*? Well, I'll *tell* you why. I hear around the town that it's *all* a big success. Well, *isn't* it?"

This you can't very well deny, so you say nothing.

"Yes, I thought so," he goes on, the leer fading a little now, but still there all the same, some of it. "I *thought* so. I thought

97

that's how it would go. The big untouchable heart-throb, Holland's answer to every maiden's prayer—and the irresistible Mr. Wharton. Must have been *quite* a little collision, I'll bet."

Then he deliberately sips at his drink, but eyes you all the time, the leer as much in those snake-eyes of his as ever it was, and on that great lecherous mouth. To think that half the young things around town are launched by *that*; corruption must come pretty easy, that's all. But he's put down his drink again.

"Why?" he says over again, the leer back on his mouth. But almost immediately it's gone again, and you don't think you've ever seen anyone look at you with so much hate in your life before. It almost makes you flinch. "I'll tell you why!" he says, nearly spitting it in your face. "In the first place, your precious Dutchman can be as *untouchable* as he likes. But he should learn how to say No with a few good manners, shall we say."

You don't have to know the details; you can guess what happened. And you can just imagine how Cor would brush off someone like Sid Needham if he made any advances. But now Needham is talking again:

"And you, Mr. Wharton; you should learn that this is a *very* small town, and you can't go around calling people names, like 'that insufferable little cradle-snatcher' and so forth. Things like that . . ."

And you know exactly what he means; you can even remember when you said it. But you can't believe that either Roy or even young silly Andy for that matter would ever rush back with it to someone like Sid Needham; they loathe him as much as you do. No, that wouldn't have happened; but what might have happened, what very likely happened, is that young Andy probably passed it on to someone else, just for the heck of it, without even thinking, and then that someone else passed it on again. And so it would do the rounds until, eventually, it go to Sid Needham himself—who now says, almost as though he knows what you've been thinking:

"You see? *Everything* gets back to Siddy Needham, sooner or later."

"So just why *did* you bother to introduce us, seeing that's how you really feel about both of us?"

And as soon as you ask, before he even starts to make a reply, you already know, somehow, from somewhere deep down inside you, that what he is about to say will be one of the ugliest things you've ever known in your life. And you're not far wrong.

"Why? *Why?* Oh, come now! Surely Mr. Ray Wharton can see the reason. Anyone could see that if either of you two were ever going to go silly about someone, then it could only be for each other. It was a cinch. And it must have been some collision, eh? Well now, how *nice!* How *very* nice! *And now I can just sit back and watch you two tear yourselves, and each other, to pieces . . .*"

You can hardly believe it. You suppose you must be looking at him with a kind of horror, it's so incredible. Well, you're horrified all right; but not so much horrified at what he has said as that anyone, even Sid Needham, could have a mind capable of thinking up a thing like that. If ever anything has nearly made you sick—sick physically, you mean, and sick generally of the whole goddamn queer set-up—then this is it. And this time you hardly can restrain yourself from wiping off that leer, that sort of vicious glee, from all over his face.

But you do manage to control yourself. Somehow or other, you do manage not to hit him, there and then. God knows, you've had enough temptation today to hit somebody. But you still manage not to do it. Instead, you just compose yourself as well as you can; you even manage to look Sidney Needham straight in the eye when you say:

"Well, I hate to disappoint you, but it'll never be like that, not between Cor and me."

And then you walk out.

But as you go back to the office—back along the street with its merciless traffic, the chill wind blowing wet dead leaves and papers all over the pavement—you can't help wishing to yourself that you could feel as confident about the matter as you hope you had sounded.

18

BACK at the office, you think about it and think about it until you nearly go crazy. You can't concentrate on anything, can't think of anything else. Even Barbara seems to sense that there's something wrong, asks a few questions and then keeps out of your way. You can't exactly blame her, the way you must have snapped her head off.

There's really only one thing you can do; you've got to see Cor. So you ring him up, at the club; a thing you've agreed you'll never do, but you do it anyway. You've just got to see him. Someone answers off-handedly at the other end, then keeps you waiting for ages, hanging on. Finally, you hear Cor's voice. Just hearing it, you suddenly feel that everything is all right again. You even feel as though everything that has happened this morning didn't really happen at all; it was just in your imagination. You ask Cor if he can meet you somewhere for lunch, anywhere; but of course, as you might have guessed, he can't get away.

"We're so busy on the moment," he says; and then: "In any case, Ray, I'm going to see you tonight, aren't I ?"

"Of course," you say. "Of course."

A little while ago you felt as though you couldn't possibly wait that long. But now, now after having just spoken to him and heard his voice, you do feel that it *is* possible for you to wait till tonight before seeing him. You even feel as though you don't want to see him until tonight. There'd be no sense in trying to talk about a thing like that in some restaurant or somewhere, having to keep your voices down all the time in case people hear you. Far better tonight, in the office. So you ring off and, somehow or other, you get through the rest of the day—even though at times it seems more like a year.

But when he comes, he's not only an hour late, he's drunk—not just a little drunk, but damn near sloshed. It gives you quite a shock; you've never seen him like this before, never thought you *would* see him like this. Then you remember how he said he had once been an habitual drunkard. It hadn't really hit you before, but now you can see it. And you say to yourself: Yes, this is what he must have looked like, night after night, week after week, after Henk had left him, and he was doing the rounds of the Amsterdam bars.

"I—I'm sorry, Ray," he says, swaying in the doorway until you catch him. His breath nearly knocks you over. "I suppose you're mad at me, for—for being a bit drunk on the moment. You see, Rob—Rob Hamilton—he's been seeing Mia a fair bit lately. And, and—oh Ray, he's persuaded her to go back to Holland——"

He can't say any more. He suddenly collapses so that you have to put him quickly in a chair. He just slumps into it. And then he does something you can't bear to see a man do—he starts to cry. His head falls forward on to his hands and he sits there and blubs, eyes and nose watering, dripping between his fingers. It's a thing you can't stand to see, normally; but this time you can understand. You know what you've been through yourself today, and no doubt he's been through a good deal more. So you put an arm around his shoulder and tell him: "There, there. There's no need to *cry* about it." Just like talking to a big kid; or a *little* kid. "No need to cry about it, boy. We'll work out something."

But he just shakes his head, shaking some of his tears and the water from his nose through his fingers on to the carpet. If anything, he only starts to cry louder than before—and you can't help it, you feel the unexpected beginning of a kind of contempt. It's not only some of your admiration you feel slipping away from you, but also some of your love. Of all things, you don't want it to happen, but you can't help it. You even start to hate yourself a bit for feeling that way, but still you can't help it. All the same, you can't very well be rough with him, or tell him, as you were just about to, that he must pull himself together. No, you've just got to let him go for a while. After all, he's had more than enough to cope with by the look of it.

So: "We'll find a way, boy. Don't you worry yourself about it," you say. But you can't make yourself sound too confident about it; so it's not so much of a surprise when he says:

"You don't know *Rob*, Ray. When he says he's going to do a thing, he does it all right. And he's got plenty of money to do it. A few hundred pounds mean nothing to him, not a thing. And what makes it worse, Mia is just the same. When she makes up her mind, nothing can stop her either. And Ray, she's made up her mind to go back. So she'll *go* back."

"I know, I know, boy," you say. "I know. Rob Hamilton has been to see me too."

"He told me he was going to, but I didn't think he'd do it. What did he say?"

So you tell him about it. In a way, you almost enjoy telling him. But after a while, it's as though Cor has become bored with the matter; you can hardly believe it, but that's how it seems. And then he says this incredible thing:

"Did he say anything about *me*, though?"

Well, you suppose everyone has got a certain amount of conceit in them, but you had hardly expected to find it like this in Cor—not quite like this. Why, it's almost what a woman would say. Doesn't want to hear the main gist of the matter; just wants to know if anything was said about her*self*. *Him*self, in this case. And you think: Oh God, don't tell me he's turning into the usual little nancy. You would never have believed it possible; but on the other hand, you would never have thought it possible that he could become so snivelling and helpless as he is now. But he starts to say something again, in between all the sniffles that seem so impossible, coming from behind those big hands of his.

"Ray, I don't know what to do. I don't want to leave you, truly I don't. But Mia's determined to go. I've asked her to see you, to talk with you, and then she'll soon see that you're much better than Rob Hamilton. But she won't. She just says she's going back to Holland. And Ray, I *can't* let her go by herself. Not when she's going to have the baby and so on. I just can't . . ."

"I understand," you say. "Truly I do." And you feel that you really mean it; you feel that you do truly understand. All the same—— "Maybe she'll change her mind?" you suggest.

"Not Mia," he says. "You don't know her like I do. She says we've got to go. She says if it was just someone that didn't mean anything to me, it wouldn't bother her. But after what I've told her, she says she won't put up with it. She says she won't be second fiddle to anyone else, man or woman. And I suppose she's right . . ."

He trails off again, not snivelling so much now, but still sometimes sobbing a bit, like a kind of hiccoughing—deep and sharp inward sounds that make his whole body shake.

"Well, we've still got plenty of time to think of something," you say, more for the sake of just saying something, anything, than really believing in it. After all, you haven't the faintest idea just how much time there is left. But you soon find this out.

"We haven't got long, Ray," he says. "Rob's booked our passages on a ship sailing in just over a week. Paid for them and all. Mia's given her notice at the hospital. She said she had to anyway, with the baby coming. But ordinarily she wouldn't have done it quite so soon. They said she could stay on longer, they're so short-handed. And—Ray—I had to give notice myself today, at the club. That's—that's why I'm drunk. They were all buying me drinks and that. I suppose I needn't have drunk them all. But Ray—you *will* try to understand, won't you—I *needed* them. I couldn't help it. Oh, Ray, I can't believe I'm going to have to leave you, just when I've found you. I can't. I can't . . ."

This brings on the weeping all over again. He's not only half out of his mind, he's drunk into the bargain; the two together aren't exactly easy to handle. You wish you had some coffee or something; but you haven't, not in the office—none left, just when you need it. And you don't want to go out for it either, not in the state he's in. There's really only the one hope of sobering him up, of his pulling himself together. So you decide to undress him and put him under the shower.

But before you can get him there, you find him difficult to handle. You can see yourself soon getting soaked through, having to hold him up all the time. So you finish up getting yourself undressed and under the shower too, half holding him up, half clinging to each other. And of course anyone would know what that would lead to.

But after that he seems much better, just resting there with his head on your shoulder. You don't even talk. And everything can go round and round in your head, the same thoughts chasing each other, like a squirrel chasing itself in a squirrel-cage. You feel as though you've been just lying there, thinking, for hours, so that you're not at all surprised when you find he's gone to sleep, snoring gently alongside you, as though there wasn't a thing in the world to worry either of you.

Then suddenly you start up, realizing you've also been asleep. You feel sure it's been for only a few minutes, so that it's a shock when you reach over to get your wrist-watch and find it's after four o'clock. Four in the morning. You've got to get him home, get yourself home. Good job you did wake up then, and not sleep on until the cleaners came in and found you both in the morning, naked together.

Driving home in that strange nether-world you've really got to know so well, the rain has stopped again. But the wind has come up. It seems funny for it to be blowing at that hour of the morning. It's almost as though you had expected it to go off somewhere to sleep too. But it's almost blowing a gale. The rain has stopped, but in the trees that sometimes reach overhead, the leaves are still all fraught with rain-drops. And every now and again they clatter in such ferocious little blasts, right onto the wind-screen, you could swear that someone had thrown a handful of stones at you.

When you arrive at Cor's place, he says he'll call you during the day, see you tomorrow night. Then you both realize that it will already be tonight, not tomorrow night. And you find that at least you've got over things enough to be able to joke about it, even if it is only half a joke. It's not until you drive on, alone, that you realize again just how little time you've got left—that's if he does go. But right now you can't bring yourself to think about that. After all, the dream isn't over yet.

19

COR sticks to his promise; you've hardly back at the office in the morning when Barbara puts him through.

"Mia's changed her mind," he tells you, and of course you leap to the inevitable conclusion.

"You mean, she's not going after all?" you say. But:

"Oh no, Ray. I wish that was true. No, I mean she's changed her mind about seeing you. She says she wants to, now."

When he says that, you think he must have had time to have a good long talk with her, to talk her round into seeing you. And you wonder whether he got any sleep at all after you dropped him home, or did he wake up early and talk to her then? Silly, but it's little things like that—quite irrelevant things really, come to think of it—that somehow or other you just want to know.

"She was still waiting up for me when I got home," he tells you. "No, we didn't have a row about it. Just talked things over. And now she says she wants to see you. Will you come?"

Well, in a way, you suppose you really are drowning, so why not grab at any old straw?

"Of course," you tell him, and you look at your appointment book. "How about two this afternoon? I'll have almost an hour then."

"What are you doing for lunch?" he asks.

Well, you hadn't exactly planned on anything, except maybe to go somewhere quiet and think things out, before you go to see this Mia of his. So you find yourself agreeing to have lunch there with them, to give you all more time. Well, you suppose it might take two hours or so, that's if it doesn't take only two minutes . . .

Preconceptions of people, you should have realized long ago, are practically useless. If it was a shock when you first set eyes on Rob Hamilton, then it's nothing compared with the shock you get now, meeting Mia. From what Cor had told you about her, right from the start you had thought of her as being someone rather noble. And when you think of someone that's supposed to be noble you naturally think of her as being rather tall and dignified, perhaps even beautiful. You'd think she'd have been someone like that anyway, for Cor to have married her. After all, being so good-looking, if he really wanted to marry a woman, he could have done a fair bit of picking and choosing while he was about it.

So that's why you get such a shock when you first see Mia. In the first place, she's little—really tiny—only just over five feet or so. Looks no more than a child, really. And yet, in the second place, she also looks old. You know she's about the same age as Cor, because they went to school together; but she looks a good five years older at least. At the same time, strangely enough, it seems to be only in her face. Her over-all appearance is still that of a child, a misshapen child. Of course, her pregnancy has got a lot to do with that; and yet, even without it, she'd still look misshapen. Her shoulders and chest are too narrow, skinny; but at the waist she suddenly bulges out, not only in front with her pregnancy, but also sideways, as though her hips are blown up like the tube of a motor-tyre. Then again, her legs are all wrong; they're just like a couple of sticks; and her feet on the end of them seem kind of ridiculous. A bit like her hands; they look ridiculous too, stuck at the ends of those long skinny arms of hers. She's got dark hair done up incongruously in Shirley Temple curls on the top of her head; you almost expect to see little pink bows tied in them. And the craziest thing you've ever seen on anyone, she's got purple eyes—really purple. And freckles—freckles the size of sixpences everywhere; on her face, on her neck, on her arms—so that you wonder if they're all over her, you can see so many just where her dress lets them show. Freckles and purple eyes. But that's not all about her eyes; they stick out, pop-eyed, great big goitrous eyes like Bette Davis's, with little crows' feet of wrinkles around them. Her mouth pouts, as though she's always got the sulks.

All in all, she's the last thing you would ever have expected. Cor must have been so keen on men that, when he got married, he just didn't know one kind of woman from another. You really can't imagine anyone wanting to marry this one. And you can't help it, you don't exactly hate her, you just loathe her right from the start. You couldn't bear her to touch you; it'd make you sick if she did—and you're not all that afraid of women. Like Barbara, for instance. In actual fact you get quite a kick out of pinching her, or goosing her or something, sliding a hand over her to make her shriek a bit; you really do. But you couldn't do it to this Mia, and you can't imagine Cor wanting to do it to her either, let alone sleep with her. It makes you almost want to throw up at the very thought of it.

But you've got to at least try and be polite, get along with her somehow—for Cor's sake; yours too, if it comes to that. So make an effort, there's so much depending on it . . .

She just about takes the wind out of your sails right from the start. After you've been introduced, and things are still a bit stiff between you, she keeps on looking at you with those great big old-woman's eyes of hers, staring. And then she says:

"Yes, he's *just* like Henk all right."

And in just that instant you know exactly what she means, and everything that goes with a statement like that. You know it without even having to think about it. It's just as though it all suddenly appears on a screen, flashed before your eyes, and you can see the whole picture in just the one gulp, and not only the picture, but also all it implies.

You think she's not going to say anything more, but will just leave you hanging in the middle of the air, for, turning to Cor, she says: "Mia want a cigarette." She says it in the sulking, pouting way of a little girl.

But she hasn't dropped the matter at all. After she has inhaled, she turns those big goitrous eyes on you again and says: "You see, Mr. Wharton, we have seen you before—before you actually met Cor, I mean. It was in the city. You were walking along the Terrace, and we were coming the other way. I felt Cor's hand tighten on my arm, and when I looked up, there you were. For a minute *I* thought you were Henk too. Cor *has* told you about Henk, hasn't he? Yes, I should think so. Well, now you know what I mean. I don't think there's any need for me to say any more, is there?"

She has been toying with her cigarette, looking down at it, smiling to herself a little, as though she was trying to deliberate whether to extinguish it or not, perhaps just for the fun of it. She keeps on toying with it as though, now that she has it, she no longer wants it. Then she goes on, looking directly at you again:

"No, I don't think so. That's why I've decided that we must go back to Holland, Mr. Wharton—Cor and I. You see, once I used to say that if it was just another man, I wouldn't worry. I know people are, well—that *way*, Mr Wharton. Homosexual. A lot of people, not just a few. I know about Cor too, of course. But I've always said it wouldn't matter to me, just so long as it didn't make any difference to things between *us*. Once I wouldn't have tolerated it, Mr. Wharton, if it had been another woman who was involved. But now"—and for a moment she again studies, intensely, the tip of her cigarette—"now I have learned a little more. In fact, I've changed my mind completely. Now I wouldn't be at all concerned if it *was* another woman involved. After all, it's hardly likely that there will be, is it? But now I know that when another *man* is concerned"—and she turns those enormous eyes of hers on to Cor, who, choosing to avoid them, looks down at the floor—"I have very little chance. And when that other man looks so much like Cor's first love, Henk, as you do, Mr. Wharton, then I know that I'd have no chance at all."

She is looking directly at you again when she says this, still toying with her cigarette as though it is something she is about to crush out of existence.

"No chance whatsoever, Mr. Wharton," she goes on, "unless I do one of two things—either resign myself to the situation, or else remove both of us from the source of temptation. And that is what I am going to do, Mr. Wharton. I'm sorry if you thought that by my asking you to come to see me, I might be going to change my mind about this"—and now you can see that even Cor is astounded by what she is saying —"for I'm not. I just wanted to see you again to make quite sure that my first impressions were the right ones. And I find that they are, Mr. Wharton. You do look so much like Henk that I know Cor will have no chance of getting over it. If anything, it will probably be even worse for him than it was then. And I think *I* know, Mr. Wharton, just how bad *that* was." Then, incredibly, hardly even pausing for breath, she turns to Cor and says, suddenly a small and petulant child again: "Mia want drink of water!"

So Cor gets up and, without saying anything, leaves the room to go and fetch it for her—leaves the two of you just staring at each other. It would be impossible to say who despised the other one the more at that moment.

You just sit there, stunned, not knowing what you can say to a woman like this. Even if you *could* think of something to say, you feel that you just couldn't be bothered saying it. In any case, no matter who she is, or what she is like, you just wouldn't want to say anything anyway. You know that everything is hopeless now, finished. You can hardly believe it, can hardly bring yourself to realize it, but you know it all the same. There might have been some hope beforehand, before you came to see this Mia of Cor's; but now it's all gone. There's no hope at all.

When Cor comes back with the glass of water, you can see that he must feel the same—stunned, helpless. Over Mia's ridiculously curly head, he looks at you like someone half in a trance, or as though he hasn't quite got his wits about him, weak. It's a terrible thing to see, those strong features of his suddenly sagged into a look of such despondent weakness, almost idiotic. Those near-oriental eyes of his look, somehow, suddenly as though they're crossed, or as though he has one wall eye, which you've never noticed before. You know this can't be so, but it looks like that. And you have to turn your own eyes away somewhere, anywhere; you can't bear to look at him any more.

Mia drinks, sips with little gurgling and sucking sounds, just as a child would do, or a bird. And you can't bear to look at her any more either; you feel as though you might kill her if you do. You can almost feel yourself getting up out of the chair, putting your hands around that skinny white freckled neck of hers, and squeezing, squeezing until there's no more struggle or breathing or whining, and she's just lying limp and crushed in the chair, dead at long last, a mere lump of clay you could throw in a river. Those hideous eyes would be closed. It's so vivid that, after a few seconds, you can hardly believe that you *haven't* done it, and, when you *can* bring yourself to look at her again, those huge and awful eyes are fixed on you once more, bulbously, like the transparent but frosted eyes of a fish, yet still staring and vicious as though it's not possible for them to close. She puts down the glass and: "Mia want a cigarette," she says.

Oh for God's sake! Does she have to say it like that?— like a little child with the sulks? Mia want *this* and Mia want *that*! You know what Mia *really* wants, and it would do her the world of good. Find her a truck-driver or something . . .

How funny it is! It's not so long ago that you'd thought: How *noble* she must be!

And while you've been thinking of this, and looking anywhere but at either Mia or Cor, you've been looking around the room you're in. It's like seeing it for the first time, just at that moment. Of course you had realized when Cor had first shown you into it that it was small and, yes, a little dingy. Yet it's not dirty; to the contrary, it's spotlessly clean, and modern, or as modern as a room in such a house could be. Walls painted grey with heavy dark-blue drapes over the windows, and over what looks had once been an old-fashioned fireplace. They've done it up themselves, obviously—or Cor has—even the furniture, in that austere yet aggressively modern style. You might have expected it; he's probably quite the handyman as well. It's not what you could say was exactly a pleasant room, let alone attractive; but it's probably as pleasant as anyone could make it with limited resources. It must have been absolutely hideous in its original state. And small; terribly small—almost suffocating.

She stubs out her cigarette, and again you're reminded of someone squashing the life from some insect, zealously. Then: "Mia's tired," she whines, and yawns as though to prove it, only half-covering her mouth with the back of her hand. "Mia had to work late last night. While *you* two"—and could anyone look more pointedly, and so suddenly?—"Well, *God* knows what you two were doing!" Then she heaves herself up out of her chair. Her pregnancy makes her look like some skinny sort of python that's just swallowed a pig. And that's *life*, you think to yourself. *There* is the beginning of God alone knows what kind of life . . .

"Mia's going to bed," she grizzles. "Mia doesn't want lunch. You'll have to get it for yourselves."

You think she's about to leave you both, without further ado, and you're glad, terribly relieved. You can't stand it in this terrible room much longer, not even with Cor there. Stifling. But at the door, she stops again, and turns those huge scavenging eyes onto you.

"Cor's quite good at getting meals anyway," she says. "Much better than I am. But I suppose he should be—it's a *woman's* job, you know!"

And only then does she go.

After a few minutes, Cor comes over and puts his hand on your shoulder.

"I'm sorry, Ray," he says. "I'm terribly sorry. I hadn't any idea she was going to be like this. I mean, it's not like her really. She can really be very nice if she wants to be . . ." But then his voice just trails away, and you're left waiting there, stifling in that terrible room.

"Let's get out of here," you say. "We can have lunch in town or something. Anywhere."

But even outside, driving away in the car, you can still see those fearful eyes, that pouting mouth, freckles—and that huge swollen lump of life cached so awkwardly in her belly. It's Cor's child, you tell yourself. But something else tells you it's like something already rotten and foetid inside her; decay setting in before life can effect its own birth. You've never felt like that about a pregnancy before. But now it makes you feel sick. Cor's child! And you can't help wondering if he wants to be a father; if he's proud of it. He could be such a wonderful father, you tell yourself.

And that's not all. At lunch, in a city restaurant, it's as though she's still with you. For you can still hear that whining voice of hers: "Mia want salt, Mia want pepper. Mia want this, Mia want that. Mia want . . ."

". . . Mia want *Cor*! Mia *got* Cor! Mia *keep* Cor!"

And it will be only eight days, you remember, until Mia will be quite sure of keeping what she wants.

20

LOUSY trick or not, you make up your mind to make the most of it. You've got eight days. Well, that's much better than eight hours, or even eight minutes. And that's all some people get. Some people don't even get that much. Some don't get anything at all. You've heard of people that love someone all their lives, and don't even touch the person they love, perhaps never even speak to him, but they go on loving him all the same. Well, at least you and Cor have had more than that. What's more, you've still got eight days of it left, so make the most of it. That's the least you can do.

Neither of you ever talk about how the eighth day is coming all the time. You never mention it. In fact, you don't even let yourselves think about it, if you can stop yourself. You try to pretend to yourselves that that eighth day isn't coming at all, that it doesn't even exist. You just pretend to yourself that what you have now—this thing that is so precious between the two of you—will never end, can't ever end. And it's as though for the first time you know what the word 'precious' means. It has never had much meaning before now. And other words too, like cherish. Cherish becomes a very precious word.

Eight days. You let the office go hang, you let most everything go hang. You look after the essential things, of course; you've always got to do that. But as soon as you can, you get away, meet Cor, go for drives in the car, out into the country or somewhere. You even make love with each other out in the country, not always in the car—sometimes just on the ground behind trees or rocks or somewhere, behind a brook that sings so much you could swear it lives too, and what's more that it knows it. Lunches. And dinners. The cinemas, and the two of you holding hands down low in the seats all the time. When you're crossing a road, he sometimes cautions you with his hand on your arm or shoulder, and you don't give a hang who sees it. He's pretty careful about that sort of thing anyway, and so are you of course. But the main thing, the most important thing, is that he always knows when to do it, and how to do it, so that there's only the two of you that ever know about it. Anyone else would have to be pretty alert and sort of snoopy to see it. They'd have to be the type that would be watching for that sort of thing all the time; and that type doesn't matter.

And there's the office, of course—every night. Sometimes you don't even bother to go home. You even buy blankets and pillows to use there, to make yourselves more comfortable, and you have to hide them in an old locked cabinet that Barbara never uses any more. At least, when those eight days are over, there won't be a single part of each other's bodies that you won't know everything about. Not only what they look like, feel like; but also what they look and feel like inside as well, as though your bodies are only just functioning —living—for the very first time.

You don't stop to think how Mia must feel, being left alone nearly all the time. She probably sees Cor only when he goes home to change. And you know she must be packing up, preparing to go. It must be pretty hard for her, alone, and her having the baby and everything. Maybe Cor does help some of the time. Or else maybe Rob Hamilton has thought of that too, paid for that too, and has men come in to pack everything for them. That's probably how it is. For Cor tell you that Rob is taking Mia down to the ship—and you're taking Cor, of course; Cor and the one case he has for himself. That's all you can think about, or *will* think about. You won't let yourself think about Mia, or her baby, or Rob Hamilton, or anything like that. And you can't think about that eighth day that keeps on coming and coming . . .

Probably Cor doesn't let himself think about it either. It's only a few times that you suddenly find him crying quietly on

114

your shoulder; just a few times when you suddenly feel him shaking and crying against you. Only three times, if you remember rightly; twice on the very last night.

21

Spring; and of all the cruelly ironic jokes, a glorious morning. It was raining earlier, quite heavily at times. But then the sun had to come bursting through, all bright and warm and even sort of joyous, as though it thought the day was a happy event. You could have sworn it would rain all the time; be all grey and dismal, drizzling. But no—sunshine. There are even birds singing; just another dirty trick. It would have to be a really fiendish mind to think up something like this . . .

The ship sails at noon. Passengers on board between nine and eleven; visitors ashore at eleven-thirty. It's nearly eleven before you and Cor get there. Mia and Rob Hamilton must have been there on the stroke of nine. Cor can hardly speak to either of them—and you, of course, can't say a damn word to them. You just can't; they look so sort of triumphant or something. It's funny how sometimes a man and a woman, not at all related to each other, and probably not even caring one whit about each other, can look so much alike as do Mia and Hamilton.

Cor says he'll see to his case, and that he understands why you don't want to go on board. You don't want to see him taking his case on board, so you say you'll go for a walk down to the end of the ship or somewhere, the bows, and wait for him there. As you turn away, you feel his hand squeeze your arm. But you mustn't stop; if you do, you won't be able to help yourself from suddenly blubbing like a big kid. And that you won't do. Which is another thing: everybody else—everybody else that's normal—they can blub away and fall all over each other as much as they like. But you—you've just got to stand there, and make yourself look as though it's only a business acquaintance or someone that's going away. *You* can't show anything; people would only sneer if you did, sneer and jeer their little pinched souls out, laughing at you. That's why you've got to get away somewhere, anywhere. Walk down to the bows of the ship. Alone. Down there where the quay and the cranes and the loading junk are all misty and remote. And they'll be a damn sight mistier if you don't fight back those bloody tears in your eyes. Maybe, if anyone does see you, they'll just think you're losing a wife or a sweetheart or someone. Maybe it'll never occur to them that it's a man you're losing, just as it never occurs to them that a man can love another man—yes, sexually and all—because they're taught and told that it's something you can't do. The hell you can't! So they'd never guess that for you it's just like the end of the world.

Five minutes, ten; a quarter of an hour. Cor still hasn't come. There won't be much more time left. You won't go back to the gangway, but you keep on looking. Where is he? People are even beginning to come off again, and yes, you can hear the voice over the amplifying system: All visitors ashore! All visitors ashore! Where is he, for God's sake! And then you can't help yourself; you *have* to go back. You can see Hamilton coming down the gangway. Mia is up on the deck, watching, and sometimes waving to him. Whenever they look at each other, those two, they've always got that smug little smirk of conspiracy on their faces. Well, they've both got what they want, so good luck to them, and you hope they'll need it.

Where is he? He must be somewhere down here. Look around you, look all around you, for he must be here somewhere. He's just *got* to be. He's not up there with Mia, and he's not coming down with Hamilton. He's not anywhere along the decks. So it just can't be that he's been delayed and then found it too late to come down. He must be down here somewhere. He just must be.

Streamers. You never thought of them. But people are already throwing them to each other, catching them down on the wharf, or catching them up on the decks, groaning if they miss and the streamers fall into the water. It's all crazy, crazy. Anyone would think it was Christmas or something. And what can a bloody streamer do? Is it anything like touching each other's fingers? Does anyone really feel as though it's like being able to stretch your fingers for a hundred yards or so, and you can still feel each other? Just bits of paper, with crazy colours. It's all mad, mad; but you can't help wishing you'd thought of them all the same. Just one would do. But where *is* Cor? Where *is* he?

Maybe it's been too much for him. Maybe he couldn't come back; he's just broken down in the cabin or somewhere and can't come down. In which case—*in which case*—you'll never see him again—never. But no, that just can't be. It just *can't* be, that's all.

You push through to see a little better, and somebody snarls at you for snapping their streamer. You can't see him anywhere. Push a little farther, but you still can't see him. He's not with Mia. She's just standing there, smiling, smug. Hamilton's down at the bottom now, and Mia throws him a streamer. Why don't the two of you go and get married or something, for Christ's sake. Push a little farther. You've snapped another streamer; you didn't know a mere woman could give such a filthy look. But you don't care. He must be somewhere. Even if he can't come down again now, even if you'll never *touch* each other again now, you must be able at least to *see* him.

You can't help yourself. You go up to Hamilton and say: "What's happened to Cor?"

And he just looks at you with that smirk of his.

"You don't think you're going to see *him* again, do you? Mia's seen to that!"

Then he turns away, and it's all you can do to stop yourself from wiping that smirk from his face. You can't stay there any longer; you've just go to get away. So you turn and walk as quickly as you can, pushing through everyone, pushing towards the end of the shed to go back to the car.

What a wonderful good-bye that was! You don't even have an address to write to him. And maybe that's it; Cor's decided to do this: just to go. And it will be up to him to write, if you're ever going to hear of each other again. So he probably won't ever write—he'll just go. You don't know how he could do it, not after all that's been between you. You really don't, unless—unless it's a sort of defence mechanism or something. If *he* leaves *you*, maybe he thinks he won't feel so bad about it; because he couldn't stand it a second time, of having someone leave *him*. Maybe that's it, but you don't really know. You'll probably never know. All you'll ever know is that he's gone. Gone . . .

When you reach the end of the shed, and you should turn to go to the car, out of sight of the ship, you just can't do it after all. You can't go another step farther. You just have to turn round again. The ship has already started to pull away from the wharf. Streamers are snapping. People calling out to each other. It's a fair while before you can find Mia again, and when you do, it's just at the precise moment when *her* streamer snaps. You watch the end flutter down into the water. And it's as though something inside of you has also snapped, and as though the very last chance of your ever seeing or hearing anything of Cor again has snapped with it. You're all dead inside —quite dead. You watch Mia wave down to Hamilton again, and he waves back. Cor still isn't with her; she's alone. And then, as though it was arranged between Mia and Hamilton beforehand, she waves once more then goes inboard. Hamilton turns and goes too. Neither of them even gives a look for you.

You know that now is the time that you must go. You must get back to the car before you make a fool of yourself in front of all those people. You must. Yet still you can't. You've still got to torture yourself by waiting until the very last minute; you can't help it.

From stem to stern, up and down all the different decks, from railing to railing, fore and aft—but he's nowhere; you feel quite sure that you'd be able to find him if he was. He just couldn't be there, somewhere, waving his arm off to you, and you not see him. A thing like that just *couldn't* happen. That would be the dirtiest trick of them all. No, he just isn't there, anywhere. It's all over. So you might just as well go home—if ever again there *is* such a place.

But again, just as you're about to go, just as you've nearly found the courage to turn and go, you can't. And it's then you see Mia come out again. You're about to look somewhere else, because you had thought you had seen the last of her, when something about her makes you watch her. She runs to the railing, pushes between people; then she backs out again and runs down the deck a little. You can tell there is something wrong. Maybe she's left something behind; that's probably it, and she wants to shout out to Hamilton about it. But Hamilton has already gone, so she can't. She runs a little farther, pushes into the railing again. She's just like a small frantic bird, fluttering up and down against the wires of a cage. Well, if she *has* left something behind, you can't help hoping, petty as you know it is, that it's something she's going to miss one hell of a lot. You're almost glad, just watching her, all anxious and frantic, looking down and around everywhere. You even nearly start laughing to yourself; at least it helps to take that other thing off your mind.

But then the ship has pulled away too far for you to see her any more. You watch the last streamer, at the stern, until it snaps and, like all the rest, flutters sadly down to drown in the water. Gulls swoop around it. On the wharf it's all waving arms and handkerchiefs—a form of mass madness, waving when you can't see the person you're waving to any more. And yet you know all too well, if you yourself had seen Cor just the once more, or knew even approximately where he was, you too would be waving your arm off.

But you didn't see him, and that's that. And at long last you can make yourself go back to the car—back to an empty car, and an empty life.

But it's just before the car that you have to stop. You have to stop and hold your hand over the sudden pain in your chest, deep inside it, it's such a shock. So now you can give yourself illusions, can you? Hallucinations. But you might be wrong, must be wrong. It must be someone else's car, the same model and colour as your own. Or it's someone else sitting in it by mistake. It couldn't be Hamilton, surely, wanting to have the last vindictive word of all. No one could do that much, not even Hamilton. And it can't possibly be the other thing you thought of, for just a second or so. It's impossible. No, it's an illusion after all, and you'll probably have a good many more of them as time goes by. You'll see him on every street and corner, in every passing face, everywhere you go. You won't have to dream about him to see him; you'll never stop seeing him . . .

And then, thinking about it, you start to laugh. Or do you cry? God knows; you yourself can't tell. You go to the car, almost wanting to believe in this mad hallucination, and you jerk the door open and almost fall inside, the pain in your chest is so bad. But it's true; the case is still there. And, oh God, you can't believe it but yes, yes, it *is* Cor sitting there, waiting for you. And what's more, when he sees the state you're in, he's damn near crying himself too. You want to fall all over each other, right then and there—forget the whole damn world just for once. But all you can do is suddenly, desperately, grip each other's hand. What more can you ask for? Could anything else say any more?

But yes. Cor says:

"You didn't really think I'd leave you, did you?"

Somehow or other you do manage to drive. And also you just keep on nodding somehow, when Cor goes on:

"We mean too much to each other, Ray. That's all,"

That's all! That's all . . .

Part Two

THE WAY OUT

I

WELL, after someone has done as much as that to be with you, you don't suppose there could be anyone who could now have any doubts about the matter. None whatsoever. Past lover or not, and no matter how promiscuous he might once have been, you surely couldn't ask for any more proof of the way he feels about you. What you want to say is, there are lots of normal people who would never even dream of doing half as much to be with their so-called lover; lots and lots of them.

Of course the only place where you can take him to begin with, after you've left the ship, is to where he was living before. It seems a terrible thing, taking him back to a half-empty house with all its memories of Mia, but there's nothing else you can do. Besides, Cor himself suggests it. The other couple who were sharing it with them are still keeping it on, he says, and he knows they will be only too glad to have him back, to share the rent as before. You don't like the idea at first and suggest a hotel or something, even a boarding-house, just for a while, until you can sort yourselves out. But it's Cor who says no, you'll have enough expense as it is, later on, when you both find your own flat somewhere. Better to save as much money as possible for that. Besides, he says, there's nothing in the house now to remind him of Mia; she took everything of their own with her, naturally, thinking he was going with her. The house was furnished originally, but with such old furniture and china and all that sort of thing, curtains, that they just packed most of it away and used their own, brought out from Holland. He had to put all the old things back again; and when you take him into the house, you see exactly what he means.

You can hardly believe it's the same room. If anything, it looks even smaller and dingier, with its old-fashioned furniture and pictures, the quite hideous curtains at the windows. You wonder how he could even think of living in a place like that, but he just smiles and says: "Oh, I hope it won't be for long. And any place is wonderful, Ray, if I can be with you." And he also reminds you that he's got to go easy for a while on expenses, until he finds another job, although he's pretty sure of being able to get back his old one.

So, he's got his own sitting-room, his own bedroom, and the use of the kitchen and the rest of the house with the other couple.

"We can even do this place up a bit," he suggests, "seeing the rent is so cheap."

But you don't exactly fancy having to share your life together with this other Dutch couple—a normal couple, that is—no matter how much Cor assures you that they know all about everything, and it doesn't make any difference with them. That may be all right for Continental people; but you, an Australian, well you just haven't been able to adapt yourself that far as yet. After all, how could you? There's no place in the country, hardly, where you could have the chance to. So:

"No, Cor," you say. "We'll find a place of our own, in town or somewhere. As you say, this'll do until we do find it. We might even come here sometimes, *geliefde*. Although we've still got the office, of course."

"Just as you say, Ray," he says. And that's something you get to hear a good deal as time goes by, that *just as you say, Ray* of his.

You're about to tell him of your plans for taking him into the office, but something or other makes you hold back. Everything has happened so suddenly, you feel that you want a little time to sort things out a bit, see if the firm's earnings can take an extra man. But you don't have to worry about this for long. Once you've celebrated this miraculous reunion in that cramped little bedroom of his (it just has room for the double-

124

bed, a wardrobe and a dressing-table, leaving, as Cor laughed, hardly enough room for anyone to change their mind, let alone anything else)—well, once that's over with and you're back at the office, you've hardly sorted out the mail and so forth when Cor rings to say he's already been to the club, and yes, he's started working there. He's started again that very afternoon, he tells you, because they hadn't yet been able to find someone else with his ability and experience, they told him, and so they were desperately short-handed. They even took him back without any stoppage of salary or anything, or without asking him to refund his accrued holiday-pay which they had paid—which at least shows how much they thought of him.

The only thing about it that he doesn't like, he says, is that he'll have to work that night until ten o'clock. But he'll get away as soon as possible afterwards. Well, you've missed a whole morning in the office yourself, and the lord knows there's enough to catch up. So you tell him that you'll work late as well, and wait for him there. When you put down the phone again, you can hardly believe that going down to the ship, and all that you went through over it, was only this morning. It already seems months, years, eons ago.

2

IT REALLY does seem so long ago that, when he does come to the office that night, around just before eleven sometime, and although you'd made love only that afternoon, in Cor's room, you both want it all over again. After all, you're back with the old carpet and radiator and everything, although it's not quite so cold as it has been during the winter, now that spring is so definitely on the way. And doing things just as you've always done them before is much more like a real reunion. Then it's nearly three o'clock before you realize it, and you know that you've both got to go home. Driving him back, and then going on to your own place, make things seem just exactly the same; it's as though all the nightmare of the last ten days or so had never happened.

But they've happened all right, and you can't help feeling a bit curious about Mia. So you talk to Cor about it. He sort of hangs his head a bit, and naturally you'd expect him to feel a little upset about it; after all, it couldn't have been an easy thing for him to do. It wouldn't be an easy thing for anyone to do. One thing, he seems to have spent quite some time thinking about it before having decided to do it, for he tells you:

"Oh, Ray, I suppose it was a terrible shock for her, at the beginning. But I figured out that she'd soon make friends on the ship, and there's a doctor and a nurse on board for her to go to and so forth. Her family will meet her in Holland, and she's going to live with them. We both were, if I had gone too. And it's not as though she really loves me. I didn't tell you, but she's been writing to an old flame of hers in Holland for several months. He wanted her to marry him before, but she always said she was waiting for me. As *you* say Ray?"—and he smiles at you—"Christ knows why! You know, Ray, you sort of swear quite a lot, don't you? Even for an Australian. Still"—and he smiles again—"we Dutch are pretty good at it, too. You should hear some of the things *we* can say, that you can't very well translate into English. Especially things from Amsterdam. I suppose, in a way, it's a bit like Cockney in English. '*Amsterdams*' can be quite rough at times . . ."

You think that it doesn't take him long to forget Mia, or be side-tracked by other things, even little things. But it's not so; one thing you have to say for him, as little as she really does mean to him, he still thinks of her a lot. He sends her a cable for one thing, and writes to her at the different ports where the ship is calling. He also says that he must send her some money, until such time as she divorces him, perhaps, and marries this other Dutchman.

"Another reason, Ray, why I must live as cheaply as I can on the moment," he says. And never, never once, does he suggest that you might help him in this respect. And you don't offer. He seems so proud about these matters that you're afraid he would only be insulted. Well, not exactly insulted, but humiliated a little, perhaps even hurt. So you leave him to look after his own affairs himself. You feel that if he really needs help at any time, then he'll ask you for it, and it'll be time enough then. But what you *can* do, you tell yourself, is to help him a little in ways that shouldn't be too noticeable, like always paying for lunches and dinners and so forth, and taking him for drives in the car. You even buy him some decent clothes.

And yes—at last you think of something that can mean almost as much as do the cuff-links he gave you. It's funny how you come to think of it, and it's only because he's Dutch —or a Continental—that you can give it to him. For most Continental men, when they're married, wear a wedding ring to show it. And it's while you're holding his hand one time, lying there on the carpet before the radiator, and you're stroking the back of his hand and his fingers, that you realize something is missing. And of course, when you look, what's missing is the gold ring he used to wear. You ask him about it, and he just says that he doesn't consider himself married to Mia any more, so he's put the ring away. When she divorces him, he says, he'll send it back to her.

So that's what you can buy for him, another ring to cover the little white band on his flesh where the first one had been. And you have it inscribed, with both your initials and, like he did on the cuff-links, the date of when you first met. When you give it to him, he's so moved by it that he nearly starts to cry about it, and that night was really an epoch in love-making. But somehow you always wish that you'd been able to think of it yourself, and much earlier. What you mean is, you wish you had been able to think of it yourself without help from any outside influence; for if it hadn't been for your noticing the absence of Mia's ring on his finger, you often wonder if you'd ever have been able to think of such a thing for yourself. And it's this which nags at you a bit; you don't seem to have quite the imagination for this sort of thing as he has. But all the same, he's pleased enough with it; anyone would think he'd been given the moon.

It turns out a bit harder than you think to find a flat for yourselves. You thought it would be one of the easiest things in the world, just to find a small flat big enough for the two of you somewhere. But the hell it is. You look at dozens of them, both of you do, but there's always a snag in them somewhere. First of all, you don't really know whether you want one furnished or unfurnished; most of the furniture in the furnished ones is pretty crappy. And for an unfurnished one, once you start pricing things around the town, you soon find that it's damned expensive to furnish even a small flat, right from scratch. In fact, it gives you a shock, and makes you wonder how young newly married couples—normal couples, you mean —can ever afford to get married in the first place, unless one of them has some money saved up. But here again, they're on a much better wicket than two men starting up together; *they* have a wedding, paid for by parents and all that sort of thing, and so naturally they get wedding presents, pretty well enough to set them on their merry little way without having to get a thing themselves. That's how *they* can do it, you suppose. You know what you yourself have given in the way of wedding presents, dozens of them. If you only had half of that coming to you now, what a help it would be. But of course, with *your* kind of marriage, there's nothing of the kind; you have to get everything yourselves.

Anyway, this is one of the snags in the first place, just making up your own mind what you want, or what you can afford. Having the car, you really need a garage for it as well; and a telephone, instead of being able to rely on the family's at home. And then everything from dishes to cutlery and beds and things, chairs, cupboards, and the hundred and one things you seem to need for cooking and so forth, brooms and all that, even down to dish-washers, things for the toilet. Once you begin, there never seems to be an end to it, before you even start on groceries and things to feed yourselves with.

Sometimes the flat itself would be all right, but the district would be no good; or else the building would have a lousy entrance so that everyone else living there could see your every coming and going; or windows of another flat would look straight into your own, and you'd never be able to do anything anyway without always having first to see that you'd pulled down the blinds or drawn the curtains. You'd have no privacy. You'd only have to slip once, just forget yourselves, and give each other a kiss or something, and you'd give the whole game away. It'd be like living in a fishbowl; not much good for the kind of life you both want to lead.

Well, there's all of these things to think of, apart from the usual things of how long you can have it for and so forth, which is very important. After all, you don't want to go to the trouble of moving temporarily, breaking off from your own family life. And that's going to be another thing; that's going to be quite something, of course; but nowhere near as much as what Cor has had to do, you keep having to remind yourself.

A couple of times you find something that is so close to what you want, you almost decide to make do with it and forget the disadvantages. But then you always get the feeling that, if you wait just a *little* longer, you'll find the really perfect place for the two of you. Maybe it's the distance from the city that puts you off; some little thing, anyway. And on those occasions, you can see that Cor is pretty disappointed when you decide no, you'll still wait for a while. In fact once you thought it was almost going to lead to your first row, but it didn't. One thing, though; it made you realize just how much lonelier it must be for Cor, having to live alone in that half of a house of his, than it is for you with your family. But on the other hand, it's this having to eventually break away from your family that makes it so much harder for you.

And yet—yet somehow—you still seem to just let things drift. You don't mean to, but somehow or other you just can't

129

help it. There's always a fair bit to do at the office for one thing; there just never seems to be much time left for anything these days, between the office and seeing Cor so much, at all sorts of hours. And so that, you suppose, is how things get to drift. You don't ever mean it to happen that way; it just does.

3

BUT if there's one thing that soon brings you out of a drifting period, it's a bombshell of some sort. And the first bombshell that hits you is something you really should have expected. Just exactly as he did before, Hamilton comes to see you.

When he comes through the door, he's all charm and smiles as though he's coming to tell you you've shared the winning ticket in a lottery or something. But you know it's all just put on for Barbara's sake, and this you can understand. In a way, it's a good job he does put on such an act. It has fooled Barbara all right; in fact it looks as though she even likes him. It's easy enough to see how she could; he's got this act of his, like he's the one and only little man so bravely making his way through a world of giants. It might even have fooled you, if you hadn't known him better. But of course there wouldn't be too many who would ever know him as you do.

As though to prove your point, as soon as Barbara has closed the door, all the charm and smiles drop from his face, like a mask that's just snapped its ear-strings and fallen to the floor. And then there's the real Hamilton—quite cocky for his size, really; and especially after the reception you gave him last time. You've got to hand it to him; he's about as cocky as they come. Which probably explains after all how he's become a company manager; sheer persistence.

This time, before you've got a chance to say anything, he says:

"All right, Wharton. Don't get up. And no, I *won't* sit down this time. I think I warned you last time what I'd do. And I suppose you thought I was just talking for the good of my health. Did you? Well, you'll soon find out whose health I was talking for. When I found out what you'd made Cor do, I—I—why it's the filthiest thing I've ever heard of anybody doing. But don't think you'll get away with it, Wharton. Don't think you'll get away with it for one moment."

He pauses then, to glare at you. And you're about to tell him he's been watching too much television by the sound of him, but just as suddenly he goes on again.

"Well, I warned you, Wharton. Don't say I didn't. So now you might just as well start packing this little show of yours right up. For you won't have it much longer. And what do you think you'll do then, Wharton? Live on your little Dutch boyfriend's tips?"

He can get his face into so many contortions, you'd think he'd once been on the stage or something.

You tell yourself you're not going to let him get away with that, but just as you're about to say something, make a retort of some kind, of all things he spits clean on to your desk and then heads for the door. It takes you so much by surprise, you can't move or even speak. And there he is at the door, opening it, all charm and smiles again, and you can see Barbara smiling back at him, as sweet as can be and putting on the cute-looking act. And you know she'd never believe it if you ever told her what had really happened in the office; she'd think you'd gone mad.

But after he's gone, you calm yourself down a little. You tell yourself that it's all just bluff, all just hysterical bluff. He wouldn't do anything like he suggests; he wouldn't dare to. Like the old saying 'it takes a thief to catch a thief', he'd soon realize that other people would start looking at him curiously, if he told them about you, for they'd soon be thinking to themselves that it also takes a queer to spot a queer.

Who hasn't heard that before? Even the police. You've heard they often use it; tempt the ones they catch with promises of being let off and protection and all that sort of thing, and then send them out on the streets at night to pick up some more for them. Pretty little operation—especially when you think that the poor bastards who fall for it only do it because they're so goddamned frightened, desperate, scared to hell out of their wits every time they think of the future, and trying to look for another job somewhere . . .

No. Mr. Robin Hamilton is just bluffing all right. He wouldn't have the nerve to go running around shooting off his mouth. He'd be giving himself away as well. When he got around to thinking of that, he wouldn't have the nerve for it. Just wait and see. Yes, you can forget it all, all right; just put it clean out of your mind and calm yourself down. He's not worth worrying about.

So you tell yourself; buy by God he must work fast. That very afternoon Barbara brings you in a memo, delivered by their own messenger, from the Bingo Biscuit Company. It's short and to the point: they regret to advise you that they find your suggested campaign inadequate, and are therefore constrained to cancel their order. That's all. About the biggest order you've ever had. And the money you've spent on it, apart from the money it would have meant to you. But the main thing is, you just wouldn't have believed that Jack Bennett could ever have done a thing like that, you've known him so long. You wouldn't have thought he'd ever have done even half as much, no matter what anyone might have told him. But he's done it, all right. It's even his signature—no, just initials—on the bottom of the memo.

Well, it's only one account, you tell yourself. But almost immediately, you tell yourself, no. It'll be more than that. When a lot of the other accounts hear about it, they'll probably pull out too. They'll start thinking that there must be something very wrong with your work or something about you for Bingo Biscuits to have pulled out, and then they'll take their business somewhere else too. It'll soon get around; start to snowball; go through the TV and radio stations and everything, the press. No, Hamilton doesn't have to tell anyone else; he couldn't have picked a better one. Just had to work what he wanted in that one direction, and he's worked the lot. You have to hand it to him; he certainly knows how to operate.

But then you tell yourself no, you won't let it go at that. You'd only be admitting it if you did. What you've got to do is to act as though you haven't got the faintest idea in the world why Bennett should cancel his order; just like any normal person would. So you tell Barbara to get Bennett on the phone, and while you're waiting for him, thinking out not so much what you're going to say as how you're going to say it, you tell yourself you'll work things out somehow or other. You've just got to.

Bennett comes on over the phone; at least he didn't refuse to speak to you. But it doesn't take long before you realize he probably didn't know who was wanting to speak to him. As soon as you say your name, you can feel his voice freeze at the other end of the line. You can't explain it, but you can feel it; no doubt about it. His voice freezes clean into complete silence. Then he just says: "Sorry, old chap, but we have our reasons." And puts the phone down. You're just left sitting there, the receiver still in your hand, like some kind of bird or dog you picked up to pet a little, and as soon as you did, it just died in your hand.

But you're not going to give up yet, not by a long shot. When you think it over, what Bennett had said hadn't sounded *too* unfriendly. A bit cold, a bit distant, perhaps; but not really unfriendly, not as though he suddenly loathed even the sight of you. So what you'll do, you'll get right into the car and go out and see him. If nothing else, it will at least show him that you're not afraid to show your face.

So you go out to tell Barbara where you're going, tell her to cancel any other appointments for the afternoon. And you give her the memo. While you're putting on your hat and overcoat, you watch her, and you see her face almost fall down on to her typewriter.

"Pretty, isn't it!" you say to her, still acting, or *trying* to act, as normally as possible, as though you don't really know what the hell it's all about. And you can see that it's also got Barbara puzzled.

"But why? Why?" she asks.

So you shrug.

"But it's the best layout you've ever done, Ray," she goes on.

And so then you say: "I know, I know. But you can read, can't you? And he's not saying much more over the telephone either. That's why I'm going out there," you tell her, still keeping the big act going, "to see him personally. I smell a rat in this somewhere."

She still just looks dumbfounded, as though she can't believe it. And watching her, you know it's definitely got nothing to do with the quality of your layouts or anything. It's Hamilton, all right. So it's all the more essential for you to show your face.

And then Barbara says: "It's not a very happy day, is it?" And for just one instant you wonder if she had possibly overheard Hamilton earlier. But no, you tell yourself; no. The door is nearly soundproof for one thing; and for another, with her typewriter and all, it's always pretty noisy out in the outer office. No, she just means the Bingo account, that's all. Bingo! God, what a laugh! But you must keep your *own* little joke going.

"Babs, old girl," you say, "you've hit the nail right on its goddamn head. You know, you ought to be a carpenter or something. You'd make a real good one, you really would."

There's one consolation; at least you can still laugh at yourself.

It takes you half an hour to drive out to the Bingo Biscuit factory and offices, out of town; half an hour to bolster your confidence, think out what you're going to say, get a grip on yourself. But when you get there, the receptionist sort of smiles at you, and then tells you: Sorry, Mr. Bennett has just gone out, and won't be back today.

There's nothing you can do. You know it's a lie of course, but there's nothing you can do about it. You know Bennett's car, a big black Jaguar because he likes to think of himself as still a bit racy. And the car is standing there right in the Bingo Biscuit car-park. You couldn't miss it; you'd parked your own car right alongside.

4

You decide not to tell Cor about it. At least when you're together, and there are just the two of you, you couldn't be happier. And it would be a pity to spoil any of it, you feel. At least that's something you've still got. No matter what anybody else may do to you, at least you've still got that much. But even as you think it, you find yourself wondering just how long it might be before they take that away from you too. You'll lose Cor. But no, you can't even let yourself think of a thing like that.

So you decide not to tell him, but it's as though he knows what's happened all the same. It's only a few nights later, when you're lying together—in his place for once, not the office—that he says:

"Ray, something's worrying you. You haven't been happy the last few days."

You still try to keep it all from him, it's so ugly. And in any case, you might still be able to work things out somehow. You've just got to. So you say:

"Haven't been happy, for Christ's sake! What the hell do you think this is!"

But you can't fool Cor. You learned that some time ago, you can't fool him at all. You can't hide anything from him either. He's only got to look at you, and he knows somehow just exactly how you're feeling. And now he says:

"It's not because of the way I—the way I left Mia or something, is it?" And then you can see that he's so worried about it—that he's also got worries of his own; a good many of them, come to think of it—that you can't let him go on thinking things, anything, that aren't the real reason. So you tell him everything that's happened.

When you've finished, you don't think you've seen anyone look so full of hate and fury in all your life before. He's so worked up, you can feel him shaking and trembling against you.

"I'll kill him!" he says. "I'll kill him!"

The way he says it, you feel that he really means it. He seems to mean it so much that it scares the wits out of you; you can almost see him doing it. And this really frightens you. So you lean over him, pacify him a bit by running your fingertips over his eyebrows, the edges of his lips.

"Oh no you won't!" you say, just before you kiss him, as though to thank him for the thought, or even for just the way he feels so strongly about it. And then: "Oh no you won't! This isn't Holland, you know. There's still capital punishment in this country. In *this* State, anyway. You'd only finish up hanging for it. And someone like Hamilton just isn't worth it. So you forget anything of that kind, baby boy. Just forget it altogether."

But: "I could *kill* him on the moment!" he says again, still shaking against you, but not quite so much now.

"Oh no you couldn't," you go on, "because if you did, and they took you and strung you up, what in the hell do you think *I'd* do? Do you think *I'd* want to go on living, without my Dutch baby?"

Then he quietens down again, even laughs a bit. It's a funny thing, but he rather likes a bit of baby talk. At first you thought it was a bit soppy; but when you saw how it brought you much closer together, you even got to like it yourself. Now you do it most of the time, but only when there's just the two of you of course; never in front of anyone else.

So now he just lies there. You think he's forgotten it, or at least dismissed it from his mind for the moment. But he hasn't. All the time he's been lying beside you, one hand gently caressing a muscle in your thigh, he's still been thinking about it.

"Ray?"

"Yes?"

"What are you going to do about it?"

"Mmh? Oh, I don't know, baby. I'll think of something. Just don't *you* worry yourself about it. That's all."

"Ray?"

"Yes?"

"Ray, I think *I* could do something."

"You?"

"Yes. I mean, the whole cause of this business on the moment is just because how he feels about *me*. And if I—well, if I sort of gave him what he wants, just every now and again, maybe he wouldn't do all these things to you. Maybe he'd——"

It's almost as though an iceberg has fallen on you. You can't help it; you suddenly go all stiff, cold, just thinking about it. You start to tremble, you can't stop yourself, you're so shocked and sort of sick-feeling about it.

"Are you suggesting what I think you are?" you ask him. And you can't help it, you can't stop that cold edge coming into your voice. You can hear it yourself as plain as anything.

"Oh, Ray, you know it's not that I *want* to do it," he says quickly, holding you closer, finding it now his turn to pacify you. "Besides, it would only have to be once a month or something. Or even once every two months. He can't do it any oftener than that, Ray. He's already getting quite old..."

Oh, God, he's even got it all thought out!

"No!" you say. "No, no, no! What the hell do you think I am! How do you think *I'd* feel, thinking of you doing everything with a little shit like that. Or anyone, for that matter. No! Don't even say it again. Do you hear me!"

It's only then that you realize you've been shouting at him. And there's really no reason to. After all, what he was suggesting, he was going to do only for you. And could

137

anyone offer anything more than that? Oh, Cor, Cor, Cor! Sometimes you nearly *kill me* with your love, you really do.

So: "I'm sorry," you say. "I'm really sorry."

And he holds you closer again, smiles.

"All the same," he says, "I wish I *could* do something."

But you're all right again, now. One thing about it, it's brought you just that much closer together again, just when you thought it couldn't be possible for you to be any closer to each other.

"Don't you worry about it," you tell him. "I'll think of something. Something'll turn up. It's bound to. Just you see."

His hand goes back to that muscle on your thigh again; his face moves closer against your own, all warm and sort of solid-feeling beside you.

"There's only one thing, Cor," you have to say. "We'll have to forget about having our own flat for a while, until I see how things go."

You prepare yourself for whatever he might say next. You know it'll be a terrible disappointment to him, he's wanted a place of your own so much. But no. No, not at all. So you know what he does? He just says:

"Well, Ray, I guess we'll just have to do this place up a bit. This is enough for us on the moment, isn't it?"

And after all you know it means to him, you can hardly believe it. But what's more, when you lift yourself up to look into his eyes, those deep and entrenched yet so warm-looking eyes of his, he's actually smiling. Sometimes you think this love of yours will make your flesh burst into a thousand pieces.

5

ANOTHER account goes, then another. In just over a week, five of them drop you altogether. They're only small ones, you know; but they all add up. Hamilton has really operated in the right direction, all right. The snowball's started rolling, and you just don't know where it's all going to stop. You can see it's got Barbara worried too, puzzled. And she can need to be worried: if many more accounts go, you won't be able to keep her on; she'll have to look for another job. It shouldn't be hard for *her* to find one. But if it gets to the stage when *you* have to—well, that's another thing. Don't even think about it. Just work harder on those accounts you *have* got left. At least your work is good, a pretty high standard. Even you know that. And no matter what a person's like, or what he does, there's always someone wanting what he can do if he does it well enough. And so you try to reassure yourself, hoping. But it's the small fears that eat a man's life away—just the small ones.

6

COR gets these old curtains the Club was throwing out, and he has them dyed, a midnight-blue he calls it, and then he cuts out some shapes and things from an old sheet, and stitches them on himself.

You can't believe it when he shows them to you, for of course he doesn't let you have the faintest idea of what he's been doing until he's finished them, and they're all hung up and everything. Just looking at them, you'd swear they were something very expensive from one of the big stores. He's even hidden the fire-place again with one of them. He's put a pot-plant up on top of it, trailing long and delicate clusters of leaves down the dark blue and stark white patterns he's made. The old-fashioned lightshade is gone, too, and he's made one of those modern-looking shades out of a kind of old sacking. You don't notice it in the day time; but when the light's turned on, at night, it throws a soft and diffused kind of glow all round the room. And he's got some old shelves from the Club and hacked them about a bit, and then painted them, some black and some white, and arranged them at all sorts of angles. Then he's stacked a few books and things on them, just here and there, all rather casual looking, though you can tell it's all been carefully thought out and arranged. It's really staggering. He's had so little to work with, practically nothing really, and yet he's made the room look not only respectable, but sort of cosy as well. It even looks bigger than it did before. You're so amazed, you can hardly believe it.

"Like it?" he asks you, obviously proud of his handiwork.

"Like it! It's a miracle, that's what it is!" you tell him. And he looks even more pleased than ever. After all, it doesn't take so very much to please him, really; and not so much more to make him happy—keep him happy.

He comes and folds himself all around you somehow. And he says:

"You see? We don't really need so much, do we?"

"Not the way you can do things," you tell him. And then suddenly, almost heavily, you feel guilty, or just sad that you don't seem able to do and arrange things so well yourself. You try hard enough, God knows. But somehow it just never seems to come off, or work out—never. Especially at the moment—*on* the moment, Cor always says. And it gives you a kind of silly feeling that you're not able to do anywhere near as much as he can, and does. It always seems as though he does all the big things in your lives; the way he made sure of getting you in the first place, the cuff-links, giving Hamilton back all his things, leaving Mia like that. And now—well, it really isn't such a big thing as the others, but somehow it seems big. You suppose that making a home always does seem a big thing, whether or not the home itself is large or small, grand or humble, it's still a *home*. What really worries you about it is, you're not so sure that you've got anywhere near as much of it in you as he has; not even half as much. But God knows, you'll try—you really will try from now on. For after all, what else is there?

7

THEN comes the day when Barbara brings you in this all too curt little letter from the University, saying that it, too, is dropping its contract with you when it is due for renewal in a few weeks' time. It's not such a big account, nothing like Bingo Biscuits or one of the petroleum companies for instance, but it's still fairly sizeable all the same. What you had liked about it most of all was that it was fairly regular, and didn't demand too much in the way of thinking out layouts and things, like most of the commercial concerns do. This time the excuse of layouts being inadequate can't very well be used, so you know that it's nothing else but Hamilton's snowball still rolling along, just as you were beginning to think that perhaps it had finished.

This time you feel that there *is* something you can do about it. The letter has been sent by the bursar, who usually just pays the cheques when they're due, but the fellow you usually deal with is a man called Parkinson who handles public relations. He's pleasant enough; you could almost say amiable. There's a joke in the Uni that even this particular Parkinson has a law of his own too, that of 'a diminishing rate of attainment and prestige in proportion to the increase of effort and amenities', or something like that. He has a very dry but amusing wit, always detached and impersonal, which makes you think that he would be the last person ever to be affected be merely a malicious whisper. He'd be quite understanding about the matter, you'd have thought. You know he's a married man, with two or three children, but there's always quite a bit of your kind of life among the academics. So you figure that a man like Parkinson would be well aware of this other half of life, and would be the type to ignore or perhaps even condone it. One thing you would have thought attributable to him is that he'd recognize such malicious gossip, whether true or false, as the emotional blackmail it is.

Well, even if that's not the case after all, one thing you feel sure you can do about it is to ascertain that Hamilton's little game really is the reason for it, and that it's not just purely some uncanny and ironic coincidence. For Parkinson, you know, is quite a buddy of Bruce Farnham's, and old Bruce would be the one person you could rely on to tell you the truth of the matter. Even if he didn't know it himself, he'd make a point of finding out. So yes, that's what you'll do; get in touch with old Bruce. It's about time you saw him again anyway. One way and another, you've got quite a bit to tell him.

At first you think you'll just talk to him on the phone. But then you think, no, he'll only ask you to have dinner at his place, and he's always doing that, bless him. It'd be rather nice to ask *him* for a change; and you can do it now, at Cor's place. Cor will be more than delighted to cook a dinner for the three of you; he's almost as good at it as old Bruce himself. Besides, it seems rather fitting that old Bruce should be your first guest since the two of you were *married*, so to speak. It will probably tickle him no end.

So you ask Cor about it first, and, as you expected, Cor looks upon it like a special birthday treat or something. Even though you have to ring him back and tell him it's pretty short notice, for it has to be that very night. Cor himself is working day-shift that week, finishing at five, and Bruce tells you it has to be that night, otherwise he's not free for nearly a fortnight. "Academic matters and all that, old thing," says old Bruce, "and not even time for a slice on the side if I could *find* one." Same old Bruce. So you tell him just a little over the phone about what the trouble is, and almost immediately you can hear the tone of his voice change. "I did hear something about it, old thing," he says, the jauntiness all gone from his voice now. "I'll have a bit of a chew with old Parkinson about it, at tea this arvo, and give you the gup tonight. Apart from that, things are still going fine? Between you and Cor, I mean."

"Couldn't be better," you tell him.

"Miracles will never cease!" he says, all jaunty again, the same old Bruce. "Well, congratulations and all that, old thing. But why in the hell didn't you ask me to the wedding! I've got a new tulle job I've been just *dying* to wear for ages! See you. Tonight then. Get out all the wedding photographs . . ."

And bless him, bless him for the old friend he's always been, when he arrives at Cor's place, he's not only got a bottle of wine for the dinner, but also shoves a great parcel into your arms and another that is only slightly smaller for Cor.

"Wedding presents!" he grunts perfunctorily. "Don't see why *we* shouldn't have such things too!" And he pretends he's suddenly absorbed in Cor's handiwork with the curtains. The only clue he gives to his real feelings is when you start to open your parcel, and he says:

"Take it easy, Dad. They're likely to avaporate on exposure."

And it's nothing less than a whole set of crystal glasses; pretty well the entire shooting match. You can hardly see them after a few moments; you're not even sure that you can stop yourself from blubbing like a great stupid kid.

"It's too much," you protest. "Really, Bruce, it is."

But he just says: "More for myself than for you, old thing. You know I like a decent glass to drink from, and you'll find me inflicting myself on you two a good deal from now on. My old digs get a bit quiet on it sometimes." His old digs! You think of that flat of his, compared with what you two have got, although you have to admit that Cor *has* made it look a good deal better than it was. Which reminds you, old Bruce had something for Cor as well. Trust him to give something especially to Cor, instead of just the one parcel for the two of you. And then:

"*God ver domme!*" from Cor, plunging into his own parcel and tugging out—it really is too much—an electric frying-pan. Cor looks at you, not knowing what to say, and old Bruce sort of sniffles and shuffles around a bit, trying not to look at either of you, trying not to be too embarrassed.

"Oh, get along with the both of you," he says suddenly. "It's not much to an overpaid and oversexed old bugger like your old mother here."

Cor doesn't say anything. Instead he does something that you think to yourself, yes, only he could do it in such a way. Without any self-consciousness whatsoever, he goes over to old Bruce, squeezes his arm, and then, leaning forward, kisses him on the cheek. It's just a brush of the lips really, but it seems to say all that he wants to say, and much better than you yourself, you realize, ever could.

Cor has really excelled himself with the dinner that night, and it becomes such an hilarious affair, you haven't the heart to bring up the one matter that's really on your mind. Old Bruce doesn't seem ready for it yet, either. He's obviously impressed with Cor's cooking, despite his own prowess, and you all finish up nearly laughing yourselves sick. The two of them start swapping recipes and things, furiously, just like a couple of old housewives. The wine flows, and then you produce some more of your own. And every now and again you can't help looking at the glasses the three of you are using, the carton of those still unpacked from their paper wrappings, and the three wine-glasses you're not using, but which Cor has

144

placed on one of his shelves, just as though the space was especially made for them.

And looking at these, and at Cor and old Bruce enjoying themselves so much together (would you ever think of old Bruce as a professor or something now for God's sake?), you can't help thinking to yourself: Is there anything really so wrong with this kind of life? Are there so many so-called normal people who can live their lives so well, and mean so much to each other? And, Hamilton aside, isn't it always these so-called normal people who are always trying to deprive you of your own chance of some kind of life together, amongst yourselves?

Snap of fingers before your eyes, and old Bruce says: "A penny for 'em, old thing." But you just shake your head, grin a bit, and pass the grog. The usual solution.

Cor says to leave the dishes to him while you two talk. And as soon as you've all taken the last of the things out to the kitchen, old Bruce straightaway drops his previous gaiety, as though it's suddenly 'gone out of style' as he says, and starts in on the matter you want so much to know about. No preliminaries. Just:

"Well, it's Hamilton all right, old thing. Christ, that boy's really got his hooks into you. But I suppose in a way you can hardly blame him." And he makes a meaningful nod of his head towards the passage leading to the kitchen—Cor. "Parkinson admits it. And I can tell you one thing, old chap, if it's any consolation to you; Parkinson doesn't like one bit of it. Doesn't like it at all. But he just hasn't got much say in the matter. You see, Hamilton didn't do his spitting in *Parkinson's* ear. It wouldn't have got much chop there if he had. No, Hamilton knew better than that. You've got to hand it to him —Hamilton, I mean—he knows his onions all right. Do you know just whose ears he has done his spitting in? Jacoby's. And you know that Jacoby pretty well runs everything and anything to do with the old shop. It was Jacoby gave the order to old Parkinson. And old Parkinson, I'm afraid, just has to fall into line. No choice about the matter. Otherwise, old thing, I can assure you old Parkinson would have just sent Hamilton back to the sewer where he belongs. That's one thing I *can* assure you about. But"—and he shrugs, extending hands of ineffectuality—"there it is."

You suppose you must have looked pretty despondent, for old Bruce suddenly reaches over and pretends to clout you gently on the shoulder. So you say:

"Pretty little operation, isn't it!"

Which makes old Bruce go on: "What really gets me about it," he says, "is the way Hamilton's been doing it. Or to put it more precisely, old thing, *where* he's been doing it. Do you know where he's been doing it? You're not in the Masons, are you? Well, that's where he's been doing it. And do you know, I think he'll cook his *own* goose eventually. You see, there's quite a few of us—oh! *that's* a bit of a give-away, isn't it! But you know what I mean—well, there *are* quite a few of us in the Masons, and if they started purging the lot of us out of it, I reckon the whole organization would collapse. Crikey, boy, just think of it! If there was ever a *world* purge or something, the whole bloody *world* would collapse! Parliaments, governments, hospitals, schools, theatres, the lot! They wouldn't know where to start to get 'em all going again. And then they'd soon find they'd have to get all of us back. Anyway, *that's* not what I was going to say. What Hamilton has overlooked in this business is that there's quite a number in the lodge who don't at all like what he's done. Even among the squares. They don't like it one bit. And of course it's made a few of us kind of a bit nervous, boy. Believe you me. I mean, when someone gets a bee in his bonnet like this crank Hamilton, you never know where it's going to stop. So what he doesn't know is that some of us dislike it so much, I think you'll soon find Mr. Robin Hamilton will be getting a transfer back to the east, as an *assistant* manager in his precious firm. And that ought to teach him a lesson if anything should. The only trouble about it for you, old thing, is that it may take a few months or so. Could be quicker, of course. But naturally it won't happen overnight, or anything like that.

But it'll happen all right. If you can only hang out until it does . . ."

Old Bruce is pretty worked up about it. And you can tell by the way he's talking that he means to have more than just a bit to do with it himself. And you can believe that. The trouble is, just as he says, you don't know whether you can hang out for several months or not, or if the damage can ever be repaired.

"Let's hope I can," you say, not wanting to sound too depressed about it. Got to show old Bruce that you've still got a *bit* of guts or something.

"Attaboy!" he says, slapping you on the shoulder once more. "Now let's clean up the rest of this grog, just so it doesn't make a stink in the place. Where's Cor's glass?"

8

"WOTCHIT, Dad!"

You don't recognize the voice for a few seconds, and then it's rather a surprise when you turn and see that it belongs to young Andy. He's breathless, flushed, as though he's been running to catch you up on the street.

"Crikey!" he says, "you walk so fast, I *swear* I can smell hair burning!"

You've got to laugh; with young Andy you just can't help it. What a personality he could have been, if he'd really been a girl!

"What can I do you for, petal?" you say. You always enjoy carrying on with him a bit, he's such a breath of fresh air. He makes you forget yourself for a while, too.

"Oh, *you* can have it free, *any* time!" he quips back. "I was just coming to see you, and now you've saved me a walk.

And I'm running a bit late for the old convent." He works in a large store, his so-called 'convent', in the men's clothing department. "But I suppose one of the other *girls* will cover up for me, that's if I *am* late. But I may *not* be now. I was just coming along to your office to give you this. From Roy and me. The bush telegraph tells us that you and that gorgeous great Dutchman have gone and—well, that you're doing things *properly*. Well, good on yer, Ray. And the best of everything. You certainly deserve it, doll. Both of you."

And after he's shoved this small package into your hand, he just says: "See you, Dad. Call around some time. Any time. And be sure to bring Cor." Then he's gone, running back along the street with his heels flying just a little too high, his arms flicking out just a little too far. He can't help it.

And when you open the package in your office, it's a little porcelain figure of Eros, quite expensive, with a card that says: "Don't throw it at each other. It breaks!" And once again you damn near feel like crying; you'd forgotten just how wonderful *some* friends can be.

9

MIA, Cor tells you, has arrived back in Holland. He says that he would show you her letter, which in any case is very short, but of course it's written in Dutch. So he translates for you.

The letter sounds like one from a child. She says that the journey on the ship was good. She met some nice people who were very kind to her. Her father and mother met her at the ship at Rotterdam. They were well, but a sister of hers was not so well. They said Cor's family were all well, too. She herself was quite well, but she was tired of carrying the baby. She would be glad when it was born so that she would not have to carry it any longer, and she could wear nice dresses again. On the ship she spent ten pounds, which she hoped Cor would send to her, but not to consider it included in the money he sent every week. She would take out the papers for their divorce and send him the bill. It was already autumn in Holland, and she did not like the idea of having another winter ahead of her when she had just had one in Australia. She hoped Cor was well and would never be too unhappy. She wanted him to send a woollen koala bear, a big one, for the baby.

That was all. No accusations, no recriminations. It's astounding, you think; she doesn't even mention the business of Cor having left her; unless, you think to yourself, she did so in an earlier letter which—perhaps because it was so bitter, as well it might be—Cor hasn't shown to you. Even so, it seems strange that the only complaint she makes in this letter is about the weather, and the only requests are for a koala bear and the refund of ten miserable pounds. If it hadn't been for that last part of her letter, you'd have thought to yourself that she was being noble again, but now that you know her, you know it's not because she's noble at all, for she can be nothing of the kind. From what you do know of her, you decide that she just can't have much in the way of emotions at all. So long as Mia is all right, Mia is about as happy as she can be.

When Cor puts the letter away, you watch him, carefully, wondering if he has any regrets at all. But if he has, he certainly doesn't show them. He looks again at the letter much as one might look at a bill or a report; and then, with a very practical air, he puts it away in his writing compendium. It is this writing compendium which, of all his few things, amuses you the most. He looks after it so carefully, and yet you suppose that he probably writes no more than half a dozen letters a year. You're still quite astounded at how he disposes of the letter with such an air of dismissal, so you decide to ask him about it, ask him what he thinks of it. But all he says is:

"Ya, it's a *good* letter. I think I shall make coffee. Do you want some on the moment?"

One thing, such a complete lack of demonstrativeness assures you that, if he ever did have any love of some sort for Mia, he certainly doesn't have it now. For you know just how demonstrative he *can* be, so far as *you're* concerned that is. In fact, looking at him as he is now, and remembering how he has been on so many occasions with you, it is difficult to believe that both pictures can be of the one person. But that's probably the way with a lot of people—most perhaps. It's just that it seems so marked in Cor, but possibly only because you've always been looking at him from such close quarters.

But there is one thing that you're almost certain he must have *some* feelings about, and that is the child she's going to have. *His* child. It's so rare, so *unlikely* in this kind of life for anyone to have a child of his own—unless you can adopt one —that you think it must be awful to have actually fathered one and then to be deprived of it before you even see it. You don't think you could stand it yourself. If there is anything you have ever regretted about being homosexual, it's that you can't marry to have children. Children of your very own, you mean. Or just *one* child. A son, perhaps. You've often thought that, if you *could* being yourself to do it, you'd like to get married just to have a son. But you know you couldn't, and it wouldn't be fair on the girl for another thing. But to be like Cor, to have actually fathered a child, and then to abandon it—this you think you could never do either. Having a child would be such a sort of accomplishment, even though it's only something that happens every minute of the day, somewhere or other—every second, probably. But for you, it can't happen even once in a whole lifetime. Much as you sometimes want it, you know it can never be. That's why you envy Cor so much, and why you can't believe he can feel so little about it. So you ask him, just to find out. But all he says is:

"Oh, I would like to see it, I suppose. But Mia will send photographs, and I suppose that is enough."

He's so perfunctory about it that you can't help wondering

if he's doing it deliberately, to cover up his real feelings about it. But when you ask him some more, he still just says:

"Oh, I suppose I'm lucky that it's mine."

"What do you mean by that?"

"Well, she had so many boy-friends, it could have been from one of the others."

"You mean, she had other men even while she was here in Australia?"

"Several."

"And you didn't object to it?"

"Why? So did I if it comes to that, I suppose. She had one Australian boy—his name was Peter something," he goes on, "who was about six years younger than her. But he must have been able to give her a good time, all right. She used to meet him in the lane at the back side of the house. She didn't know I knew about it, I suppose. But I was there myself one night, with Rob, on the other side of a tree that hangs over the fence, and we had to stay there until they had finished. I must say he was pretty quick about it. Probably he was afraid of being caught. If he only knew it, *I* didn't mind. I was only too glad there was someone to keep her happy. It takes quite a bit of doing, you know; she's such a glutton for it."

This time you're really astounded.

"Then you're not sure it's your child?" you can't help asking him.

And of all things, he says: "Oh, it's mine all right. I can be sure of that, by the dates. Peter had left her, and she hadn't yet found Bill. Or was the next one Eddy? I can't remember on the moment. Anyway, it was me all right. She'd been at me so much, I got sort of angry and tried to hurt her with it. But the man just isn't *born* that can hurt Mia. Not that way; she loves it. You should have seen her face. You'd have thought she was in paradise or somewhere. I was glad when she found another boy-friend. But yes, it's my child all right, Ray. And to think she didn't even know she was going to have it, until it was too late. And she's supposed to be a nurse and everything. That's women for you . . ."

Somehow it seems a little brutal. Something inside you, really deep down inside you, shrinks away from it, sort of shrivels. You can't quite explain it; you can only feel it. It's another one of those little doubts, a sort of nagging fear, as though you don't quite know the person you're in love with after all, and you suppose you never will. You even begin to wonder if anyone ever does, anywhere.

10

SUMMER comes, lifting the leaden-weighted skies from off your head and, whipping them up into packs like mad frightened sheep, or sometimes just into long, tormented streaks across the sky, whisks them finally over expanding, expansive horizons. Blue skies and earth green. Green, green everywhere. Sun-glitter in the leaves. And the beaches calling with their long and sensuous surfs, the flex and writhe of white-muscled water, wrestling playfully with your slightly shocked body. Green and chill-cool underneath, and little fountains of underwater dust. Beyond, the water always green and then green-blue, then blue so deep it surely *must* be black under there. Cor wrestling with you in the water; and the tide, playful as a pup, tugging and nipping at your legs, tumbling you over so that you come up laughing and threshing and spitting out salt water. How hard and warm is his brave young body, beneath that extra skin of water.

And thank God for the car which can take you to such lone and far-off places, to swim free of girding costumes and afterwards, with little beards and vests of warm white sand, to lie basking in the sun. Legs spread with the sun soaking into your back, your thighs and your buttocks, the back of your head. Sun glinting capriciously on the short crisp hairs of his legs.

Secret little world of your own scooped out of sand and salt-bush, long sword-like rushes. Miniature desert undulating beyond your eyes. Cor's arm round your shoulders, warm and heavy, and your hand burning in the cleft of his thighs.

What a sheer miracle life can be, from the huge blue dome of the sheltering sky to the mere but exquisite architecture of an eyebrow. If it all ends now, it's been worth it. Worth every minute of it. Because you've got that feeling again that you're going to just burst or something. Hold on hard with your grip on the world. Sometimes it seems to spin so madly, you swear you'll slide, and skid, and then maybe slip off. Clean into the void. Tighten your hand and make yourself believe it all really exists: this flesh under your fingers, that smooth plane of shoulder, green swords of rushes waving just beyond focus, minute and frantic little planets of sand, the impossible beauty of a lip, the flaring wing of a nostril. To be a sculptor, to be able to paint! To be able to make even some sort of no matter how pathetic a reproduction of all this impossible creation, or just one infinitesimal particle of it. And if God had *not* created woman, would it ever have occurred to man to conceive one? For here He is, right before you, conceived in His very own image—Cor—with an ant on his shoulder to prove it. So what else is there? What else can there possibly be?

Drift of sand, drift of water, drift of a clean wide blue sky. So drift the weeks from under you, boundlessly. October, and gone is a whole quarter of an oh so precisely dissected little calendar. Quotidian intercalations, all garnished with public holidays. A whole three months gone—drifted. You can hardly believe it, but they're gone all right. Gone so quickly, with Cor beside you all the time. Cor. So precious, your Cor. If only there was some way that you could take out your heart and put it in his hand.

Yet it may all soon go stale on you, or so you've heard it said. They say it so knowledgeably, you'd think they couldn't be wrong. But they're *wrong*, all right; nothing's gone stale for you. Always there's something fresh and brilliantly new and exciting that comes up. Little things. Simple things.

Something new he's cooked. Something new for the room. Or like now, for instance, Cor getting up and playfully sitting on you, his firm thighs straddling your own, his hands making capricious little clouts at your chest and your unresisting jaw. Makes anything seen possible . . .

If there's anything stale at all, it's having to go back always to that room of his—those two rooms of his—or to leave them, to go back at all sorts of hours to your own place. Place? Don't you think of it as *home* any more? It would be all right, Cor's place, if you had it all to yourselves. But fitting in with the other couple for the kitchen and bathroom sometimes isn't your idea of home. And the one toilet. Hiding smeared towels until the laundry comes. Again just little things, but at times they seem mountains. Any kind of lovers, or all kinds, have got to have a place of their own, you suppose—just as Cor says. He's right again, as always.

For sometimes, when passion carries you clean out of the world on its tumultuous tides, you forget the creak of a bed, squeak of a floorboard. Or sleeping, half-sleeping afterwards, you hear the *other* couple's creak of the bed, squeak of a floor-board. Giggles. You can't help it, much as you hate it; you just can't help giggling. And it's then that it all seems kind of cheap or something; the magic rubs off. Sordid, a bit. It's then you know you've *got* to have a place of your own—any kind of place, anywhere. You've just got to, that's all. Cor's always so right, so right—one more giggle when their goddamn night-table gets kicked over makes you quite certain of it; that and the sometimes haunted, hurt look in Cor's wistful eyes. Nothing can accuse so much as his eyes.

II

So you leave home. You've been there so seldom lately that it's easier with your family than ever you would have thought. Of course, they think that you've been having to work so much lately, they quite understand that it would be easier for you if you did have a flat much closer to the office. It's really so easy that you can hardly believe it; you'd always thought it would be near-impossible before; thought there'd be hurt looks from your old man, tears from your mother. But it's not like that at all. It's all done very sanely and practically, and no emotions out on the sleeve. They quite understand; were really going to suggest it themselves, they say. The car coming in and going out at all hours of the night--oh, they know you really can't help it, in *your* line of business—but Father sleeps so lightly these days, you know.

It's then you can see it all. It can't have been so wonderful for them either in the last few months, the way you've been. They'd never say it, of course, but probably they'll be even glad to see you go, although they assure you, naturally, that if the office quietens down a bit, later on, and you feel you would like a bit of home life again—a bit of *real* home life, they mean—then of course your room will always be waiting for you. But as things are now, yes, they really do think it would be for the better. Father must have his sleep, or his health will crack up. Of course, if there's anything they can do . . .

Really, life can be so ludicrous at times, how can you ever keep a straight face?

Things at the office seem to have settled themselves a bit too. Only a couple more accounts have left you; but then you nabbed another one, a big one. Things aren't quite back to what they used to be, but they're improving. At *least* they're improving. And neither of you has heard a word from Rob Hamilton in ages, or so it seems.

So you look at your bank account, and Cor tots up his wages after what is left when he's sent his remittances to Mia, and you work out a budget. It'll be a bit of a squeeze for a while, and the bank account will be practically cleaned out when you buy what you need. But who doesn't have to face things like that when they're starting out? It'd cost you a darn sight more if you were really getting married—to a woman, you mean. And she mightn't even be able to go on working either—like Cor. If things get too tight, you could always sell the car, you say. But this makes Cor look so down in the mouth, because it would literally be selling off all those wonderful week-ends, that you have to promise him no, you'll never do that. You'll manage somehow.

Somebody 'up there' must be looking after you, you've decided; or at least for some of the time. You find a flat right in the heart of the city, in a great modern block pretty well half-way between your office and Cor's club. It couldn't be better if you'd hand-picked the spot. No garage, but a parking lot. Partly furnished, but mostly with old junk you'd want to throw out; until Cor says he can do something with it, if you'll buy him a brush and a few tins of paint. You load up the car with the few things he's got in his old place, mostly just the black-and-white curtains, the shelves, the pot-plant, old Bruce's glasses—the most dazzling possession of all—and young Andy's little porcelain Eros. While Cor sets about arranging things, you bring up all your own stuff from the house, even books and things, anything to fill up space. Besides, you've learnt long ago what Cor can do with even an old jam-tin or something, so you bring the lot. The kitchenette has gas, and there's the electric frying-pan old Bruce gave to Cor. Cor's even got a couple of pots and some dishes and things—not much, but enough to make do for a start. And your mother sorts out some things she says she's got two of, and you take those too. She finds an awful lot, really; some of the things you're almost sure she hasn't got two of. But she wants you to have them, so you take them. She looks at you a little oddly, almost as though you're going off overseas again instead of just into town. And when you get the place fixed up a bit, you decide to ask her to come along for tea or something; meet Cor. You don't know whether she'll put two and two together or not, she's such an innocent old thing when it comes to matters like that. But you don't really care; it's *your* life. If she gets along all right with Cor, you could have her over quite often; even the old man, too, when things start to work out. Packing things into the car, you begin to feel almost enthusiastic about it all; even when you feel a bit tired at times, a little washed out.

So you move in. You close the door and pull the curtains across the window and then you and Cor make it really home, for the very first time. And for the very first time, too, you get a feeling of seclusion at long, long last—and security. If only you weren't so tired at times.

When Cor's done as much as anyone could with what was in the flat, you tell him to go around town, when he's not working during the day, and get the rest of the things you need, chairs or something. He says, don't you want to go too? But you tell him you haven't the time, not during the day. There's so much you've got to do to keep the office going, find new accounts all the time. Again he looks a bit hurt at first; he wants you to choose everything together. Well, that'd be pretty nice all right, but you explain again how you just haven't the time. And at night, when you could go window-shopping together, he's often working till pretty late—you both are. But he at least has got some days free, when you still have to be at the office, so you leave it all to him. You feel that sometimes you seem always to be leaving things to him; but the way things are, it just can't be helped. He ought to understand, you say; and then he smiles and says of course he does, and everything seems O.K. between you again. Not that things aren't always O.K. between you; it's just that at times they're not quite so perfect as at others. It's certainly not that the gilt is coming off the gingerbread, or whatever the saying is—definitely not. That way, life couldn't be better. It's just that things might have been a bit much for you lately, you're always so tired. Sometimes you feel as though you could just lie down and sleep for a whole month or something; you really do.

12

IT's all right when Cor is at home too, nights, to cook for you. It's when he's working at nights, and you come back to the flat alone, that it's pretty rough. It's not so much the having to cook for yourself—you're not that helpless—it's just that it seems so much bother, just cooking for one. You just can't be bothered somehow; just scratch around and get anything. You don't even do that sometimes; you stay at the office or bring work home. It'd be different if you had Cor to cook for too, even if he just ate it cold or warmed up when he got home, late. But he always has food at the club when he works at night.

So when you get home, there's only yourself in those four dead walls to think about. Not only the walls, the whole flat seems dead without Cor there. Sometimes you wonder if you can stick it there, alone, waiting for him. You feel as though you want to go out. But where? And why? Lord knows, you've got enough work to get through always. But it's the loneliness that gets you, when he's not there with you. Makes you decide you could never *live* alone—never. You'd soon go dotty if you did.

And yet it's not only the loneliness. Why does everything seem to be so much of an effort lately?—things that you wouldn't have even been conscious of once. Now they sort of nag at you for hours before you can get yourself around to doing them. Getting old, perhaps? Reflexes slowing? Cheerful thought! Or too much on the nest maybe; that's probably more like it. After all, you *have* been rather wallowing in it a bit; *must* take something out of you—text-books say so. At times you feel like something filtered through a nylon handkerchief, no kidding. And lately there have been those nights when you can't get up a hard. You're not worth two pins as a lover any more. So maybe you do need to lay off it for a while. And yet it doesn't seem to have affected Cor at all; he's always ready for it—always.

That's the maddening part about it; makes you sort of jealous or something—envious—seeing him ramping for it all the time and you limp as a wet dishwasher. That really gets you. It makes you so furious, so frustrated, you try to work yourself up with pig-headed fury, sheer determination, just because Cor can keep on with it. You tell yourself it's stupid on your part, but you can't help it all the same. You can't help the way you feel about it, not even when Cor says he understands, and that it's not necessary all the time. And the silly part of it is, you know that he does understand, and that it's not necessary—not with him it's not. But it is with *you*; that's the *real* silly part about it. Some mad, unreasonable quirk inside you makes you want it all the more; you just can't help it. And so you keep on trying; even though you know it's only making you worse, you still keep on trying.

Then the night comes when you know you just can't do anything at all; you have to give up. And when you're sure that Cor's asleep, you find yourself weeping into the pillow like a petulant child. It's about all you can do to stop yourself from crying out aloud. And yet you know it's all really so stupid on your part; all you need to do is to just let yourself sleep for once—sleep a few nights running—and then you'll be all right, you tell yourself. You know all this, but you can't do a thing about it somehow. Just try sleeping next to someone who's always potent as a powerhouse and then see how *you* feel. Sometimes you could stick your head in a gas-oven or something; you really could.

Yet at the same time, you can't help wondering if it's so much the sexual side of it that's wearing you down as perhaps the mental part of it. Is there ever a second—just a single second—when, no matter what you're doing or saying, or supposed to be keeping your mind on, that you're not also thinking to yourself: you musn't let it show. Whatever you do, or say, or whatever gesture you make, even in a casual or offhand moment, you must never let it show. There's not only a law against it; people will leer at you. Ordinary people. Which is even worse. You try to dismiss it, try not to think of it at all. But always there seems to be some sort of isolated cell in your mind that keeps twitching away at it. Watch your step in front of Barbara. Watch your step in front of your clients. Watch your step in front of your family, ordinary normal friends. Watch your step when you're on the street. Watch your very step itself, the way you walk. It goes on and on. No matter what you do to try and turn it off sometimes, it still goes on. You think you've turned it off, even got rid of that one isolated little fiend of a cell, but it soon comes on again from some other part in your head. It's just like some sort of flea; you slap a hand down on it and you think you've got it, so that you can exterminate the damn thing, only to find that it's popped up somewhere else. It wasn't where you slapped at it at all. And no matter where you slap at it, it still keeps on just popping up somewhere else. Over and over. The faster you hit at it, the faster it slips through your fingers. And always there it is, somewhere else, but still there, throbbing and leering at you. Watch you step. Pffffft! Watch your step. Somebody is always bound to be watching you, waiting for just that one little slip. And then everything of normality will skate away from your feet, skid clean from beneath you. You try over and over again to tell yourself that things aren't really that way, but this one isolated little cell hopping around like crazy all over your mind all the time keeps leering back at you that there *is*—there *is*—you've got to watch it all the time. Watch your step. Watch it. Watch. In front of Barbara. In front of clients. Talk about *women* or something—*chasing* women and *making* women—*bedfuls* of them. Don't ever let yourself think about the *one* thing you can't stop yourself from thinking about—Cor. But he's built like some hermaphroditic stallion, pulses like a powerhouse. Nothing to do with the outside world, or the office. Got to keep the two of them apart, those two worlds of yours. But that one little cell seems to make it impossible. Maybe because it's that one endlessly twitching fiend of a cell that's *more* than just a cell—it's a *link,* a link between the two worlds—between Cor and normality. And it won't ever let you forget either of them, not for one minute. Concentrate on one, and it just jiggles at the other; rattles it around in your head like a bag of old marbles. Or it creeps up on you quietly, with the stealth of a snake. And isn't that a phallic symbol or something? Or it oozes itself into you, squelching. Watch your step. Not only *where* you step, but *how*—always. Sometimes you think it'll drive you crazy or something, you really do. Who wouldn't think they were going crackers when, in the middle of displaying layouts and things, you suddenly find yourself wondering if you'll be *able* to that night, if you'll be able to cope with that powerhouse that always seems to be grinding and grinding beside you. And you have to pull yourself up with a jerk, suddenly, wondering if it not only shows on your face, but also wondering if you've actually *said* something about it, just a moment ago, just then, because you can almost hear some sort of words that you feel you *must* have said, the way they keep echoing and reverberating, rattling around and around somewhere in your head. You tell yourself that you couldn't possibly have said anything; but that fleet little fiend of a cell just pops up again and says: Are you *sure*? Are you *sure*? And that's the one thing you can't be—sure. No matter how much you try to be, you just can't be sure—ever.

Maybe if you talk about it to someone you'll get rid of it. It's supposed to be a cure for all that sort of thing, you've heard—somewhere. So you try talking to Cor about it. If there's anyone you should talk about it, then surely it must be Cor. Who else? But he seems not to hear; he's always concentrating on whatever he's cooking, something he's making —anything at all, anything but what you're trying to talk to him about. And when at last he does seem to register something, he just shrugs if off; says you've been working too hard, you need to relax. He comes over and starts to massage your neck or your shoulders or somewhere, and that only starts it going all over again. Because you can't stop yourself thinking: If you try it now, will you be able to? So you have to push him away, and then learn *not* to push him away if you don't want him to get that hurt look on his face that he seems to get so much lately. You don't exactly push him away; you just let him pet and pat you a bit until, when you think it'll be O.K., and he won't turn on that hurt look of his again, you can extricate yourself, take yourself off into a much safer range. Or *out* of range. And somehow you manage it. But all you've really managed to do, so far as the *real* matter is concerned, is to realize that you haven't communicated a single word to him—not one. He doesn't understand one iota of it. He just thinks you need more love and petting, when now that's the last thing you need. And you start to wonder: When will the next pat come that will be the last one of all, the one that'll skid you clean off the rocks? This one? The one after?

If only it wasn't so difficult at the office, perhaps things would be so much easier between the two of you.

Or: If only it *was* so much easier between the two of you, things would be all right at the *office*?

Which?

These are the cartoon sketches and blurbs for Planet Candy Bars, stills for the press of course, and animated with gremlin goblins for the TV spots, three different voices saying WOW! WOW! WOW!, one voice a little boy's, one a little girl's, and one an older boy's. Cor's voice would . . . See? There it goes again. Why, *why*, for God's sake! Because Cor will be wanting it again tonight? And maybe you can't? . . .

Or when you're there together, and you're thinking you can start leaving off one of the blankets now, and would it be any better if you slept in separate beds or something, and you're nearly seared into shreds with Cor's hand just resting lightly on your belly, just scratching a bit, and for once you know you *can*, and so you go to, and then it's all going all right because what you need on the TV spot is some sort of animated animal or something to say WOW! instead of two *boys'* voices—and see? It's gone again. You can't. You just can't, and you've got to turn over. And then for an hour or so you can feel him just lying there, thinking it's something that *he's* done or said. It's nearly four o'clock before you can go to sleep. But is it ever sleep?

What the trouble really is, you tell yourself then, it's been too much of both. Lay off it a bit—and stop worrying about the office. You're not starving yet, are you? Well, *are* you? So? What you need is a break from it all—just one evening would be a help. So next time Cor's off at night, go out somewhere—anywhere—out of these four walls squeezing you all the time. Always it's either the walls at the office, or those at the flat; but always four walls.

So one night the two of you go out for dinner—a small restaurant where the food's always good, and it's quiet. No one who you don't want to is likely to see you. And Cor's so happy about it that you try to listen to everything he says, you really do. But somehow or other a layout or that *other* thing keeps scratching and scratching at you. And the walls of the restaurant are just four more walls anyway. You'd have thought that the wine would have helped, two bottles of it. And it's while you're trying to make up your mind whether or not you'll make a hog of it by ordering a third, when Cor says something that nearly bowls you sideways:

"I'm glad it was a boy," he's just said. You could swear he did. In any case, he must have, for he goes on to say: "Having parents separated and all that is easier on boys than it is on girls."

So, "Who are you talking about?" you have to ask him.

And, oh God, have you done something *so* stupid again? Was it really *so* stupid that his face has to nearly crumple up the way it does? Was it so bad that he has to get the sulks

163

about it, pout his bottom lip out and look all over the place, anywhere at all around the restaurant, anywhere but back at you? And then just say:

"Oh, nothing!"

So you try to be pleasant.

"No, Cor, tell me," you say. "I'm sorry, I wasn't listening just then."

"That's the trouble. You never are."

"Well, maybe I've got a few things on my mind."

"Who hasn't!"

"Let's skip that." Smile at him; say something. *Can't* hold his hand. "Come on, tell me. Who *were* you talking about?"

And then, of all things, he sort of looks at you as though he's only just beginning to believe that you *didn't* hear him. He looks at you as though you're almost *nutty* or something, which really hurts. And it hurts all the more when, for just a few awful moments, a few really awful moments, you almost feel that he's not going to say anything more at all. But he does. And that's when the shock really comes.

"About Mia, of course. And the boy, our child. Who do you think?"

You're astounded. What a way for anyone to tell you!

"But Cor, how was I to know?" you say.

And again he looks at you in that funny sort of way, from the side of one eye. But then eventually he does look you straight in the eye, looks at you with his eyes screwed up and his mouth pulled tight into a hard little line of—oh God, yes— it's almost hate . . .

"Because I *told* you, that's why."

"Told me! When?"

"A week ago, when Mia's last letter came. I even showed you the card she sent me, one of the ones she's had printed."

Maybe you're suddenly blind, deaf, and dumb; everything is crazy. You could swear he never said anything about it, on a Bible if necessary, you would have heard it if he had. You just can't *not* hear a thing like that. Or could you? Could you? That damned blind spot in your brain somewhere, that's what

164

it is—not just a cell; a blind spot. Must do something about it; you really must. But first you must do something about Cor—now. So you reach out and—to hell with the restaurant, or even whoever wants to see it—you put your hand on his, on the table.

"Cor, I'm sorry," you say. "I really am. I just couldn't have heard. Honest. I must have been thinking of something else at the time. Maybe it was when——"

But there's no time for more. He just pulls his hand away, looking at you as though you're almost inhuman, an animal. You can hardly believe it, but that's just how he does look at you, and you wonder if you'll ever be able to forget it. But you haven't much time to think of that now. For just as you're about to say let's celebrate, let's order another bottle of wine, he just gets up and doesn't give you time to ask for the bill, let alone pay for it, and you can't believe it but he's already half-stumbling, half-staggering across the restaurant towards the door. And yes, then he's gone—he's actually gone. And all you can think of are those last words he flung at you, just before he left the table. At least, you *think* he said them. He must have. You can still hear them so clearly, still shrieking around somewhere, somewhere inside you.

"Why don't you go and *live* in that damned office of yours!"

That's what you heard, all right. Yes, you can be sure of it.

Somehow you ask for the bill, pay it, get up, walk out. Try not to show anything. At least, not until you're outside, where no one'll see. And you look up and down the street, expecting it to just fold up and slide clean away, out of sight somewhere. Anything could do anything at all now and it wouldn't surprise you any more. You look for him in both directions, but he's gone. Christ, he must have been quick! How could anyone be so quick in a goddamn city; all those people . . .

But when you get home, there must still be someone up there looking after you—or so you tell yourself. At least some of your luck is still holding, for there he is. He hasn't run out on you after all, much as you probably deserve it. He's lying there on the bed, still fully dressed. But at least you've got a whole ten hours to make it up to him.

13

THE way things work out, you don't have to tell Barbara to find somewhere else; she goes. You could have stopped her, you suppose, with just an apology; it wouldn't have taken much effort. But you couldn't do even that much. Or maybe it was really because you didn't want to do anything about it; you really wanted to see her go. After all, it's one responsibility less, despite all the time she's been with you, and the way she's always been so loyal and worked well and all that sort of thing. But she's gone now, and it's probably for the best. It means just that much less you've got to earn now, somehow or other. Pity it had to be like that though, with all those hard feelings and bitter words. And over such a little thing, too— stationery expenses. But it just hit you the wrong way: that was all. You had been able to cut down some of the over-heads, but the income seemed always to be diminishing at twice the rate. Hence the blow-up over stationery expenses— and now no Barbara.

Then after she's gone, it suddenly occurs to you: Why keep the office on at all? Why not work at home in the flat? It'd save paying two rents for one thing, and a lot of time in going backwards and forwards for another. It would even save the time of just getting dressed. There's room enough in the flat for you to work if you take out a couple of chairs from the living-room, and put the desk and your drawing-table in there. A bit cramped maybe, but you can do it—at least until you get things back on to their feet again. You've just got to, that's all.

You ask Cor what he thinks about it, and he says he thinks it's a good idea, that anything you want suits him, you know that. And yet he says it in a sort of way that makes you feel he might resent it somehow. It's hard to tell. After all, you suppose it is your *home* you're messing up. Still, lots of men you know use their homes as their offices—normal men at that, with wives and kids. And with you, well, there's just the two of you. After all, it's not as though it's for ever; as soon as you've got things going really well again, then naturally you'll want a proper office, a really swanky one next time, one that'll knock all their eyes out. And when the time comes, no doubt you'll laugh yourself sick, instead of worrying yourself that way, at how much you actually did worry about the things that are happening now.

It's a pity about Barbara though; you'd become quite fond of her, in a way . . .

14

OF COURSE it's soon apparent that you've made yet another mistake. At least, before, you did have two sets of walls; now there is only the one. The same four walls to sit in, night and day, day after day. It might be a lot cheaper so far as overheads go, but it's much more expensive on the nerves. Before, when you had to go out to the office, you did at least get outdoors sometimes. Now you just move from your bed to the table, from the table to the bed. Or so it seems. What should have been a home, and now an office as well, has become nothing more or less than a cell. But it's too late now; too late even when you realize that you're actually missing some business by not being right in the city, in your old office. People

167

go there, or phone, to find you're no longer there; so they go somewhere else.

On the other hand, Cor seems happy enough with the arrangement. And yet that's just where another snag comes in. You'd completely forgotten that on alternate weeks he works only at night, and is at home all the day. He makes a point of not interfering with your work, of keeping as quiet and out of your way as possible. But that's it; he makes too much a point of it. Try as you will, you're always conscious of him being there, somewhere in the flat, either doing or making things in the kitchen, sleeping or reading in the bedroom, or even reading in the same room. Reading, but mostly just watching you. Wherever he is, you're conscious of his presence all the time, and somehow you don't seem able to concentrate as you should. You don't know which is the worst place for him to be; in the room with you, or out of sight somewhere. In the bedroom, you suppose; for he will lie there reading in just his underpants, that great body of his stretched out all over the bed. And that starts you wanting again; one thing, you've still got that much left between you. You've only got to see him and you want him.

Sometimes you just can't help yourself. You think it'll be for only half an hour or so, and then your mind will be free of it again. But it's always more than just half an hour you lose—much more—what with a shower afterwards, getting dressed again, and then he wants to sort of *mother* you all the time, making cups of coffee and so on, cooking a batch of scones just because you once said you liked them, even just asking you if you want a cigarette. It all eats into the day. But then at least he does have to go off for the evening, from five to eleven, and then you too can work at night—if only you weren't always so tired.

And another thing, your mother keeps dropping in, now that she knows you're working at home. At first you were so glad to see her; you hadn't realized until she came just how much you really missed being at home. She always brings something, cakes or a pie or something she's cooked for you;

168

and as good as Cor's cooking may be, you know then, too, just how much you've missed *her* cooking. It's different somehow; sort of homely. And she's probably right when she says all the time that you're looking so much thinner. You haven't even had time to go out and weigh yourself, but you don't need a weighing-machine to tell you. You can tell by the way your trousers just hang on you now. And yet Cor doesn't seem to look any the worse for it; if anything, he seems to thrive on it.

A strange thing, though, is that no matter how many times she comes, somehow your mother always manages not to come when Cor's there. Except once. But then Cor was lying on his bed, as he so often does, reading in just his underpants. So you had to close the door and say he was sleeping. And she said she wouldn't stay long; she knew you were busy and she had a lot of shopping to do anyway. But it was as though, without even seeing him, she knew she wouldn't like him. Or else she had just made up her mind *not* to like him. That was more like it, probably; she didn't want to meet him, she hardly ever mentions him, which makes you think she probably knows more about it than you ever thought she did. But you can't help that; it's still your life—no one else can live it for you. There are some who always *try* to live it for you, but thank God she's not one of them.

On the other hand, Cor doesn't seem to want to meet her either. That first time, you did go in and suggest that he might dress and come out. But he just looked at you, his face set into those heavy lines you've got to know so well lately, and his eyes seeming to be even more deeply entrenched than ever. And he says no, making the excuse that he would have to shower first before he can get dressed, and that means going out through the living-room to the bathroom—true enough—and he doesn't want to meet your mother like that. So you say sure, and go out and tell her he's still sleeping. But you can see she doesn't believe that either, and shortly afterwards she says she really must go.

It was a bit awkward that time, and when you suggest to Cor that you arrange a morning or something for her to come to tea, he agrees to it of course, but he doesn't sound at all enthusiastic about it. So you just let it drift, like you do with many things these days. You always seem to be just letting things drift.

How different it is when ever old Bruce drops in. You'd think he and Cor were long lost brothers. They laugh and talk with each other, open one bottle after another, and swap recipes as though the end of the world is coming and they won't have time to cook all the things they want to. They even start cooking things none of you can possibly eat, because it's the middle of the night. Or at least, they can eat them; you can't. Just the smell of cooking is enough to make you feel sick, sort of queasy.

And that's another thing: once you really loved your food, but now you've only got to smell it and, instead of getting hungry like you always used to, you get this nausea all the time. It's not as though you eat so much these days; you just don't seem to care for food any more. Even liquor makes you feel off-colour, and the next day you don't exactly have a hangover, you just look and feel about ten years older. Your face looks all grey and sort of lined, too. There's no doubt about it; anyone, if they could see you then, would take you for at least forty-five, not thirty-five.

One thing, old Bruce never fails to cheer you up a little, he's always so bright and breezy. Yet even this is depressing too, for it makes you suddenly realize that you need cheering up, which is not like you at all. You were never like that. *Wild and Woolly Wharton* they used to call you once; but there's nothing much either wild or woolly about you now. Well, just woolly perhaps. 'Woolly' is a pretty good word for it, the way you feel most of the time. Still, old Bruce does brighten you up a bit, you must admit. Yet he always seems to put you back down in the dumps again afterwards, almost without fail. He never seems to be without some pretty depressing bit of news to tell you, just as he's leaving; so that when he goes, he leaves this nasty bit of news or gossip hanging in the air like a bad smell, or dirt in your mouth.

The latest thing he tells you comes near to home.

"Have you heard about young Andy?" he asks you.

You tell him no, you haven't seen Roy or young Andy for weeks now. Come to think of it, the last time you saw either of them was when young Andy stopped you in the street that morning, and gave you the little porcelain figure—Eros over there.

Old Bruce rolls his eyes around in his head as though to emphasize his concern, or stress the sensation of it.

"Young Andy'll be in the jug this time," he says, "that's for sure."

And horrified, you listen to him tell how young Andy is up on a charge for importuning. It seems that young Andy went into a public lavatory somewhere, for just purely innocent reasons for once, old Bruce says, and this tall bloke was standing there, half in the dark, showing himself.

"Well, of course," old Bruce says, "young Andy couldn't help himself. He soon fell for something as easy as that. So he moved over. Just touched the bloke. And as soon as he did, one of the privy doors flies open and another bloke comes out, and they nab him. He didn't have a chance."

"Who do you mean by *they*?" you have to ask. And old Bruce looks at you as though you're still a child.

"Coppers, of course. What do you think! That's their new little game. Gets 'em more arrests—and *hence*, dear boy, promotion."

That really makes you sick. You can't stop yourself from thinking about it for days. And something inside you literally aches for young Andy; it's so damned unfair. If he'd actually gone there looking for someone, then there might be some justification in it; or if he did actually make a pass at someone. All the same, anyone can always say no. And it wouldn't take much to repel young Andy's advances; there's certainly nothing much of the brute about Andy. But no, young Andy would be just the type they would pick on, small and slight for one thing, and shit-scared into the bargain for another. Oh, they're great big wonderful men our policemen, all right.

171

What's the worst of it, though, is <u>they</u> probably enjoy doing it. The one who showed himself would *have* to enjoy it, even if it was only to get himself excited by it for one thing; otherwise he wouldn't be able to lure types like young Andy on. So who's the worst pervert in a case like that?

It's not long afterwards that young Andy comes up for trial, and gets three months. *And* the infamy of course. Where in the hell is he going to get another job when the comes out again? In a gay night club in another State as a belly-dancer or something? That will really put him on the skids, even if the three months in goal don't. For anyone knows what happens to youngsters, even the normal ones, once they get shut in goal with a lot of sex-starved men. And not only from the other prisoners, you've heard; the warders are supposed to be the worst. Of such is *life* . . .

And whenever you look at the little figure of Eros—Eros, of all things—you can't stop yourself from thinking of young Andy, and sort of aching for him—and of how, if it had happened to you, you'd probably cut your throat. After all, it'd take a lot of guts *not* to.

It's after old Bruce tells you about this, you really feel like getting pie-eyed. You're half-way there in any case, with what the three of you have drunk already. And none of you have to work in the morning. So why *not* make a night of it? Old Bruce is willing, and Cor too. So out comes the bottle of Scotch you've been keeping for some occasion or other—it's some *occasion*, all right. By four o'clock or so you're all pretty tight. What you mean is, you're stinking. You can even see *double*, for God's sake. In fact you can't even stop yourself from seeing double when you try to, and you really do try, especially after you get sick and have to hang over the toilet for what seems a goddamn eternity, and you think you'll hawk your whole flaming guts up all over the place. You can't take any more after that, and you're only too glad to let Cor and old Bruce undress you and somehow or other lump you into your bed. Then you pass out cold.

In the morning you think you must still be drunk, the way

you feel. Your head feels as though it's been hacked into at least two separate pieces, your body feels like a sewer. You ask Cor what he's got in the way of something for hang-overs, but he's still asleep; just grunts and rolls over. So you lie there a while longer.

But it's not long before you can't stand it any more; you've just got to get yourself up and find something, no matter how tired and weak you feel. So somehow or other you trip and stagger to the bathroom, and it's only when you look at yourself in the mirror that you know you must be ill. You're *yellow*, for God's sake—yellow as a flaming Chinaman—eyes and all. At first you think it's just the light; you even pinch yourself on those crazy yellow cheeks of yours, to see if you're awake. But you're awake all right; you whole lousy body tells you so. And there's no mistake about it, you're as yellow as an egg-yolk.

15

SIX something. You don't know what it's six of, but at least there is one thing you do know; there's a six in it somewhere. But whether it's six weeks, six days, six hours or six minutes, you haven't the faintest idea. It's long enough for it to have been six years in any case. For what means is there for measuring disaster? Unconditional. Complete.

The doctor was perfectly right; you just have to lie there, flat on your back and hardly ever moving. You don't need a doctor to tell you that; your body tells you so. It's sick, it tells you. You just have to lie there for six . . . but six what was it? Anyway, there's nothing else you can do. Just lie there. The doctor said so, plagiarizing the words and simple facts of your own limply mute body—which knew it all the time. He also tells you you're not to eat fats, no alcohol. He's heard your body say this too. Your body wants bitter things, oranges and lemon juice; weeps all the time for water; shrieks for sugar, wanting to retrieve its lost energy. It rejects everything else, and is content with so little, just lying there. Rest, and the pictures in the ceiling.

You don't think about the fact that you're sick—so bald a fact that it's silly anyway. Don't think about whether you could be more sick than you are, or should be less sick; or wonder why you're sick at all, or even why you shouldn't be not sick. It doesn't have to think about it, your body—it knows. You're sick, and that's all there is to it. Your body is in a different state from usual; needs different conditions and circumstances—that's all. When the phase is over, the body will know that too; but not until the time comes when the phase *is* over—only then. Now it just knows that it's in a very different state than usual. It needs different things, and needs *not* to have a lot of things. Food, love, movement; all of those must go. Just rest, water, sugar and something bitter. And the pictures in the ceiling.

How endless they are, those pictures. There in the stark white blankness of its limitless canvas, the pictures evolve and resolve, form into vague thoughts and sayings, images, without shape or form or anything, no words. Colourless. Move effortlessly and endlessly, in changing patterns, and series of patterns, and patternless series. Clouds and great distances, beautiful. Peace. Animals and their sharp little eyes, teeth. Whole skies and the galaxies slowly wheeling, slowly and so inexorably. A tree of your childhood; you used to have to walk under it every day, to go to school; every day. Countless leaves, countless just because you want to count them all. And the boiled egg, the plain bread and butter your mother always gave you whenever you were sick, so that now a plain boiled egg always reminds you of sickness—never fails. White egg in the wheeling patterns of ceiling. But no butter on the bread, and your mother's fingers searing chill on the shivering heat of your brow, her eyes sharp as the fox's teeth in the right-hand corner, over there. Beyond the tree and the expanding wheel of planets revolving the Milky Way. Africa depending from the huge white rump of an aerial whale, clear as anything, the island of Madagascar and all. Street names. No, they're towns. But names anyway. Like Bingo Biscuits and WOW for a Willies. Chocolates. Revolving with the letters M and W, and a horizontal 8 formed by the mouth of a small boy crying. Books are being written up there; look at all the pages. And pictures too, in the ceiling.

Nothing else. Not yet.

But it comes all the same. What you think about when you're sick is not that you're being sick, or how long it will take to get well again, or what is being done for you so that you *will* get well again, or who's doing it. No, none of that. What you think about and think about and go *on* thinking about is what you would be doing if you *weren't* sick. What you *should* be doing if you weren't sick. Work, and getting new accounts, working on the old ones. All that you *could* be doing, and can't. Can't at all. Don't want to anyway. But you must, you need to so badly, so desperately. Who else will do it if *you* don't? No one else *can*. Only you. And *you* can't. So none of it's done, none of it at all, and the whole goddamned world is falling, sliding to pieces. In a circular motion. It will all be gone by the time you can move again, or do something again. All of it, gone. Not a shred left. And then?

But *now*. Your body just lies here, gasping. Yellow, and sick. Half-dead. Yet never quite dying. Just half-living, in low gear, at a snail's pace. And even that's too quick. Let it all revolve slowly, effortlessly, taking its own sweet time, germinating. Like the pictures, so many of them, up there in the ceiling.

Most of the time it's the same hands that bring you things, water and things bitter, plain bread. Tablets. The same hands with the same eyes on their fingernails move just above your face and plunge down deep *deep* DEEP into your forehead. In *there*. The same hands with the same voice endlessly saying the same words: "It's Cor. How do you feel?" So what! And who's Cor? The hands move and mercilessly ruffle up all the

175

pictures in the ceiling, cast a stone to make ripples, resounding a thunderous silence, like doom, in that deep white, wide canvas. Stilled. And everything clear and concise as mathematical tables, in chronological order, predictable to the split second. Six times six are thirty-six, always have been and always will be. Shadows. Like shades of unmeaning. White woolly elephant with a woolly white eye, gliding through silky thick pine-trees. Should be gone soon. Because it takes only six, usually. Same hands twisting the patterns and pictures, up there in the ceiling. Accounts made out, ready for cheques to be written, but cheques that will never come in. Not any more. When you *can* do something again, you will have to do something else. But what, for instance? Q.E.D. six? Wish you could remember who/what is Cor. A name perhaps for the hands with the eyes on the fingernails. Such deep eyes, now just *beyond* the fingernails. Tablets. Water and something bitter. Genitals always so lax.

And the pictures in the ceiling.

Now that's life for you! Something you can always grasp hold of and understand . . .

Simple!

16

THE day you can sit up, Cor tells you that the doctor said you weren't really sick enough to be put into hospital. It would have had to be the infectious diseases hospital anyway, and then you might only have contracted something else, the doctor had said. What was it you had? Infective hepatitis or something; the old-fashioned name for it was jaundice. You just had to lie still for six weeks and have very little to eat, lots of water, pills. Your mother didn't take you home after all, because Father might have caught it, as he's not been so very well lately either. Besides, she says, Cor didn't want you to leave the flat, he wanted to nurse you all the time. And you couldn't have had anyone better, she says, almost friendly-like. It's easy to see they've become rather good friends, but in an obliged kind of way on her part, still with limits and restrictions, reserve.

Slowly you begin to realize things, to learn what has happened. The doctor tells you it's a liver disease, contracted by virus. You've been physically run down, he says, so that your body had little or no immunity, which is the usual case. A strict diet is required, not only during your illness, but for several months afterwards, and no alcohol of course. For several months you may not feel yourself at all; you'll feel lethargic and perhaps nauseated at times, tired. Soon have you on your feet again. But what we've got to find out, he says, nodding and wagging an omniscient head like some presumptuous child, is the cause of the matter. What he means is, why you should have been so run-down in the first place. Have you been worrying about something? That's the usual thing. And also it's usually something that's really nothing to worry about at all. He thinks a psychiatrist. But don't be alarmed. Nothing to be alarmed about in seeing a psychiatrist; it's not as though you're nutty or anything silly like that. It's just that you've obviously been worrying about something that you shouldn't worry about at all. It's nearly always that way. Takes a psychiatrist to ferret out what it is, bring it into daylight and put it in its proper perspective, stop you from worrying. You'll even laugh about it, eventually. Soon have you on your feet again. So stop worrying about anything, anything at all. He'll make all the arrangements. And—sly wink of just *how* much perspicacity, you wonder?—you're in very good hands. Very good hands. Couldn't have a better nurse than your *friend* here . . .

For of course it's been Cor who's looked after you all the time. And your mother, too, of course. She came when he had to be at work. She says she will still come when Cor has to go to the club, because of course you must still rest for a while, for a long time yet. And you're not to worry about anything. "It's so silly to worry, darling," she says, "especially about things that really don't matter . . ."

Things that don't matter! That nearly kills you. It really does. So it's a psychiatrist you're supposed to see now. The hell you will. And tell him the whole box of tricks of what has *really* been worrying you? Tell him that you love another *man*, and that you worry yourself sick that you'll lose him, worry yourself sick about the people who have had their whole lives changed—broken, almost—by your loving him; worry yourself sick about what will happen if other people—the *normal* people, *outside*—ever find out about it? Tell him all that? The hell you will.

You suppose you'll have to see the psychiatrist, though. After all, you can hardly refuse, not without seeming a damn fool. So you'll just have to find something else to tell him, and not tell him what had really been eating at you—eating away your whole mind and body, like corrosion from an acid.

Well, you've got something else to tell him, all right. You've been worrying about your business, earning your living, accounts slipping away from you, being taken from you when the lord knows it's a competitive enough field in just ordinary circumstances. That's something to worry about all right, and to tell to any psychiatrist. But even then—even *then*—you can't tell him the real reason why you should be so worried about it. You can't tell him about Hamilton, for instance. Because then he'll want to know *why* Hamilton should have started such a campaign against you. And then out will come the whole box of tricks anyway. So what *can* you tell him? Nothing! Nothing at all. You'll just have to say that you haven't even been aware that you *have* been worrying.

How wonderful for the normal person; *he* can just spill the lot—have one bloody great catharsis and no one will think anything of it; because, no matter how bad the situation might be for a so-called normal person, it would at least be considered as *normal*. With you, it's different; they'd just go from

178

one thing to another; and if they did find out what had really been worrying you, that wouldn't be the end of it—not by a long chalk. Afterwards, they'd try and cure you of that too; say it's just a matter of reorientation or something, readjustment. Readjustment, hell! It's *you*, your whole *being*. Personality, mind, soul, conscience, consciousness—call it what you will, it's still *you*. Not merely some sort of skin you can tear from your body—or have torn off for you. No, nothing like that. It's in the very depth of your flesh itself, as deep as anything can be. It always has been, always will be no matter what they try.

Working too hard—that's the only reason you can suggest, within the margin of safety. Once slip just an inch outside that margin and you're finished—a known nancy for life. Which you're not; not a *nancy*, you mean. Not like a little *trish* or something. There are so many of you that aren't like that, and never will be, couldn't be if you tried, and you could never bring yourself even to try, let alone want it.

Don't they ever realize? Don't they ever think? No. It's not *their* life. So why should they? The only time they ever think about it at all is when some crazed lunatic rapes some little kid, a little boy, or molests schoolboys or something—the exception, the poor bloody exception who, by his very repression, has been pushed clean over the edge of sanity. And then *that* side of it comes out all right; it can't fail to. The press loves it. And then all homosexuality—the love of one man for another, fellow beings created exactly in the same image—becomes something heinous again, hideous. Something to be despised, and stamped out. If it's just because you're different, do you also stamp out anyone else because they're different? Everyone with red hair or something? But yes, you suppose they do—they still do. Jews, and negroes . . .

Anyway, this isn't what's really worrying you. You *know* all this. You've known it for ages, and been prepared to accept it, to face up to it. For what else can you do? Suicide is also a shameful thing—and so melodramatic, so hysterical. No, that's not what worries you at all. For even though you're still pretty weak, and there's nothing much these days to give you a sense of humour, or even to keep a sense of humour going, there's still that flippant old saying of yours which still holds good. 'You're perfectly adjusted to your maladjustment.' You've got all that worked out all right. All you want is to be able to walk around with your head up, and with your self-respect. And to work at something in this crazy so-called *normal* world, to do something which is really a service to the normal world. For where would the normal world be *without* your kind? Everything from politics to fashion, anything you can think of—particularly the arts.

Here you've seen your whole business slip away from under you. Because yes, it's all gone now. While you've been lying on your back, ill, for six weeks, the last of your accounts have gone elsewhere. Could you ever get them back? In how many' months, how many years? Even in another town perhaps.

So now what do you do? You've not only got to earn a living for yourself, you've got all these doctor's and medical bills on top of it. So what *can* you do? Go out and crack stones or something, you suppose. Yes, there are probably quite a number of people who'd like to see you have to do that—go out and crack stones.

17

COR'S deep dark eyes are looking at you again and, from somewhere even deeper and darker in that carefully moulded head of his, he plucks out a thought. It's something you can almost *see*, it takes such an effort.

"Ray?"

"Yeah, bub?"

"I don't know why you've been worrying so much on the

moment. If your work doesn't bring in anything, I've still got my job. We can live on that. And you'll get going again soon, when you're better again. I mean, ordinary married people have to—you know, support each other. So why can't we?"

For the first time in ages, he almost makes you cry. But you don't. That's the worst part of it, the part you've only just begun to realize. You can't, not any more. When your business slipped away from under you, and your health skated off, something else went slipping and skating off too—Cor, and your love for him. Something happened to that as well. You can hardly believe it, but it did. You can feel it. The only explanation you can offer is that you suppose worry takes up so much of your mind, occupies it sort of, that it doesn't leave much room for anything else. It pushes everything else out, even love, and just takes over. If your love *is* really dying, then it's the worry that's done it. And it's the ordinary people—the whole goddamn world of ordinary people, outside—that have caused the worry. Without them, or if they were all like you, the worry would never have existed. It could never have even started in the first place, and then the two of you—you and Cor—would have been damn near the perfect lovers, you suppose. Was there ever anyone who could have loved so much? Anywhere?

But now something has happened to that too. And it's not just medical. You know the doctor said you won't feel like that any more for a while, wanting sex or anything, he said. Not for a while. You won't even be able to, not until after you're quite better again. Then things will get back to normal, he said. So don't worry yourself about that either. But for a while, now, you won't even feel like it. And yet, surely it's not just the sex side of it that has brought you together? And kept you together? Surely it's been much more than just that? But the thing is, now when you look at him, there's never even the same old thrill as before. Something's gone. Before, whenever you looked at him—well, just *remember* how you used to feel. And now there's nothing at all like that any more. You can't explain it, but there just isn't. If anything, at times he seems to you as just someone you know only casually or something. At times he even looks kind of stupid, the way he's always watching you, sort of cow-eyed. And his mouth—that mouth that was once so exquisitely sculptured to you—now looks sort of loose-looking and almost idiotic. You still let him kiss you, of course—because you owe him that much. But that's the point: before you always wanted it, now you have to let him. You submit. And you know that it's really so damn little that he ever asks for, now, and after he's done so much. What *has* happened to you for God's sake . . .

What did he say? Oh, yes. You remember, and you hear yourself answer:

"You don't think I'm just going to lie back here and be *kept* or something, do you?" You know it's the wrong thing to have said as soon as you've said it. It's a pretty lousy thing to have said, but you can't help it; it's what you meant. "Don't start thinking of me as your *wife* or something, who you've got to pay for. Or even a husband, if it comes to that—out of work. I can't stand it, Cor. I tell you I can't!"

And he looks away, turns away—hurt—goes away; says he has to do something in the kitchen. But just before he goes, you can see the hurt come out into his eyes, forced out in hard little tear-pricks, but brushed away fiercely. And you could damn near kill yourself, you feel such a heel. But you can't help it; you can't *help* the way you feel.

There are so many slow and sudden silences between you now, sliding; long minutes of saying nothing that seems hours, when before there had been hours of saying nothing, not in actual words you mean, but you were always saying everything even with your flesh, with the very bones in your hand come to think of it, and the hours drifting by had seemed only minutes. Seconds—and such precious things. That had been the time when you had known the meaning of the word 'precious'. And 'cherish', words without meaning any more. Now just silly little boxes of sound. Words that had once blossomed so beautifully, now somehow seem vulgar, or great monstrous things like cauliflowers. Or all petals of emotion, only to wither a bit—fade—now like pressed dead flowers you kept once in a schoolbook. Sad and dead replicas of their former selves, only the sight of them ever refreshing their memory. Brittle and crackling at the touch, just like most of the words between you now. Stale. Most things ᵤ. m to turn brittle and crackling when they go stale. Even bread. The bread of life—joke!

But sometimes you do try to do something about it. When he touches you, you let the touch remain there, heavy and burning, but sort of a bit insolent or something, there on your flesh. But you let it stay there; you owe him that much at least. And debt's always such a long-winded thing, like regret. But you do make an effort sometimes, and try, by touching him back. And then comes the most pathetic part of it; he's always so grateful for it, just like a dog or something, that you can hardly bear to look at him. Just pat him a few times on that intimate-smelling warmth of his sleeves, feeling underneath the flesh so firm and so willing, but constrained by necessity. Just a few little pats. But it's always on the last one, or even just before you let the last one fall, that you realize how meaningless they really are. Forced. Or worse, pretended. And somehow you feel that he can sense it. You never *could* hide anything from him—not from Cor. So how can you expect to now? Especially something like this, when it probably means so much to him. But at least he doesn't show it, or tries not to show it. At least he does that much. And with those big transparent eyes of his, you can tell he's just waiting, and will go *on* waiting for a long time yet, for it all to come back. And even this very patience of his seems—well, sort of cow-like.

Ever since you've been sick, you've slept in separate beds. But they're not really separate somehow. There's probably three feet and eight and a half inches between the edge of your bed and that of his. But it might just as well never exist, once the light's out. It's as though he's right next to you again, his body firmly imprinted against your own, consuming it, devouring it, just as it always did. Even from over three feet away, you can still feel it, at all hours of the night, knowing he's probably awake too and just lying there, so far away, yet hard up against you.

Once you even make the gesture of getting in to his bed with him, just as in old times, just to lie there, holding him a little if only for old time's sake. It almost makes him delirious. You even feel something of the old feeling creep back into you, but it soon goes again, leaving you even emptier, drained, than you were before. Yet for a moment you had almost thought you would be able to do something that time. And of course he could have. Have you ever known the time when he couldn't? That goddamn hot-blooded Dutch powerhouse of his, reared and buttressed with milk and cheese and butter and such. At times you can almost feel it, and smell it in his flesh, in his blood. The right diet for a good strong wholesome never-failing sex-life, you suppose. Australians drink too much tea, probably. Bursts through the pores in a sweat of expired energy, like masturbation. Milk stays in the body, consolidating, building up a kind of storage or something. And with that storage of his, he's always ready for the slightest little gesture for his whole body to start consuming, demanding. And your whole body shrinks away from it again. After what you think is a decently inoffensive period, you get out of his bed and go back to your own. Small duty done, obligation fulfilled. But it's never enough, not for Cor. He knows it's just a duty. And what you know is that again you've hurt him, and this time more than you've ever hurt him before. But you can't help it, can't do anything about it; that's the way it goes, that's all.

Then it soon settles into the next stage. Lots of things about him, that you never even noticed before, you can't stand any more. Little things, silly things. Used razor blades left where you nearly slice a hand on them. That old toothbrush of his, flattened and squashed, curly, and sort of pinkish-looking. A Cor-smelling singlet left on the end of the bed after he's gone to the club. Congealed dishes in the sink, or a glass pungent from stale beer. Because, of course, he can still drink, and says

184

he needs it at times—which he probably does. Can't exactly blame him, but . . .

The dishes get left because he will moon around you so, and then at the last minute has to dash off to the club and leave them, because you haven't any work to do any more, and haven't anything else to do anyway. Little things. Even just the way he sits sometimes. When a love starts to die, its decomposition sets in so fast, you can detect it long before the actual death.

It's probably all your fault, you tell yourself; you just haven't got anything else to do.

18

As soon as you're well enough, you go through the wreckage of your business, just a few pathetic bits of flotsam and jetsam, to see what's left, what you can salvage. But there's nothing—nothing much, anyway. The few jobs that are left outstanding, and which you can still do, aren't worth either the effort or the return, so you pass them on to someone else. It's no good trying to pick up things from a few useless odds and tatters; you'll have to take a job somewhere, if you can get one. Start looking around; after all, there's no desperate hurry about it. And even if there was, you couldn't do much about it yet. You still don't feel up to it, or that it's worthwhile. So take your time. After all, you've still got a little left in the bank; you can always sell the car.

So every day you start looking through the newspapers, job-hunting. Something in advertising again of course. Some big company perhaps, who want a man of their own to handle it. Right up your alley, that would be. Or if not advertising, then something like it, or associated with it. Public relations or personnel handling or something. Anything like that. After all, you haven't got any qualifications for something else; haven't got qualifications for anything at all—just the personality, and perhaps a little experience. But even that much is often enough to carry you through, somehow or other. Look at lots of other people you know.

There are one or two ads you think might be suitable, but it's even an effort to answer them. You manage one or two, and expect to see yourself soon walking through wide glass doors into a shiny new office somewhere, and just hold out your hand for a pay-cheque every week. After all, lots of other people can manage it—why not you? But you might have expected it; all you get, after waiting for days, weeks sometimes, is a polite and oh so impersonal acknowledgement of your application with thanks for tendering it, and that you *may* hear from them again in the future. But when you do, *if* you do, it's only to say that the position has already been filled. Etcetera.

But you keep on trying, almost every week-end.

One consolation, old Bruce tells you that Hamilton can't do you any more harm. Not that he needs to, for hasn't he done more than enough already? But Hamilton has been transferred; old Bruce isn't exactly sure where, but he thinks to another dead-end branch over east somewhere. Anyway, it doesn't matter; at least he's out of the way. And Mia, Cor tells you, has got her divorce. Must be able to do things like that pretty quick in Holland. But she's got it. Not only that, Cor tells you, but she's married again, just as he thought she would, to the bloke she'd been writing to for a while before she went back. So Mia's all nice and cosy again, settled. And even though she's so far away, you can almost hear her, sometimes, saying Mia want this, and Mia want that. And getting it, though probably still whining. And those big goitrous eyes of hers all the time; you can just see it. Smug in her motherhood too, and probably crowing to herself if Cor has ever told her what's happened to you both.

Does he have pictures of the child, the child he's never seen?

If he has, then he's never shown them to you, never said anything about it. Strange, you'd think he would say something,
even if he didn't get any photographs. But he keeps to himself
these days, more and more. Suppose you can't exactly blame
him; you really *ought* to try a bit more, be a bit more congenial or something. You really should. But you've still always
got that sort of *tired* feeling; somehow or other you just can't
be bothered. It would be false or forced if you did. And Cor
would soon know it. One thing about him, you still can't *hide*
anything from him, or pretend either. So what's the use of
trying?

One week you get so close to almost getting something,
handling the advertising of a new insurance corporation, that
when you're called for a second interview, let alone a first, you
start thinking to yourself yes, this is going to be it. Very soon
now you'll be walking through these doors every morning, day
after day, weeks on end, for years maybe, and taking the lift
up to your own floor, joking with the liftman on the way, and
saying a few words to the different ones you'll be getting to
know, nodding to others, getting out of the lift and walking
along a very shiny passage to your own door where you'll go
in, perhaps even have a secretary to say good morning to, and
then go on to your own office, your very own office again, and
sit at your very own desk with layouts and blurbs and things
scattered all over it. You'll sit down and just start into work as
usual, hungry for it. And if ever you do think back over this
period, before you started the job, you'll only think of it as
some sort of off-tune transition period. You really will. No
more than just a sort of enforced holiday. And at the second
interview, you can see it all as clearly as anything; can sort of
feel it in your bones, as though intuition comes out of your
very flesh and blood, not just your mind, and is like some
kind of vapour that releases itself through the pores of your
skin.

Then this fellow comes in, right in the middle of the interview; he looks at you oddly, and for just a second or two
there's a clash of eyes; or rather it's like both pairs of eyes,

187

yours and his, are carefully measuring the distance between you. And *his* eyes seem to find the distance not far enough for his liking, they look so cold and suddenly hostile. But then they turn away again. He speaks to the personnel manager w o's been interviewing you, and with whom you've been getting along so well, just like old buddies, until this fellow asks him can he see him a moment. So they go through a door into another office. And while the door is closed between you, you suddenly know what is happening, and you're not even surprised when the personnel manager comes out and, all apologetic and everything—you have to give him that much— he says he's sorry but the matter has been taken out of his hands; an appointment has been made by one of the higher-ups. He almost falls over himself to apologise about it, and you can see he's so genuinely upset you feel quite sorry for the guy, knowing he really can't help it or do anything about it. So you just smile and say that's O.K., and shake hands—yes, he does shake hands with you still—and you go out into the street again, knowing just exactly how it feels to be a leper or something.

It's funny, but when a thing like that happens to you, and you walk out afterwards on to a perfectly innocent street somewhere, and even on a perfectly innocent morning, and you know that nothing of what you're thinking can possibly be true, yet it just *seems* that all the people you can see around you have somehow managed to have their backs turned to you. And again you think to yourself, you will *have* to crack stones or something, eventually, even if you do go to another town.

You walk along that stiff hostile street, the morning sunlight beating and basting itself down and around you all the time, and even the buildings in their two prim little rows seem stiff and hostile towards you, all eyes and tight-lipped mouths. And for the first time you realize that what you're really doing is just running a kind of gauntlet, an endless gauntlet. Nearest temporary refuge? A pub for a beer.

But it's only when you get inside that you remember that it's got to be only lemonade or something; you're not allowed to drink. Even the luxury of getting drunk is denied you. So you drink about half the glass of lemonade and, if you think anyone's looking at you, whether they think they know you or not, then you just don't look back at them; you don't want to talk to anyone, not about anything. And then you go out again into that harsh flood of morning air and jeering traffic and just walk aimlessly around the town a bit, not going anywhere in particular, feeling it all familiar around you, and yet at the same time as though you've never seen any of it before either, it all seems so removed from you, as though it's not a real city at all, but just something glowing on some kind of big screen around you, and likely to be flashed off again at any minute of the clock. Once you even lean a hand against a block of marble in a wall to see if it's real, all that beautiful grain and rich colouring and everything, and it just about starts to feel like really something, there, under your hand, all warm from the morning sun and flashing back weirdly stretched glimpses of the street and traffic, cars and things—until suddenly you look a little closer into it and you can see your own distorted reflection staring back at you, the features all stretched and strained, drooping in great tremulous pendants that hardly look like a face at all and yet are unmistakably your own features. But if there's one thing you just don't want to look at right now, it's your own face.

So you take yourself off to a cinema and find yourself sitting in some bleak row in this sort of half-world of dusk and shadows, dim lights, with just a handful of other people with nothing else in the whole world with which to fill the vacuum of a week-day morning but vacuous drivel from Hollywood. It's supposed to be a real-life drama and all that with this young blond and blue-eyed piece draping and posing himself all over tobacco fields or something, and nothing else but one little glittering piece of Hollywood glamour after another clawing and drooling her way all over him, and he always just standing there, looking all blue-eyed and bewildered, until he must have realized he's supposed to *act* or do something, and he makes the phoniest imitation of a clinch you've ever seen.

You could do it better yourself, you reckon; you really could, even with a woman. And you can tell that it all looks so phony and awful because if this blond, blue-eyed beauty is so used to making *other* kinds of clinches, *off* the screen, that he can't do it with women even when he's supposed to, just for a movie, not even for his living. It's all so phony and stupid you can't sit it out any longer, and you lurch up the aisle and get yourself out of the cinema before it makes you puke.

Outside, you buy a paper. But all you use it for is to beat your thigh with as you find yourself just walking around and around all these alien and impersonal streets. Then you suddenly find yourself in front of the old office building, where you used to have your own office once. Seems like a million years ago by now, and you don't know how the hell you got there, but you have, and you step back a little, right back to the brink of the pavement so that you can look up at the window where your office used to be. You can almost look clean through the window and see yourself working there, or how you used to be—you and Barbara. Don't even know where she is any more. And at night, you and Cor, in front of the radiator, on the carpet. What's happened to all that? If only you knew. If only you *knew*. But right now you can't look at it any longer, can't bear to be in even the same *vicinity* any longer. And just like a snail when something comes whamming down a bit too close to those feely-fumbly horns they have, you retract yourself quickly and hurry off into your own little shell, hollow and cavernous little refuge that it is is from the rest of the world.

The flat. And there you stay, lying on your back on the bed, smoking one cigarette after the other, even if they do taste like straw or the bottom of a cockey's cage. Until somehow or other the rest of the day has sort of wrung itself out to the last miserable drop, the door bangs, and you've got something else to contend with—Cor's home.

" 'Lo, Ray. How do you feel?" he always says. And now he can add: "How did you get on today?"

And all you can say is:

"Lousy." To both questions. What's the use of trying to say anything more?

"Anything come out of that insurance place you were going to today?"

One thing about Cor, he can at least be consistent when he wants to be—never varies.

"Yeah, sure thing," you tell him. "Nothing!"

So he just looks at you for a minute or two. It's really nowhere near as long as that of course, it just seems it. And then he sort of shrugs, his arms all loaded with the parcels he's bought on the way home, and for the very first time you can remember he starts to go on through to the kitchen, without coming over to kiss you or anything, not even just the usual light smack on the forehead. And you don't know what comes over you, a sort of great gust of panic or something, you don't know what it is; but you're suddenly shaking all over, terrified. For you know he's just going to go straight in to that kitchen of his and start cooking, and for the very first time there'll be this breach between you. It's just a little thing, this quick smack of a kiss you're used to giving each other, whenever either of you comes home. And you suppose it doesn't mean so very much really. But if ever you stop doing it, you realize now, you might never be able to start it again. And then where will you be? Things are difficult and strained enough as they are, without letting them slip altogether. You know it's *you* that's been doing all the slipping. You certainly can't blame Cor—to the contrary. And if you let him go through to that kitchen of his now, without the usual, habitual, ritual, doesn't-really-mean-anything-but-means-a-whole-goddamn-lot little gesture you've both been so used to, then you might as well admit right now that everything *is* all washed up between the two of you. And that's what you panic about. For suddenly, astonishingly, you find that it just isn't like that at all.

"Cor?"

Even just to say his name seems to bring back some of the old magic.

He stops, turns, looks at you. And then there are parcels and things all over the floor, swilling around your feet and getting trodden all over. But it doesn't matter—nothing matters. There's just the two of you, holding each other again, rocking together in the middle of your very own room. And it seems years, *years* since things have been like this.

All the things he's done for you. How could you ever have forgotten it? You can't really blame him for crying the way he does.

"Oh, Ray," he says. "I thought you'd got to hate me."

And you think to yourself, you hope that what you're feeling this time is what you're *really* feeling, and you're not just letting a bit of panic delude you into feeling something that isn't there at all. But it must be there all right; you haven't felt like this in ages. And somehow or other you can actually bring yourself to tell him how sorry you are.

"Oh, Ray," he says, "it's just that you've been so sick and that. And you do worry yourself, you know. But it's all right now. Things are going to be all right. You'll see."

He's always been so right about things before, you can only hope he is again this time.

19

ANYWAY, *something* works—works like a charm at long last. The very next day there's this letter in the post, from one of the places you'd written to, and it's been so long ago you'd almost forgotten it. In fact you still have to think a bit to remember just which interview it was, what the fellow looked like, where it was that you went to see him. And then you remember where it was, in one of the city hotels where he was staying, over from the east just to interview you. And a few others too, of course. It all comes back when you see he's staying again at the same hotel, where he wants you to ring him and make an appointment. You'd thought at the time that you were almost sure this guy was also a 'member of the club', although he never made a pass at you or anything like that, never even said or did anything that would give himself away. You just felt it. But everything was kept on a purely business-like level, so much so that, as you hadn't heard anything more about it, you naturally thought it was just like all the rest, that nothing would come of it.

You still think that probably nothing will come of it; tell yourself not to build up your hopes too much. It gets a bit monotonous, to say the least, having them all knocked down again. So you ring him up and you can remember his voice all right, and yes you're almost sure now that he *is* a member of the club, quite likely to be anyway, being in the advertising racket. But it doesn't make any difference. Neither of you would be the other's cup of tea, you suppose. At least, you can speak for yourself. Seems a nice enough guy though; says he wants the interview straight away, if you're still free to take the job, so that he can fly back east again that night if possible. He's pretty nice about things, all right; he even asks you to lunch.

So you ring Cor straight after and tell him the good news, and the two of you are crowing to each other over the phone, you're so glad and relieved about it. You tell Cor how this bloke had said the advertising agency, an international show, wanted a manager for one of its branches. So they probably mean right here. In which case it would mean not only a job, without all the worry and responsibility and everything, but you'll still be your own boss more or less. Things couldn't be more perfect. So you tell Cor to keep his fingers crossed, and he says, laughing, that he'll keep everything crossed that can be crossed, and to be sure to ring him as soon as you can, he'll be waiting to hear.

You really feel on top of the world again when you go to the hotel and see this bloke waiting for you, in the lobby. It must be obvious to him how you feel too, for he doesn't beat around the bush at all. Takes you straight into the dining-room where there's a table waiting, saying he remembers how you're not allowed to drink and so forth, so you'll just eat straight away if that's O.K. with you. You don't mind if he has a Scotch-and-soda at the table do you? Mind? And he then tells you straight off; the job's yours.

You're so sort of dizzy and excited feeling, you don't know whether you're going to laugh or cry or jump out of a goddamn window. You hardly listen to what else he's saying, you're just seeing yourself already starting work again, in some new office somewhere, and even before that, telling Cor about it, over the phone, and the two of you having so much to talk about, you don't know if you'll ever be able to get it all finished. Food of some sort is placed before you, and you eat with the right utensils and all that sort of thing, say yes and no when you're supposed to. And then you do try to make at least one half of that crazy brain of yours listen to what's being said to you, it's all so important.

It's important, all right. If the charm is still working, then it's suddenly working in a very different direction. All this talk, suddenly, of how long will it take you to get your passport renewed do you think, and your taxation clearance, all that sort of thing. You suddenly realize that this branch you're to take over from someone or other isn't here in the city at all —not even a country town, not even another city in the same country. Normally, you'd jump at a thing like this. But how on earth are you going to tell Cor about it? And what will you do about him anyway?

Because this branch that they want you to take over is clean at the other end of the earth. A three-year contract with six month's leave after it, all passages paid of course, before they renew the contract—that is, of course, if renewal suits both parties. Maybe some other place in the world afterwards. You might even have to take over somewhere else before the first contract has expired, if it's necessary, it really is such an inter-national show. They like to move you around as much as possible, see the world, get to know it. The more you know of the world, the better use you are to them and all that.

Of course, he says, he realizes that you need a bit more time to think it over. Will a week be enough? Sooner, of course, if you can. The sooner you get started, the better. You'll have about three months in London first, at the head office, and then out you'll go to take over your branch. You ought to feel pretty flattered, he says. The company's taking on six new men altogether, but six from all over the world. You're the only one to be offered the job from this country, because of your past experience in your own business, and your travel overseas.

Yes, you can't deny it; you feel pretty flattered about it. At any other time it would seem as though the whole wonderful world had been dropped in your lap. But now—now what worries you is how are you ever going to tell Cor? And what *are* you going to do about him?

Who'd ever have thought, even just a few minutes ago for instance, that you'd soon be packing up to go clean across to the other side of the earth? Because the branch you're taking over eventually is, of all places, Hongkong.

20

THERE'S no use in beating around the bush, you tell yourself, or in putting things off; you've got to tell him sometime or other. Even if you still haven't made up your mind or anything, it'd be better if you at least talked it over with him. You'll have to do that much anyway.

So, just as you said you would, you go back to the flat and ring him at the club. Naturally he's so excited when you tell him you can have the job if you want it, you can hardly get a word in sideways. But even when you can, you can't quite bring yourself to tell him about it's being in Hongkong—not over the phone like that; it'd be too brutal. Knowing Cor, you wouldn't know what he might do; he always takes this kind of thing so badly. So you leave it until he comes home, even though you hate yourself for it. You know he's going to be so glad about it, all through the day, only to have it all smashed down again when he gets home. But what can you do? If you don't take this job, and the lord knows you want it badly enough, how long will it be before you're ever offered another? Or will you ever be offered another? Not in this town, you tell yourself; you can be pretty certain of that, the way things have gone so far. In any case, you'll be glad to get out of it; glad to get away and shake off its lousy parochial dust—*dirt*—and be free of it for a while. You really will. No, you're going to take this job all right. If it wasn't for Cor, you'd ring that bloke back straight away and tell him—if it wasn't for Cor . . .

You don't quite know what to expect from him, once you've told him. Disappointment of course, perhaps even shock. But after that, what? Tears? Accusations? Hysterics? Recriminations? Or just a kind of posed but sullen indifference? You never quite know what to expect from his these days. Did you ever?

When he first comes in, his impatience rattling the key around in the door, his very steps impatient as he comes down the short passage and into the sitting-room, he's almost bursting with excitement, like a big happy kid. He even starts talking about it before you've had a chance to tell him any of the details, let alone the main one—about where it is. Or rather, he's not so much talking about it as firing questions at you all the time; even wanting to know what you had for lunch, for God's sake. Cor always wants to know all the details, no doubt about him, even down to the little things that don't matter a damn; not to you they don't, anyway. Things you would never even have thought about, if it hadn't been for him wanting to know all about them.

You've just about come to the end of all you can tell him,

before you must tell him the main thing about it of course, and you're trying to fashion or formulate some sort of way of putting it to him, fumbling around with it on the very brink of your lips, when he gets up suddenly and, still all excited and a bit awkward and careless of things in the room, he says: "Wait!" and goes into the kitchen and comes back again with two glasses, a can and a can-opener.

"Grapefruit juice!" he says, those deep eyes of his now warm and glittering, his smile restoring the old shape of his mouth. "But we can *pretend* it's champagne."

It's that sort of thing about Cor that always gives you a twinge deep down inside you somewhere; something you've never known with anyone else, not with any of the others. And it takes just a little thing like that to make it all the more difficult for you. But now you know you can't hold off any longer; it wouldn't be fair to him if you did. So this time it's your turn to say wait. And then you tell him.

Everything seems to just slide from his face, slips from it. It even seems to slip from his body, the way it sags. And from his hands. From one hand when he puts down his glass and then just lets it hang there, suspended over his knee. And from the other which had suddenly clenched at his breast, and now the fingers are slowly unfolding, as though the very life itself is seeping slowly from out of them. Slowly, so slowly, it comes down and down, until eventually it settles in rest, curled upwards, on the limp wrist of the other. An upturned hand—from which the world has fallen. Just that slow and despairing movement, the coming to rest of his hands, tells you everything; you're very glad you didn't watch his face.

For now, when you look up into it, you don't think you've ever seen a human face so ravaged by emotion in all your life. It's a terrible thing to look at. It looks suddenly old, drawn, heavy. An ugly face. A mere parody of what Cor's face usually is, or as though it's suddenly been deflated of whatever kind of force has supported it before.

He doesn't look at you. He just stares out through the window; beyond the window. Beyond even the other windows that obstruct whatever distance there might once have been beyond that window of yours. You can even see the window itself mirrored in his eyes, they're so still; sort of twin portraits of the model before them. And then he gets up and walks over to the window, leans and takes support from it. It's almost as though his whole body has been received into the window, and the window has taken some of his shape into itself. It's all so indelibly imprinted in your mind, you feel you'll never be able to look at that window again without seeing him there, that great back of his being received, or possessed, and finally framed by the window, just as though he was nothing more than a picture. And the curtains waft in and out, silently, like a slow, slow breath. Faint and far away, the traffic sighs.

"What are you going to do, Ray?" he says at last, sort of stifled.

You still can't bring yourself to say it, so you just let the silence between you wash and wade around the room for a while, like some slowly rising tide, cold. All the words you were going to say still fit snugly into some far recess of your mind, like a row of little boxes. But they fit just a little too snugly; you can't get them out. They'd only sound like a lot of silly noises in the air if you did. Silly empty noises, parrot-squawks. So it's better not to say anything. You don't think you can find your voice to say anything in any case. It seems to have sunk somewhere; buried itself, irretrievably. All you can do is just sit there, fumbling around with your fingers, looking at the picture of him there drooped against the window. You couldn't move, let alone get up, if you tried. Can't say anything. But you don't have to. For once again he says it for you.

"You must take it, I suppose," he says. And even the voice which says the words doesn't sound at all like Cor's. Not like anybody's. Or at least not like anyone's you know. As though he realizes this, he clears his throat, and it seems somehow to make his whole body tremble, taking root there, and he says again: "I suppose you *must* take it." But still the voice is not quite his own.

How long he just stood there, you don't suppose you'll ever

know. But it seemed ages—ages suspended there, reverberating between the two of you, hovering around like a cold, gloomy threat, annihilation. Then a hand slips; drops from the window-sill to hang, suspended, down the slack length of his thigh. The thigh shifts, feeling its own weight. Then he turns and walks straight out of the room, into the bedroom, and you hear first of all the weight of his body falling full length across his bed, and then the terrible, terrifying sound of his crying. Uncontrollable. It's so terrifying that it's some time before you can make yourself get up and go into him, stand at the door and see that body of his, that long body you have loved so much, stretched out prostrate before you—but now with grief instead of desire. And even his grief is submissive. Even the sound of his weeping tells you that he has accepted it already, just as he accepts so many things.

And somehow or other you do manage to bring yourself over to his bed, to lie down beside him, to put your arm around his great quivering shoulders, and, exactly as if he was a child, tell him not to cry, not to cry, you'll think of *something*. You mightn't even take the job, you say, foolishly, because you know that of course you will, there's nothing else you can do. And he knows this too.

"You *must* take it," he says, his voice still drenched from its weeping. And then the next thing he says, he doesn't really say to you at all. You don't know just who it *could* be that he does say it to, to no one you suppose, and yet it sounds as though it *has* to be to someone. Someone you don't know, perhaps. Someone to whom he can pour out his own private grief without any interference or intrusion on your part, cutting you clean out of it altogether.

"Oh God," he says, "I knew it would end on this way. It's just like Henk, all over again."

No matter how long you live, you'll never be able to forget the way he said that. And for the rest of your life, you know too that you'll wish it had been some sort of physical blow he had given you; you don't suppose you'll ever stop flinching from this one.

21

You have a week in which to make up your mind—seven precise and so clearly cut days, like crystal, each one following the other like seven similar, same-shaped, same-sized beads on a string; something you can almost touch and, one at a time, flip from one end to the other, except that it seems such a long time between having flipped one and the turn coming to flip another—at least until there will be only three, then two, then only one left to flip. Only then do you become conscious of some secretive process of acceleration that hadn't been apparent before.

There's been no point in the delay. If anything, you've been anxious the whole time to send off the telegram, especially towards the end when you also start to have a kind of half-fear that you'll leave it just a little too late, that the company will presume you don't want the job and give it to someone else. It's a thought that fills you with a constant and over-riding panic, even over and above that of having to make this one act of finality. For the moment you do send it, you realize, will be the very moment of acknowledging a far greater finality: that you have broken off everything with Cor. Everything will be finished between the two of you. And this is something you cannot yet bring yourself to do, not easily anyhow. The time will come when you'll be forced to do it, and this much you can accept. But enforcement will be necessary; it is still impossible for you to do it merely of your own free will. Somehow or other you just can't.

So this is one reason for the protracted delay, this kind of nameless, wordless, but monstrous fear of yours—severing yourself from Cor, to face a life of loneliness again. It will be

200

like cutting yourself in two. That's one reason; another is hope
—of all things—but hope that, maybe in this one week that's
left to you, some other offer will turn up, something here in the
country, or even in the same city, so that you and Cor will be
able to stay together after all. Almost anything will do—but
within reason, of course; you can't *exactly* go cracking stones
for a living; that's just an expression, a last resort in words
only. Besides, you haven't exactly got the constitution for it.
You'd soon crack up, you know all too well, before too many
stones got cracked. No, it doesn't have to be something with
anywhere near the prospects and money of this Hongkong job;
something in the same line if possible, but even something with
less than half the money that this offers will do. But of course,
just as you expect, nothing comes—nothing at all.

A third reason for your delaying the telegram is really
something half-crazy, it's such a preposterous sort of thing to
think of. But half-crazy or not, and no matter how imprac-
ticable it might be, you feel that you must explore its possi-
bilities. It's the last thing you can do. And after all, you do feel
as though you owe this much at least to Cor. And this half-
crazy thing you've been thinking about is the possibility of
taking him with you.

So you find the appropriate office to make inquiries, and you
have to go and feel and fumble your way with some stolid and
ineffably stupid official, to whom you can't possibly blurt out
the real reason why you're making such inquiries. You're
doing it on behalf of a friend, you say, who is toying with the
idea of just going to Hongkong on spec, to find a job and live
there. But you've soon given plenty short shrift with this one
little act of penance, as it really is. You can't go to Hongkong
—except as a tourist with plenty of money—unless you have
acquired a position of some kind before you go there. You
need an entry permit, a working permit; otherwise its impossible. You'd just be shipped out again. Hongkong is overcrowded as it is. So then you calculate your salary and try to
work out, find out from the same stolid and stupid official if
it would be possible for the two of you to live on it, instead of

just one. But there are too many considerations and conditions which need to be verified before you can even attempt it, like knowing whether your accommodation is provided and that kind of thing, and, even if it is provided, what kind of accommodation it is.

Instead of sending a telegram, you're almost tempted to telephone instead, to try and find out a little more about such conditions. You're even almost tempted to tell this guy Hempson, who gave you the job, the real reason of why you want to know, tell him about Cor and how you want him to go with you—because Hempson was not only such a decent sort of guy, but you could still swear, more than ever now, that he was the same way as both of you. What's more, you feel he'd understand; probably let you make some sort of arrangements of the kind, expenses on your own account of course. But somehow or other you just can't bring yourself to do it. If Hempson's not that way, and not at all sympathetic, then the whole game would be up once again. You'd lose the job, and then where would you be? . . .

That's the ironic part of it. If you were a normal person, married to a woman, then this would be one of the first things you *would* be able to discuss. In fact, you'd hardly need to discuss it at all; it would be presumed, from the very beginning, that you'd take her with you. It would be only the details and conditions that would have to be discussed. But when it's another *man* you're involved with, you can't discuss anything of the kind; you can't even broach it. Even if you've got all the money in the world for such a thing, you can't exactly go around saying: "I'm Raymond Reginald Wharton and this is my boy friend. Kindly accept him in exactly the same way as you'd accept a woman who might happen to be my wife." You wouldn't get very far if you did. And yet, if he *was* a woman, he'd have all his fares paid for him too, probably a house supplied, especially if there were children as well. But he's not a woman; and that's all there is to it.

And even if you did get him there, somehow or other, what could he do? He's not a qualified architect, even in his own

202

country. And he can't exactly be a barman, not in a place like Hongkong. They have Chinese for that sort of thing. In Asia, the menial jobs are done by Asians. The white man has to be the little white lord, to be able to work and live there. In the executive class, skilled—or a specialist. There are already too many hands wanting work in a place like Hongkong—especially in teeming, overcrowded Hongkong—for a pair of ordinary *white* hands to find something to do, and be paid for it as a skin, when it *is* white, must be paid to be able to live accordingly. If it was only to London that you were going, then that would be different. But it's not. And there's no use in just protracting the agony of it all by taking him there, to London, for only about three months and then still having to leave him. Although—and you do have to consider this too—he would then be nearer his own country if he wanted to go back. But you know the answer to that one; he could never go back—not Cor.

So in the end there's really no answer to it—no answer at all. Each successive hell of a day follows each successive hell of a day—days when you can hardly bear to look at each other, nights when you can't. He starts to drink, heavily. He says it's just customers at the club starting to get in the Christmassy mood, and buying him drinks all the time; he can hardly refuse. But you know it's not that at all—not quite that, even if there is a certain shred of truth to it. He's gone back to his old refuge, drink. You can hardly blame him. But it's pretty hard *not* to hurl abuse and recriminations at him when, one night, you've got good reason to suspect that he's also reverted to that *other* former refuge of his. He's started going with others. You don't know where. It could be anywhere, for God's sake, even parks or public lavatories, and with God alone knows who. But you can't very well say anything. After all, you know only too well where the blame lies. And then again, you could be wrong. If only there hadn't been that soiled handkerchief and torn trouser-fly to shriek it at you; and scratches on his back, a blue mouth-bruise on his neck. And the way he just sort of displays them, lying there, stretched out naked, and drunk. But there's nothing you can do about it. When you can see disaster coming in one form or another, there's always so little you can do to avert it; it's like trying to hold back a tidal wave. There's too much force behind it, too many extraneous forces beyond your control. You're always much too enfeebled and helpless even to try to cope with something like that.

Try reasoning with him.

"Cor," you say, "can't you see that I'm *trying* to find some way of taking you with me?"

No reply. No movement from his bed. But you know he's awake, listening. Still sober enough to hear you, and absorb it.

"Or even if I can't take you with me, to London and all that," you go on, "perhaps when I've got to Hongkong, and had a chance to settle down and look around, I'll be able to send for you."

Still no reply, no movement.

"Admittedly," you go on, not knowing whether it will be of any use or not, "it may be six months or so, perhaps even a year. But after all, lots of *normal* couples," you point out, "have to face separations like that, and it doesn't bust up everything. It doesn't stop them from still loving each other, until such time as they *can* be with each other again. You *must* know that. And if you *really* love me, as you say you do, then surely you can wait six to twelve months too . . ."

There should be something in that, you think to yourself; especially with someone like Cor. And so you wait a while, almost certain that, this time, there will be at least some movement, some reply, from the inert form on the bed. You're so sure of it that you even go over and put your hand on the hot plane of his back, feeling the warmth and strength of him, the *being* in him, so much a thing of reality and substance under your hand that you can't possibly believe that, one day, it might no longer be there.

For a moment you feel as though perhaps you're winning, winning him round. He still doesn't move. But he doesn't shrug away your hand or anything either. Just leaves it resting

204

there. And then what you knew would come, does come. A reply. But it's hardly the kind of reply you expected.

"And if *you* really loved *me*, as *you* say you do," he says, every word biting viciously, biting almost clean through the soft flesh of your nearly dead love, "then *you* couldn't think of leaving me, not even for six or twelve *days*."

And there it is. Absurd. Ridiculous. But so true. You have to admit it to yourself; there is, possibly, some semblance of truth in that retaliation of his. How thankful you are that you don't have to look at his eyes. . . .

So you take away your hand, and lose even the soft insidious jealousy that the scratches and bruise had aroused in you. And if you can lose that, then very soon there's not going to be anything much left between you at all. Except hate, perhaps. And then loathing. You would never have thought things would come to that.

You don't send a telegram. To make quite sure of your own decision, and even more certain of having acted upon it, you telephone. And Hempson tells you the company will book an air passage for you, in about three weeks.

22

YOU try to get him to look at things a bit differently, at least in one direction. The last time you both had to go through this, you had only eight days. This time you've got three weeks. But he just doesn't seem to see it that way, doesn't see it that way at all, or he doesn't want to.

Of course you do have to spend a fair amount of time seeing your family and so forth, old friends—time that Cor can't very well be with you. But you also try to arrange all this sort of thing when he'll be working, and couldn't spend that particular time with you anyway. All the same, there are some occasions when you just can't manage this, naturally, and the awful thing about it is that Cor always puts on that hurt look of his, of having been left out of things, just as though you had arranged it all deliberately—which, the lord knows, you haven't at all. If anything, it's the very thing you're trying to avoid, if he'd only take a proper look at things, be more reasonable and rational. Sometimes you feel as though you'll lose patience with him altogether. But something around the flat, or from just inside your own head somewhere, always reminds you, just in time, of something or other he's done for you, of all the things he's done for you ever since the time you first met, and then, no matter how difficult he seems, you just can't bring yourself to say anything.

Then he starts to drink again; *really* starts drinking. Sometimes he comes home so drunk he can't let himself in the door. You can hear the key fumbling and banging around at the lock and not getting anywhere, and when you go and let him in, he nearly falls flat on his face in the passage. But that's not all; when you go to grab him, just to help him, he shrugs your hand away; more than just shrugs it really, he does it so violently. And when he's like that, you know there's not much use in trying to do anything, not even when he's being sick in the bathroom.

The only times when you do manage to help him is on the two occasions when, after a fair while of staggering and lumbering around the flat, he passes out cold. So you haul him up, all that bulk of his, and somehow or other you get him into bed. And when he's just lying there, his face looks so bloated and ugly, so set into those heavy lines of his, that you almost feel a kind of repugnance. You can't help it. You find yourself wondering what on earth you saw in him in the first place, or else wondering where whatever it was that you did see in him has gone to. There doesn't seem to be much of the Cor you first met left in him now. But then, thank God, this thought soon passes again, and you find yourself seeing him a second time, and when you look at that mouth of his, brush away the fleck of spittle from one corner, yes, you *can* see again the sculpture of that mouth, the set of his eyes, even more pronounced now in sleep than when he's awake. You brush the hair back from his forehead, feeling the heat of his brow, and you tell yourself that he would never be like this at all, would never be anything like this, if it wasn't for your going away. So you can't really blame him.

One night, when you come home from seeing some friends to find him passed out on the carpet in the sitting-room, a bottle of sherry upturned next to him and soaked into the carpet all around his head, smelling the place out and everything—well, that night you have to get him into bed again, and just as you've managed it, he starts to say something, just sort of mumbling, and one hand fumbles at your shoulder. So you put your ear to his mouth, not knowing what he might say. You fully expect him to say something that will just hurt you all the more, all over again, as though you haven't got enough to put up with as it is. You even expect him to say something about that Henk of his, and make you feel as though you're really just an intruder, and have been all the time, hanging around in those four walls of the flat when you're no longer wanted, there are already the two of them in it. But what does he say? With his hand still half-fumbling at your shoulder, brushing your cheek now and again, even though his eyes are closed tight and you could swear he was passed out, nevertheless he can still manage to say: "Oh, Ray, Ray, Ray." Nothing more. Just that, over and over. And everything inside you starts bleeding again.

"I'm here, boy. I'm still here," you say, not knowing whether he'll hear you or not. Or, even if he does, not knowing whether it'll still mean anything to him. But he must hear it, and it must mean something to him after all. For his hand waves around a bit, and then seems able to locate you at long last, in its private little circle of darkness and loneliness. For it suddenly comes to rest against your face, gently, feeling and exploring your face as though it has just discovered it for the very first time. The fingers creep around your neck and, taking hold, pull your head down.

"Ray? Ray?" He almost whimpers it, and you thank everything you can think of that the name he calls out *is* Ray, and not Henk. And you let him pull you down to him, ignoring the smell on his breath. You know he wants you to kiss him, and so you do kiss him; you even find yourself liking the smell of his breath. Then when he moves over on his bed, managing it somehow or other, to make room for you, you tear your clothes off and get in beside him. He's still drunk, but he wants to make love so desperately, calling your name out, just softly, over and over again, that you suddenly think to yourself that at last, at last, the troubles are over between you. Once you've made love again, after so long without it, he'll see things much more reasonably, much more rationally, tomorrow. You feel really certain about it.

But not for long. It's when you actually start to make love, he gives himself so violently to you, his body is so greedy and demanding, that it's not long before you find yourself wondering if he knows who it is that is with him, even when he still calls out your name at the climax of an embrace. His embraces and the receiving of embraces are so desperately violent, you feel almost certain he doesn't know it is you. He may want it to be you, but thinks it's someone else, someone else he's picked up just to pretend it's with you. And it makes you also feel sort of stunned, soiled somehow. You feel as though you're not really making love at all, let alone expressing your love; it's so much a kind of bodily lust that's going on between you, almost like animals.

And then when it's over—when at long last it's over for both of you—he just falls immediately into the deepest sleep it's possible for anyone to fall into, snoring his head off. You can hardly bear to stay in the same room with him. And yet this is not only just because of the snoring. It's much more because you feel so wretchedly debased, humiliated. Soiled. But the main point of it is that you can't exactly blame him altogether for the way that you feel, because you know you're just as much to blame for it as he may be. And that's what is really so difficult to accept.

All the same, you do feel that it might make *some* difference between the two of you, in the morning. But you're wrong. When the morning comes, he's exactly the same as usual, sulking, even resentful. And distant, so distant. You'd think he didn't even know what had happened between you the night before, the way he just goes about things as usual, performing all the mundane things that you suppose have to be performed.

The resentment still continues, the drinking continues. And the same clawing and clutching at each other continues whenever he's passed out and you have to go through the same routine of putting him to bed again. If anything, you begin to feel that he's doing it deliberately, as things between you have now gone so far that the only way you can ever come together again is in these hideously violent, acutely humiliating collisions of your two determinations—that never mean anything, afterwards. In a way, you suppose there is more actual sex between you than there ever was before, even during that eight days when you had previously thought it would be for the very last time. This time, there may be much more of all that sort of thing, but it doesn't say anything to either of you, doesn't mean anything. It merely defeats its own purpose, right from the outset. More, it just seems to make things all the worse between you, increasing the distance between you further and further until, in a way, you'll be almost glad when the time comes when you know it will happen for the very last time, and then, in one last profane act of violence, it will all of it be over. And you think to yourself, this is the way all once-sacred things end. As love resolves into hate, the sacred resolves, eventually and inevitably, into the profane.

Eventually too, things get so desperate between you, you suggest to him wouldn't it be better if you split up even before you're due to leave the country? He could still stay on at the flat, perhaps even find someone else to share it with him. You'd keep on paying the rent, of course, until he did. You

209

can afford it now, for of course you have to sell the car, and it will fetch more than enough to see you through until you start drawing your salary. Besides, you add, it will be more convenient in a way for you to be back home with your family, just before you go, for packing up and all that sort of thing. Your folks would be glad to have you for the last ten days or so; your mother has already said they would. In fact, you can see that she almost expected it, and that she was terribly disappointed when you told her no, you were staying on at the flat with Cor. You don't even think she even half believed the excuse you used of saying you didn't want to have to make the two moves in such a short time, you had so many other things to see to. No, you don't think that really washed with her at all.

But when you have these second thoughts about the matter, and just mention it to Cor, his reaction is so violent you can hardly believe it. Before you even know what's happening, his hands have gripped you around the throat, and they start squeezing, squeezing, his eyes bulging from their sockets as the full force of his hatred and resentment glares down upon you. Until just as you begin to think that yes, he *is* going to kill you, you can't free yourself from those powerful hands of his—those unbelievably powerful hands—he manages to recover himself, realizing what he is doing, and his hands break away from you. You can feel your throat is all bruised and red, probably blue. And you can hardly breathe; it's quite a while before you can get your breath back, let alone say anything. *He* doesn't say anything; just looks if anything even more furious and resentful because something, you don't know what, stopped him from doing it. Certainly it wasn't you. Because if there was one thing you felt at the time, apart from the killing grip of his hands on your throat and the feeling that your very life was slowly being stifled within you, it wasn't so much the pain or the fear, although even that was quite something to contend with as well, but no—what you felt most of all was that, finally, you had become nothing more to him than just an object of such hate and frustration, it was as much as he could do *not* to destroy you, if only to give vent to that terrifying hate and resentment of his, to give him relief, release. And if he *had* gone through with it, if he hadn't been able to stop himself—or if there hadn't been that unnameable something that *had* stopped him—well, what a pretty mess it all would have been. Even as it is, it's still an awful mess. You can hardly believe that all the things you once felt for each other, had once meant to each other, could so quickly end this way, the way you've seen it all end so often, with others, but thought it would never happen to you and Cor. But it has, all right—it really has. And there's nothing much you can do about it. There's nothing much left between you now, except fear— fear that he'll do it again; and next time, perhaps, he won't be able to stop.

It's not long after this that, just by accident in the street one day, you happen to pass Sidney Needham. Neither of you have to speak; you hardly look at each other. But what he said the last time you saw each other suddenly smacks clean between your eyes, and you're glad you didn't acknowledge each other. For you feel he can tell, just by the look of you, that things are going exactly as he wanted them to. And even when he's passed you, swaggering along the street, you can hear those words of his even more plainly than you did when he actually said them: *And now I can just sit back and watch you two tear yourselves, and each other, to pieces . . .*

Yet somehow this gives you the determination still to disappoint him, if it's at all possible. If you can't possibly work things out with Cor so that, eventually, you *can* send for him to rejoin you—and despite everything, or perhaps because of everything, you still want this to happen—well, if you can't, and it won't be for the want of trying, then at least you must try to end things decently between you, eradicate all these hard feelings. For the rest of your life you'll never forgive yourself if you don't.

So you become more determined about it, seeing Sid Needham again and being reminded of what he'd said. And as though that's not all, and even though the very coincidence of it nearly knocks the wind out of your lungs, just a few minutes after, in the same street, you see Roy walking along towards you, but on the other side of the street. You're about to cross over and speak to him, and you've already started to step across the street, when comething about just the way he looks makes you stop. And you turn back, stunned; for you suddenly realize that someone else is going through something that's just as bad as what you're going through. It might even be worse, for all you know; for by just looking at Roy's face, so sunken and vacant-looking, you remember that young Andy—poor silly little Andy—is already in gaol. You don't know for which one it'll be the harder, Roy or young Andy; they were so devoted to each other.

So you hurry on again, even more determined now to do something about things between you and Cor. After all, you two can still do something about it; Roy and young Andy can't.

Seeing these two, both Sid Needham and Roy on the same day, makes you think of someone else you should see again, or at least speak to over the phone—old Bruce. You never know, he's always been able to help before, most of the time, so he just might be able to help again now. And it suddenly occurs to you that he's just the very one who probably *can* help. He moves around the world so much, he probably has friends in Hongkong who could tell you about conditions there. You become so excited, just thinking about it, that you can hardly get to a phone quick enough.

"Well, old thing, what's the trouble besides your age?" he says, jaunty as ever, always the same old Bruce, bless him.

So you start to tell him, and his voice becomes all serious again.

"Yes, I know," he says, when you tell him about Hongkong and so forth. "Cor told me. It's pretty hard on him, old thing. What are you going to do about him?"

So you tell him; ask him if he knows anyone in Hongkong.

"Know someone that's just the job," he says. "Put the phone down and I'll write off straight away, find out the lot for you. Couldn't be happier. Could kick myself for not having thought of it myself. Go on, put the bloody phone down and let your old mother here get busy with this poison pen of hers. Soon as I get a reply I'll ring you, and both of you must come to dinner. Now stop worrying yourself about things; you don't want to finish up looking like a flaming Chinaman again do you? Especially if you're going to Hongkong! They'll think you're just another refugee from Red China or something. So off you go now, and just leave things to old Mother Farnham. She'll soon have things right, you'll find. So, *eff* off with you ...

Same old Bruce. You could almost weep for joy—if only you could somehow or other bring yourself to tell Cor about it too.

23

BY THE time Bruce phones to ask you both to come over to dinner, you feel that you've got things going so well, all you need now is just a bit of favourable information from old Bruce about Hongkong, and being able to take Cor there perhaps, and everything will be on top of the world again. You can feel it so much, you're almost certain of it—certain that nothing can go wrong again now. And when the time comes for you to tell Cor about it, you can just imagine his face; it'll be almost like his being reborn again. You're sure of it.

So you feel quite optimistic about things again. Life isn't going to bust up on you after all; you feel sure it isn't. All you have to wait for now is for when you get to old Bruce's, and he tells you the gup about Hongkong. Then everything can start all over. It'll be like the sun coming out again for the first time in ages; it really will.

When you both get there, though, with Cor still rather sullen beside you, but not reeking too much of liquor for once, you have to admit that you're a little surprised to find Bruce has got someone else there as well, someone you've never even met before, another 'visiting fireman' from the east. You didn't want to have to talk over things like this before a stranger, but you suppose old Bruce just couldn't help it, he knows so many people from all over—from all over the world, that is —and they're always dropping in on him to chew the international fat. At first you're disappointed, and you're not even sure that this guy's a member of the club for a while, and you're almost sure that Cor won't be able to hold himself together, the way he's been lately. You certainly don't want any more scenes at this stage of the game.

Old Bruce is far from stingy with the drinks at the best of times, but tonight he seems determined to get you all pie-eyed. Neat Scotch to start off with, to warm the cockles of your heart, he says. And when Cor tosses his straight down, he sort of laughs it off; and to put Cor at his ease, old Bruce says: "Come on, now. Bottoms up everyone. Only your glasses, of course. If there's going to be any of *that* sort of thing, you've all got to wait till you've had dinner at least!" It's a bit coarse, but you can't help laughing; besides, it soon sets a much better mood to things, if only Cor wouldn't keep on drinking so much.

You're all pretty hilarious long before it's time to sit down to the soup. That is, just three of you—not Cor. He's still withdrawn into a little circle of his own private gloom, a little impregnable world of despondency, picking and probing all the time at what has really become, now, his own deliberately self-inflicted wound. You'd think he'd buck himself up a bit; if only for appearances' sake; it's so damned humiliating for one thing, having him sulking around the place all the time, especially in front of a stranger, even if the stranger does take it all in pretty good part. There's nothing much else he can do about it, you suppose; nothing much anyone can do about it, especially yourself. Somehow or other you know that if you try to do anything, Cor will just explode out of that tightly closed little cage he's got himself into. And then there'd be no telling just what he'd do. You know how violent he can be lately.

But eventually you all sit down to soup, and Bruce pours a bottle of white wine, and things are still going about as comfortably as could be expected of them. But then, of all people, it's old Bruce himself who has to go and put a spoke in the works. Doesn't mean to, of course. Who would ever have thought that things would turn out the way they did?

Bruce suddenly takes advantage of a sudden and rather embarrassing pause in the chit-chat to tell you about Hongkong.

"I wrote off to that friend of mine there," he tells you. "But *crikey* it's bad luck, boy. Instead of getting a reply about it all, I just got a postcard today from old Jack in San Francisco. The paradise town, *eh* boy? Old Jack always seem to be off on leave or something, or business trips he calls them. But I know what kind of *business* trips *they* are! Especially in a place like San Francisco"—and he gives you all the longest and lewdest of winks it's possible for old Bruce to give, which is saying a great deal. "Anyway, I suppose that letter of mine will either wait at his office until such time as he gets back, or else it may go chasing him all around the world somewhere. And I don't know anyone else besides old Jack to write to in Hongkong. It's tough luck all right, Ray. Sorry, old boy. But don't take it too badly"—which makes you realize that you must have started to look pretty disappointed, which wouldn't at all surprise you, you'd been expecting so much to come out of this night. "Don't let it get you down. I'll probably get a reply from him sooner or later, even if you've already gone to London. And I'll soon shoot it on to you. And then"—but then he makes yet another mistake, though as inadvertent as the first, by making a jocular kind of nudge in the ribs to Cor —"you'll probably find you can fix things to take old Cor here along with you after all, or follow you there." And then, he still has to make yet another bloomer, even if it *was* intended as just an innocent joke. "For after all," he says, "you can't very well go off and just leave your old *Dutch* here behind, can you, eh?" And he digs Cor in the ribs again.

Which is all that's needed to touch off the trigger.

Cor suddenly slams down his spoon into his soup so that it not only skits soup all over the place, and especially all over this poor guy from the east who's suddenly had it all inflicted on him, knowing nothing about it, but gets a shirt-front of soup into the bargain—well, not only that, but the force with which Cor has brought his spoon down breaks the plate as well, and the rest of the soup and bits of broken plate stream all over the table that had been so beautifully arranged. As though that isn't enough, Cor ignores what he's done and, like a child, just bursts into tears and sticks his head down into all the mess he's made on the table. You can hardly believe it, but that's what he's done, blubbering away hysterically and almost deliberately, as though wanting to wallow in his own self-indulgent misery. It's such a terrible thing to see, it makes you shrivel up with disgust. And you suddenly know, for certain, that you don't love him any more. How could anyone love somebody who carries on like that! But at the same time, you don't exactly hate him either; you just despise him, with such cold certainty that the very shock of it makes you tremble.

And what makes matters worse, Cor *will* go on and on with it, instead of at least trying to pull himself together and apologize to old Bruce. You don't want him to apologise to *you*; it's too late for that now; but he might at least apologize to old Bruce, and pull himself together; try to salvage something from the evening's wreckage after Bruce has gone to so much trouble.

But Cor still leaves his head on the table, his face and hair covered in the mess he's made, and old Bruce can't even get at the tablecloth to try to clean it. The guy from the east just sits there, trying not to look too angry as he mops at the mess on his shirt. Old Bruce puts his arm around Cor's shoulder, trying to pacify him, while all you can do is just sit there, feeling everything you ever felt for him drain clean out of you, just as though a plug has been pulled out.

You could have told Bruce that anything he might say wouldn't improve things; if anything, it would only make them worse, which it soon does. For Cor suddenly pushes his arms along the table, in front of his head, not only settling himself more and more into the mess he's made, but upsetting other things on the table as well. It's all so disgusting you can hardly bear to watch it any more. All you want to do is get up and run somewhere, anywhere, so long as you can get yourself away from that disgusting, degrading sight at the table. But somehow or other you manage to restrain yourself, the lord alone knows how, and you just sit there, even when Cor starts all his hysterical shouting.

"He wouldn't leave me at *all* if he really loved me, like he says he does," he keeps on shouting, so that you feel certain the whole block of flats can hear. "He wouldn't be *able* to leave me," Cor keeps on, now grovelling in the mess on the table. Even Bruce has given up trying to salvage something out of the wreckage; and you can hardly blame him, it's so hopeless by now. Yet Cor still goes on: "He *wants* to leave me, he *wants* to leave me. I know *his* kind. Just wants his fun, and then goes off and leaves you. I know it, I tell you! Don't tell me I don't! I've been through it all before! And he's exactly the same, exactly the same . . ."

You know what he means, and you can't stand any more of that kind of stuff. It isn't as if you *haven't* tried to do something about things. It's damn near driven you crazy. But he doesn't think of that. No, he doesn't look at things from that side at all—only from his own point of view—which is what most people do, you suppose, so you guess you can't really blame him. The only thing that you do blame him for is carrying on like an hysterical boor. It's this you think you'll never be able to forgive, not in a lifetime.

So you get up, and as soon as you move, Cor suddenly gets up too, pushing the table in front of him so that it nearly turns over, and is only stopped by the man from the east still sitting on the opposite side. But even he doesn't stay there long. You suppose if you could just see all this on a film, instead of it really happening to you, it would all be so damn ludicrous as to be even funny. People would split their sides, looking at it. But it's nothing much to laugh at, especially the way Cor jumps up on to his feet, overturning his chair, and almost slamming old Bruce through the wall. His face is so contorted with hysterical rage that you expect him to come over and start throttling you again.

But thankfully that's not what he does. Somehow or other he just pushes past old Bruce, who looks all stunned and helpless—who wouldn't?—and goes through to the kitchen, slamming the door. You all just sit there for a while, listening in stunned horror to the sobbing and weeping that goes on from the other side of the door.

Then old Bruce pulls himself together, recovers both his breath and his composure, and says: "You two stay here. Don't worry about all this. I can fix it in a jiffy afterwards. But I think I'd better see to Cor. Don't *you* come, Ray—not for a while anyway. I'll call you if I want you."

And you have to hand it to him, into the kitchen he goes.

Well, there's this bloke from the east that you still have to behave yourself in front of, so you offer him a cigarette, and he says yes, then no, and then both of you try to pass the time away—though still listening to the sounds from the kitchen—by clearing up at least some of the mess on the table. You can hear old Bruce's voice all the time, trying to pacify Cor; but it doesn't seem to be doing much good. Every now and again you can hear Cor's voice burst out all over again. But now, at least, he's got a new hue and cry to go on with.

"It's all finished on my way," he says, over and over again, just as before. His voice and accent have become as thick and coarse as his features had, just before leaving the table. And you can just picture him, still looking the same way, hideously hysterical; it nearly makes you sick.

"It's all finished on my way," the voice breaks out again, just like a record that's got stuck in a groove and can't stop. Cor's worked himself up so much, he simply can't stop himself; you doubt if even old Bruce can stop him. All you feel you can look forward to now is Cor making his final burst and come crashing through the door, glass flying everywhere, then go howling out into the night like some crazed banshee or

218

something. You can just *see* it happening, you really can; so that after a while you can hardly believe that it *hasn't* happened.

But Bruce must be a sheer miracle, for nothing like that happens at all. You still have to go on listening to Cor blubbing that everything's finished for him and so forth, but at least there's nothing worse than that, which is something to be thankful for.

It really must have been a miracle that old Bruce has worked; for suddenly the door opens and he beckons to you to go in. You don't think it's at all wise, but you go anyway. Cor won't look at you. But when you make the effort, and put a hand on his shoulder, at least he doesn't shake it off. But he doesn't stop his weeping either, even though you must admit that it *has* quietened down.

As though he's been waiting to see how things will go, old Bruce says after a while that it might be better if you take him home; leans over and says into Cor's ear, just like you would with a child: "You want to go home don't you, Cor boy? Want Ray to take you home? Of course you do!"

So you mumble something about how sorry you are, and yes you suppose it would be better if you did take him home, but you're sorry the whole evening has been busted the way it has. All of which old Bruce just brushes aside, as only old Bruce could, and somehow or other you manage to get your coats and things and, trailing a long cloud of humiliation behind you, you lead Cor stumbling out of the flat and towards the car, into the night.

Neither of you say anything. Any words between you, now, would be too awkward and cumbersome, grotesque. So you just keep silent—silent all the way in the car, the two of you wrapped in it like two separate cocoons. Silent when you arrive at the flat, with only the shame and humiliation left as some sort of bond between you, and only then because you can't shake it off, try as you will. You suppose that the shame and humiliation you feel for this evening will be something from which neither of you will ever be able to rid yourselves. At least, you know how *you* feel about it. More than those great hands of his could, this shame Cor has brought on you almost strangles you.

Still wordless, still wrapping your separate cloaks of silence around you, as though it's some kind of protection, you undress and go to your separate beds. And still in your separate cocoons of silence, you lie there. If only you could sleep. Early as it is, and without having had dinner after all, it would be one way of forgetting things, if only for so short a time.

But even sleep is denied you. You don't know whether Cor has fallen asleep or not; it's quite likely that he has, he always seems to be able to go off so quickly, no matter what might have happened. But you know you won't sleep, not for a few hours yet, if then. The four dead walls of the flat are cloying around you again. And, silly as it seems, you feel you just have to get up, dress yourself again, and go for a walk. Anywhere. Nowhere in particular. Just anywhere.

So you get up, fumble for clothes and things. You think to yourself that Cor must be asleep, and marvel at it. But just as you're almost ready to go, you find he's been awake after all.

"Where are you going?" he demands.

"Just out," you say, weary of it all, and start to go to the door.

For a while you think he's not going to say anything more. There is just the silence between you, still dripping into the room. But as you turn the handle, he nearly makes you jump through the ceiling, the way he shouts at you.

"That's right, then. Go! You can't get away quick enough, can you!"

The words rock and reverberate around through the petrified dark, rolling in great echoing waves from wall to wall. And you can't help wondering how many other people in the building have heard, and wondering what they're thinking if they have. Oh, the shame of it! On top of everything else. If anyone hears it all now, any of those normal ones, they'll just snigger to themselves: Two queers having a shindy! Something amusing to listen to, something a bit different from usual, to brighten up the dreary rut of life. Can have quite a bit of fun afterwards, telling it to their friends—the last and ugliest touch of all.

But you try to control yourself still, try still to be calm and composed when you say: "For God's sake, Cor! Do you want the whole world to know you're queer?"

But this, of course, was quite the wrong thing to say. For, louder than ever, he shouts back at you, so that the whole building can't help but hear: "*You're* the one that's queer! Not me! You! You're the one that's queer all right . . ." And falls back to sobbing again, there in his bed.

But you can't stand any more. It's as much as you can do not to put your hands over your ears and go running out into whatever sanctuary the night might have to offer. Yet somehow or other you still manage to restrain yourself from making any foolish, idiotic retort, and walk out into the night. You're no sooner outside than you hear something being smashed against a wall. And just by the sound of it, you feel sure it is the little figure of Eros that young Andy gave you. And you think to yourself: How appropriate! How very appropriate!

It's almost as though the night has eyes—and hands, to brush and finger you with its morbid curiosity. You can almost feel it sort of only opening up to let you pass when you push yourself through it, and it just stands back but still jeers at you, mocking you with a mimicry of Cor's hideous words. And you wonder how many miles you'll have to walk before those words of his will stop shrieking in your ears.

24

AT FIRST you only half hear it, and don't take any notice of it. But then it becomes more insistent in your ears, drumming almost, like a heavy but still distant rain. You still hardly take any notice of it, your mind is too cramped by so many other concerns for one thing; and for another, you don't yet realize that even rain could have anything to do with you. It's no concern of yours. It doesn't matter if it rains or not. In a way, even a flood would be welcome, and just rain would help to conceal you from the rest of the night, form a curtain around you. And the lord alone knows, you feel as though you need something like that.

You're walking on the sidewalk, down the hill towards the open sports grounds that look blanketed away for the night, and beyond them the river gleaming all dark and foreboding, although just the very blackness of it is kind of welcoming too. Even without feeling at all morbid or anything, you can just imagine someone wanting to throw themselves into it, just by looking at it. Which is what you feel almost sure must happen to some people now and again; they don't actually have any intention of jumping in, but when they stand there for a while, particularly if they get close to it and look down into it, from only a few feet away, then they get this sort of hypnotized feeling, just by the dark and slowly flowing lines of the current, and trying to see beyond the blackness of the depths by forcing the eyes to focus, with a kind of X-ray ability or something, even though you know your eyes can do no such thing. At some time or other, you've felt it several times, and the effort to stop yourself from jumping has needed to be even greater than you suppose it would have been for you to have jumped and have done with it.

But this isn't why you go towards the river—nothing like that at all. It's just that you don't want to go into the city, with all it's brightly lit shops, traffic, people window-shopping and so forth. You want to go somewhere where it's dark and quiet, where you can be alone. And there's not even much traffic down there. That sound of rain drumming somewhere forces itself on you again; so you turn around, fully expecting to see a shower approaching you down the street. But to your surprise, there's nothing like that at all. And then you think to yourself, there couldn't be anyway; there's not a sign of rain anywhere, the sky is clear and damn near trembling all over with stars. There's not even a wind. Ahead there's a garage with lots of lights burning and two blokes lounging around talking to each other, one of them horsing around with the other one. It may be all innocent, but you can never tell these days; blokes do it even subconsciously, without ever knowing why they do it; they just like doing it, that's all, otherwise they wouldn't do it. But it would probably worry the hell out of them if they were ever told to think about it. But all that you'd tell them now is not to horse around too much, they might find themselves in the same sort of mess as you're in. Which once you thought would be so wonderful, a whole new life opened up for you after so many years of loneliness. A whole new life—*hell!*

That sound of rain again, or something like it, getting much nearer. Admittedly, over towards the garage, there is a large puddle in the middle of the road, with reflections plunged deep down into it. As you get a little closer, you can even see petrol rainbows glittering in it. But the puddle's not from rain, you realize; it's from a tap left running towards this end of the garage. And yet it's not the tap that's making that noise either, and which is getting much closer to you, so close in fact that you must turn again to see if you can't see what it is by now, it seems to be creeping up behind you all the time. And it's a good job you do turn around.

What you'd thought was the sound of rain, was really the sound of feet running—and the feet belong to Cor. Now that he knows you've seen him, he stops slinking behind trees and things, and starts running directly at you, almost like a madman. So that's what you get for trying to put something out of your mind, and just as you were succeeding so well at it, too.

He's not fully dressed. He's just pulled his trousers on over his pyjamas, thrown on an overcoat. He has shoes on, you can see, but no socks. His trousers end several inches above his ankles, and he looks a sight without any socks. You don't know how anyone could go out like that, even if there aren't many people in this particular locality. But you never know. And it's so damn silly for one thing, apart from being sort of common.

You wait for him to come up to you, hoping he's got over all his hysteria and isn't going to start shouting it out all over again. Perhaps you'll be able to calm him down if you face up to him, you've decided; whereas you just know that if you ignore him, it will only make him all the madder. And then the lord alone knows what he'll do.

But all that he does to begin with is to just pull up in front of you, and say: "Ray?" He keeps his voice down all right, but it must be an effort for him, the way his body is shaking and trembling all over, and he can only just get the words out from between his teeth, almost hissing it.

"Well?"

"Are you coming back with me?"

"No. I want to walk for a while."

"I said *are you coming back with me?*" he says again. And you suppose that you should have been warned, if only just by the way he says it, a little louder than the first time, although his teeth are clenched even tighter than before. And his eyes have started to stick out, deep as their sockets are. If he hadn't had so much to drink, earlier in the evening, you'd have thought he'd gone a bit dotty by the look of him. But you can't be bothered with him just now, so you say:

"I said, I want to go for a walk."

You hardly know how it happens, there's such a blow on the side of your head. And even though it seems for just a split second, when you *can* open your eyes again, the road is so close to your face you can see all its individual little blue-black stones glinting sharply before you. Something stings on your hands, knees. And it's only then that you realize he hit you, hard enough to knock you to the ground. And yet even that wouldn't worry you so much; you feel as though you can still say something to calm him down, or else fight him back if necessary, though you hope to God it won't be, not here out in the open, to make a spectacle of yourselves. No, it's not this that worries you; it's the sound of that forced kind of breathing of his, hissing all the time, so that if you could look up at his face, you'd swear he'd be frothing at the mouth.

Anyway, you can't stay down here; it'd be too silly for words. So you go to get up.

But as soon as you do another blow lands on the other side of your head, and the sky seems to crack open with all sorts of livid lightning streaks, dazzling. And your ear feels wet, which it must be, for there's suddenly a few blobs of blood falling on to your hand.

"Don't, Cor," you manage to say. "Don't be silly. Not here——"

But you can't say any more. You just have time to hear his hideous voice saying: "Get up, and come home!" before his shoe hits you in the stomach, so hard it makes you retch. You know he's out of his mind then, and also that you've got to get away from him; he'll probably kill you if you don't.

But when you go to move, he just keeps on shouting this same thing, over and over: "Get up! Get up!" and doesn't even listen when you try to say: "I'm trying to, for Christ's sake." He just keeps on yelling at you, and then his shoe catches you on one hip, then nearly in the groin, and something else lands like a ton of bricks in the small of your back, on the kidneys. Yet it doesn't hurt much anymore. You can feel it, but by now it's all in just cushions of pain. Not sharp at all. But if only you could get up. Stop the roaring in your ears. Everything seems to be happening so slowly too, like a slow-motion film, and yet you know that there's really only a couple of seconds or so between every kick, every blow, the next thing to come whatever it might be. Good job you're at least doubled over a bit, otherwise that shoe of his would really get you in the balls.

"Cor," you say. "Cor, for God's sake!"

But what you're really thinking of are at least two other things; you've got to get yourself away from him, somehow or other, and, if you can't, what a pretty mess this is going to be. He might knock you out or something, even if he doesn't kill you, and it'll all make such juicy headlines in the paper. You can just see it. If you could only get your breath back, so that you could move, especially when that last clout lands on you, on the back of your neck. And again that merciless shoe of his nearly gets you in the groin.

"Cor, please——"

But all he ever says back to you, kicking and punching all the time, is: "So you want to leave me, do you! So you want to leave me!" And he can kick and punch so fast, you'd think he had at least half a dozen legs and arms.

But then, in between what he's yelling at you all the time, somehow or other you hear another voice come sliding in between, from farther away. It just says, "Hey, you!" and feet start running. You can hear them, running towards you. And you think: Oh, God! If someone comes, even if it's to *help* you, they'll want to know what it was all about—and then the whole game will be a give-away, which is the last thing you want. You'd rather stay there and let Cor beat you to a pulp rather than have *that*—people knowing about it all. But at least it does give you the chance to get yourself to your feet, and start running.

It's then you can see that the bloke who yelled was one of the garage attendants, and they're both running towards you. When they see you get yourself to your feet and start running, they make way for you, without actually stopping themselves, and close in on Cor. You don't know what you want to do then. You're glad of course that they've interrupted and given you the chance to get away, before you're beaten to a pulp; but you don't want them to knock Cor about, the two of them. For you at least know that he can't really help himself, he's half out of his mind. So you don't want them to beat him up at all; if they just hold him off until you can get away. For if you'd had at least some chance to fight back, you reckon you might have been able to hold your own with him. But as things were—

You haven't got much more time to think of anything like this now, though. The two garage attendants don't beat him up or anything; they don't get a chance to, can't even hold him back. You just manage to see Cor take a wild swing that

226

knocks one of them to the ground, and then he's past them, after you again. So you've just got to run.

It's all crazy—it's really crazy, you tell yourself; but you don't dare to stop now and try talking with him. You've just got to get away from him, run as fast as you can. But he seems to run like a madman, gaining on you all the time. If only you could get your breath properly and didn't ache all over, or have that pain in your groin. One street after another, flashing by, all dark streets, flashing past you in reverse so it seems. Bits of houses and buildings skid past your eyes. Windows, doorways and things. Trees and lamp-posts. Kerbs, gutters. Your own knees and shoes flashing just underneath you all the time, but never fast enough, never fast enough, you can still hear him catching up on you all the time. And when he does? Well, it'd be better if he did kill you. You couldn't stand the shame of the other thing, it all coming out in the press and so on . . .

Which is why you can't ask for help, or run for help. But at the same time, you're not exactly ready to stop and let him do whatever he wants to with you either. Much as you fear the other thing, you're still really afraid to die. You're not ready for it yet, even if it is the better of the two alternatives. So you keep on running, somehow or other.

The road starts doing crazy things now. It keeps swimming up and around you all the time, sliding away from underneath you, as though things aren't difficult enough without it doing that. Rocking and sliding all the time. Roaring in your ears. And it's not for quite a while that you realize the road can't be doing any such thing—it's you; it must be you. Something wrong with you. But you've got to keep on running. Push yourself around this tree that almost hits you in the face, stagger over to the gate, cling to it, push yourself away from that too, stop yourself from falling down when it swings open and you lurch through, the dark of a garden all round you. Fool! You've trapped yourself! You'll never be able to get out again without him catching you. Trees, shrubs, dim lawns all around you. Yet never dark enough to hide you. Some sort

227

of bush throws up white sickly flowers at you, waxy looking, or all melting or something, splashing the relief of cold drops of water on to your face and clutching hands. Sickly sweet smell in your nostrils. Camellias, you tell yourself. But maybe you can hide in them. And you scrabble yourself through leaves, twigs, scratches, branches. Claw at dark, damp earth, in thick clods under your hands. And rasp for breath. The dark clods of earth rock and slide around you, under your hands. And you think to yourself, almost calmly: So this is where it's going to be. For you can hear his steps closer to you now, somewhere, running around in circles, looking for you. But he'll soon be able to find you; the moon is scudding between thin streaks of cloud, wan and sickly. He'll find you at any minute now, and this will be the last place you'll see. Bury that noise in your ears here in the damp clods of earth; it'll be such a relief.

But somehow or other he doesn't see you, goes round to the back of the building or house or whatever it is. Tall spire over there, spinning dimly against sky. He's gone.

Suddenly you don't want to stay there any longer, not here in this damp earth, like a grave. You want to go somewhere else, anywhere else, to the river perhaps, just anywhere but here. And you drag yourself from out of the Camellia bush, the wet waxy flowers brushing against you like pieces of dead flesh. Cold and dank. But as soon as you stand up, everything spins round you. The sea roars in your ears. The earth sliding. You put out a hand to stop it, but it just spins all the faster. You can see the gate and make towards it. But for some silly reason or other, your feet just go backwards. Or else someone is dragging you backwards. So you look back behind you to see if maybe that someone is Cor, he's got hold of you again. But you can't see any one; you just keep on sliding backwards. Your head and one hand smacks against something, slides away from you, and then smacks against you again, on the head, torturing little smacks, just hard enough to hurt, but without ever quite smashing your skull in. Something keeps on pressing into your hand all the time, and the roaring in your

228

ears takes on a new note, shrill, persistent, like a thin thin thread from a lone violin, clean inside your skull, where whatever it is keeps banging against your head. Sliding, all the time——

And then, with startling clarity, you suddenly realize that the banging on your head is not something actually hitting you, it's your head falling against a door all the time. And the buzzing in your ear is mainly from your hand having fallen by accident against a button. You try to push yourself away from it. This isn't what you want at all—not at all what you want. What if somebody comes! Oh, Christ, you *must* push yourself away from it——

But you're too late. The door suddenly swings open and you fall down on to the floor, half inside the door and half out. Worn carpet under your hands, shoes and black trouser-legs not far from them, standing over you. If they're going to kick, all you can hope for is that they hurry up and get it over with. And you lie there, waiting. . . .

But the kick doesn't come. Instead, someone is saying something, calling out to someone else, and hands under your arms drag you up. Your feet fumble for a footing. Walls reel. Your eyes fly open and there's just one vivid glimpse of an oldish man's face, bald, white collar underneath, and behind the face a long, thin, naked body hanging nailed on a cross. Voices talking, making urgent little sounds to each other. The thin body, crucified, reels at an angle. Until suddenly you know what it is, and where you must be.

And "Oh, Christ!" is all you can say. Weirdly enough, it sounds more like something appropriate than a blasphemy. For it's all over now. You can just let yourself go. Now they'll start dragging everything out of you . . .

But it's not the end at all. Footsteps slap and bang behind you again. Something tears at your shoulder. Someone keeps on shouting: "Let him alone! Let him alone!" And you know it's Cor's voice. He's come back and found you again. Lunges at you. So that the hands that were holding you gasp, drop you, and you slide to the floor again, see the crucifix from a new angle. And now you can see there are two priests; the old one who was holding you up, a younger one just behind him. You see the old one get pushed in the chest, pushed against the wall, and the crucifix rocks on the one nail impaling it to the wall. The old priest looks as though he's just seen something he can't believe, but as quickly recovers himself again. The young one starts grappling with this wild thing that keeps on lunging and lunging around you all the time, feet flying everywhere. And all you can do is think to yourself: Now the massacre will really begin, knowing what Cor is like. And you can't do anything about it. You can't even watch properly. You just hear and feel it all going on around you, over you, all that thumping and banging, the yelling and lunging around, until you think that——

It stops. Everything stops. Everything is so suddenly still it's as though the film has jammed, and just the one sustained picture is left imprinted blindingly in your eyes. No sound. No sound at all. But yes, there *is* sound, faint, far away it seems, yet just over you as well—the sound of someone whimpering. And then a strange voice says: "Oh, God, what am I doing! What am I doing——"

You're not sure whether it's Cor's voice or not. But one thing you *are* sure of, it's certainly not the voice that, as though it's just registered it's self-composure, and its authority, says as clearly as anything:

"You hang on to this madman here. I'm going to call a doctor."

And you still can't do anything about it. In any case, it's all up with you now, so it doesn't matter any more.

But a crucifix is such an agonizing thing to look at—to *have* to look at. It makes you also want to give up the ghost.

25

THIS, then, is the way that most things come to an end—or so you tell yourself. First the bang, and then the whimper. You've read quite a number of pretty crappy sort of novels about your kind of life, and they're all so sort of *noble*, and the characters in the story seldom if ever get to even *touch* each other or anything, and then one of them always gets killed at the end, and nothing's ever really said about the life itself. It's always vague and all too pretty-pretty. And yet, that's not the way of things at all. There's a good deal more to it than that, all right. Most gays you know *dòn't* finish up on guillotines or getting hung or shooting themselves or jumping off cliffs. At least, the majority of them don't. Only a very few of them ever come to a sticky end; no more, you'd say, than happens with normal people. But what does happen, and what's almost as bad, is that they no sooner get started on an affair than it gets broken up, somehow or other, and they just drift out of it again—and then soon look for another, but take any casual encounters in the meantime. There never seems to be an end to it—nor to the hoping. Always hoping—and trying. And so the years go by; life itself goes by—until one day you wake up to find yourself fifty, no longer attractive, just a sad old aunty still trying to put on the brave young bright act, but can't any longer, and so you're stuck with your loneliness. No guillotines or anything—just drift—and everything such a waste.

On the other hand, there are some couples you know who have been together for ten, fifteen, twenty, twenty-five years. It's been a bit of a strain at times, now and again, but whose life isn't? But these are the lucky ones. Or else they've got strong enough character to carry them through and keep them together. For, yes, if it takes anything, then it takes a good deal of character to be a decent homosexual.

231

You've got quite a lot of time to think about all these things, back in hospital again. The ironic thing is that there's nothing much wrong with you, a few bruises and cuts, and they've put a bit of bandage around your head; but it's all just superficial and nothing serious at all. Yet you're to stay there for a week, the doctor told you—not even for observation or anything, but just so that you'll be safe from Cor.

And that's what things have got to. Even though he's in a hospital too—a *sort* of a hospital, that is; for it's really a place where they put mental cases—this doctor tells you there's always the chance that he'll break out, and try to do to you again what he almost succeeded in doing the last time. Within a few days, this doctor says, they will probably have calmed him down, with injections and things.

It's when old Bruce comes to see you that you find out, to your horror, that they had to resort to shock treatment. You try not to think of it. You try to tell yourself that it really isn't your fault, but you can't ever quite get rid of some isolated but persistent feeling of guilt somehow.

Just lying there, you wonder what on earth is going to happen to him. The way you feel about him now, you can't even contemplate sending for him, later on, once you're in Hongkong. In a way, you don't ever want to see him again; yet in another, you still do—you'd still like to try to patch things up between you. After all, you may have been through three pretty disastrous affairs before, although none of them were anywhere near as disastrous as this one. But at least you did manage to survive them. Cor has been through only the two— but a good deal else besides. You don't know if he'll ever be able to get over either of them, and it's that part of it that makes you feel sorry for him. No, more than that; you really ache for him at times, just as you did that time for young Andy. And yet it's no more than that, not any longer. You'd just like to see him get himself well again, and be able to face up to things, life. At least you wish him that much.

This doctor seems fairly sympathetic about things, seems to know all about it all although he's not one himself. You can tell that by the first look at him, without even learning later that he's married and got kids and so on. Yet he's still pretty know-ledgable and sympathetic about it. But you suppose that's just his job, being a psychiatrist—he's just got to be sympathetic, so he is. He's pretty genuine about it all, but in a way you feel it's only in a sort of *abstract* way. He doesn't ever let it get personal; you suppose he can't really afford to. It wouldn't be wise, not in most cases. If he did, he's only find a lot of the little nelly types transferring their affection from some other hopeless object to him, and then he'd soon find himself in a mess.

So that's probably why he just keeps everything on this abstractly scientific and impersonal level, knowing everything there is to know about it probably. In fact, to get your confi-dence you suppose, he tells you about some pretty desperate cases he's had to handle at times; which you suppose are intended to make you feel that you're not *quite* so far gone, but it does just the opposite. It seems to put you in the same category, or very nearly, as all those other cases he tells you about, if only because he does tell you about them. And this, you decide, is not very bright on his part, not if he really wants to get your confidence and co-operation as he says he does. But you reckon, after a few days, that he's really not so interested in you after all, probably because it's obvious to him that *you're* all right; it's Cor he's really worried about. And that's often the way, too; it's usually the hysterical types, the ones who can blurt out all their miseries, who get all the sympathy. The ones who try to control themselves, if only by deliberately bottling it all up inside them, are the ones who are considered as safe—cold, perhaps even ruthless. Your type, you presume.

Your mother takes the attitude that you've just been unfor-tunate in being kind to a *foreigner*, and taking him in to the flat with you, only to be repaid with a bash over the head. She sniffs angrily about it, and dismisses all foreigners as a kind of subhuman species. And even if you could be bothered, you know it would be useless trying to explain things to her—she's just your mother. In a case like this, she wouldn't understand.

233

But your father's attitude is even more shattering. He comes in alone one day, with this attitude of discreet intimacy between men and a your-old-man-does-know-something-about-these-things look on his face—so smug about it. And *his* attitude, with a sly pat on your knee, is: "Don't worry about it, son. You'll soon be rid of him when you leave for London. There's no fury like that of a woman *spurned*," he says, smirking all over his omniscient mouth, and licking wet again the lips that are almost always as dry as emery paper.

Those are *their* attitudes, the kind of thing that make you almost weep for Cor. And no matter what he's done, you feel that he alone can always be miles closer to you than anyone else can ever be—even your own so-called kin.

Apart from still worrying about Cor, the only other one you feel that you can at least have a little respect for is the doctor, much as you may disapprove of some of his methods. After all, he can't be expected to know the best way to deal with everyone. So you decide to try and co-operate. In any case, there's not very much he wants you to do. It's on about the fourth or fifth day that he comes in and says:

"Well, if it still interests you, your friend is out of hospital and seems to be almost himself again. But this doesn't mean you can go out yet. He hasn't asked much about you—at least, not to me he hasn't—but you never know; if I let you go home, he just might try to do something again." And then he looks at you with that hard, almost contemptuous look that gives you rather a shock, and he adds: "After all, he's got some reason for it, I suppose." Coldly. "Anyway, to make sure that nothing silly like that happens again, I'm keeping you in here for a few more days. It should be quite safe then. Even so, I'll only let you out on one condition. I understand that this friend of yours had a rather similar experience, and was left once before by someone. Well, he hasn't got what it takes to go through it all a second time. But what he *can* do—*must* do, in fact—is to be the one to leave you. It may sound a little silly, but I can assure you it's perfectly logical"—as if you didn't know it yourself. "You'll find your bill will be debited with a second-class fare for him to Sydney. Don't worry, it will be the cheapest possible, only about twenty pounds or so. He won't even have a sleeper. But it'll get him there. He hasn't got any money for it himself. Then he can find himself a new job, and perhaps"—he pauses just long enough to give you another of those long, hard looks of his—"a new life as well. I for one certainly hope so, anyway. I trust you agree to this?"

You don't want to talk to him about it, so you just nod. After all, what can you say that won't be only superfluous? Or a trifle absurd?

"Good," he goes on, neatly folding up both interview and the entire little experience—or so he thinks. "I'll see that he gets away as soon as possible. I just want to make sure that he leaves here before you do, that's all."

You nod again, wishing he would go. But he doesn't go before he makes this last jab of all.

"Whether I approve of these sort of relationships or not, Wharton, doesn't come into it," he says; and then, with a really sharply-cold edge to his voice, goes on with: "but I do think you might have made a bit more of an effort over it. Frankly, I think you might have at least considered him to be worth that much."

And then he's gone, leaving those last absurd words of his rattling around in your head like a handful of stones. For what you would like to know is, what *didn't* you do, for God's sake? What more *could* you have done?

But the answer to that one is easy! Just wipe out the whole of the so-called *normal* world to leave the two of you alone. That way, you might at least have had some chance.

26

THEY let you out of hospital the afternoon Cor's supposed to be leaving on the evening train for Sydney, on the understanding that you don't try to see him. And even then, this is because you have only three days left yourself, before you're to catch the plane for London—so nicely arranged. Just time to pack up your things at the flat, have one of those charming family send-offs, and then step onto the plane. No time, of course, to see Cor. Not even once—just to tell him how sorry you are.

So you go to the flat first, not wanting to see the family straight away, and you find it already so nearly empty it's hard to believe that, such a short while ago, or even an eternity ago, the two of you were living there. All his clothes are gone, of course. All?—the *few* he had? The frying-pan old Bruce gave him is gone, and meticulously, half of a tea-set you had bought between you—honesty to the last possible degree. Even the black and white curtains have gone and you can't help wondering where they'll be hung up again one of these days. Only *his* books are gone, but two of *your* records, the ones he liked so much. To replace them, you can only suppose, are two pieces of Dutch pottery you can now remember having once admired. And yes, it *was* young Andy's little Eros that had been smashed against the wall. The rest is yours to pack up and take away. Then the flat is free once more—for someone else to encage their lives in, and make either a go or another unholy mess of them.

You're about to leave, astonished that you can still look around at it all with perfectly dry eyes, when the phone rings. At first you think you won't answer it, it might only be Cor; it's silly, but you *had* promised that you wouldn't go there alone. The doctor had said that if you did, and Cor was there, or if he came while you were still there, then he couldn't guarantee what would happen; anything could. But you know that that's all over now, for both of you. You don't give a damn for all the medical knowledge in the world; at least you do know Cor that well enough. There's no danger any more.

So, whether it will be Cor or not, you pick up the phone, in a way almost hoping that it *will* be Cor, you want even this much of an opportunity just to say something to him again. You're almost disappointed when it's not Cor; only old Bruce.

"I just wondered if you'd be there, old thing," he says, but not quite so jauntily as usual. One thing about him though, he's still his old self when it comes to not beating about the bush. "Ray," he says, "in case you're wondering, Cor's here with me. He doesn't know I'm calling you, as he's taking a shower just before he goes. I'm driving him up to the station. I just wanted to let you know in case you'd like to see him again."

He stops, and you don't know what to say, it seems such an impossible suggestion, against all the advice you've been given —all the *professional* advice, that is. In one way, it's exactly what you wanted to happen, and you almost bless whatever providence there may be that gives you this last opportunity. But on the other hand, you can't help wondering if professional knowledge could be the wiser after all; emotion, you've found, can be such a treacherous thing. So you don't know what to decide.

Bruce decides it for you—not knowing, of course; only in what he says next.

"I wasn't going to ring you at home, Ray, when I found out you'd been discharged from the hospital. I was just going to ring the flat. And if I found you there, as I have anyway, then I figured you'd be in sufficient frame of mind to see him again. You wouldn't have gone to the flat if you weren't."

That does it. Coincidence, providence, call it what you will; but there's too much of it to be ignored. You don't even need the next assurance Bruce gives you to know that you've already made up your mind.

"And Cor's all right, Ray. I've had a long talk with him and he sees things a bit differently now. He's quite all right. He's going to get along just fine . . ."

You can't get there fast enough. When you arrive, you've got about twenty minutes before Bruce says they must leave for the train. Cor's waiting for you in the other room, he says; and he himself will just wait outside here until he might be wanted, or it's time for them to go. You don't have to thank him, don't even have to ask him if he thinks it really will be all right for you to see Cor. There's no need for words about such things with Bruce. So you open the door, and go in.

It's hard to believe, but he looks exactly the same as when you first met him. Smiling at you, and giving you that look he used to give you before, the kind of look you knew he never had for anyone else—only for you. It's almost as though nothing had ever happened between you.

"Oh, Ray," he says; nothing more. And then eighteen of those twenty minutes are something you could never tell about, not to anyone. But if you must say something about it, then it's just that there never were eighteen minutes between you as those were, in old Bruce's bedroom.

When the knock comes on the door, you sort of bump and bang into each other all the time, getting his coat done up, his tie straightened, your own things too, making sure he's got everything. And then, when you're both quite sure he's got everything, you don't kiss or anything, you've just had all that. What you do is really much more, and you're glad that things have at least finished up this way, so that you are both capable of doing it. It's such a simple thing, really—shaking hands.

"Good-bye, Ray," he says. "And—good luck."

When he's gone, you have to hold yourself up over Bruce's washbasin for quite a while, shaking and trembling like a crazy thing, before you can drive yourself home—wherever that may be from now on.

27

IF YOU'VE got any integrity at all, you'll finish the story completely. It won't take long. You find that, even in only three days, you've still got a night free, or rather a night you can make free. And so you go to the old Palais of course. You know damn well that you just have to go in. You've walked past those doors now not once, nor twice, nor even three times, but probably thirty-three times. But you don't walk past them another thirty-three times. You go in. And eventually you take the sailor with the deep eyes and the dark curly hair, and arrange with Roy to use young Andy's room. Roy's got someone to help him get over things too. He's not quite as lucky as you are. You couldn't have found someone more like Cor if you'd tried, to help you forget about him—or remember him all the more.

And so this is the way things end—just a long succession of casual adventures, casual reminders. The whimpering comes afterwards.

28

IN LONDON you get a letter from Cor after a couple of weeks, saying he got himself to Sydney all right. He spent the first night in a hotel, got out the next day and found himself a job, selling records in a suburban record shop, found a room. The black and white curtains fit in just nicely, he says. He hopes you won't be disappointed in him, but he's found someone he quite likes, a playright for television. Quite a nice guy, he says, but in the same breath he hurries on to assure you that he'll never forget *you*, Ray—he never will.

And while you're over on that side of the world, he says, you might even get the chance to slip across to Holland for a few days. No, he doesn't want you to look up Mia, or his family, or anyone connected with him; he can see that there just wouldn't be any point. But in case you feel like using them, he lists a few bars and clubs where you can be sure, he says, of finding someone who'll give you a good time there. And he finishes in almost a jocular mood:

"And if you do get there, Ray, give my love to Holland. I don't suppose I'll ever see it again. But just think, if we'd been able to go *there* to live, we would have been *legal* [the italics are his] and not just a kind of *criminal*. But I suppose it's not much use talking about things like that on the moment. So Good Luck to you, Ray. And look after yourself.

Still with love, as always,
Your Cor."

Rather nice to think that, after all, he did find a place to hang up his curtains.

But not for long. They probably still ended up in some rubbish-tin or other, somewhere or other. You don't know how much this last attempt took out of him, with the playwright, and you suppose you never will. But about six months later you get another short letter, just to say that he's marrying again, to an Australian girl this time, yes a real girl, but one who understands, he says. Her father owns a string of chain stores; he's taking her up to the north of Queensland, to manage one of them. If there's one thing he can't face, he says, it's loneliness; just the mere prospect of it frightens him to death. And he can't see anything but loneliness ahead of you in the *gay* life, not these days. So he wishes you luck, and again sends his love.

Now that must be all. Oh, no—there *is* just the one more thing you'd like to say about it, and that's how you mostly only think of him now when, in Hongkong, this little Chinese friend you've now got is a fanatic for palm-reading—apart from anything else. And it always strikes you as being rather ludicrous when he points out the great length of your life line. It couldn't be more ironic; for what on earth, you wonder, will you ever *do* with it all. . . .